Oh My God, What a Complete Aisling

To Aislings everywhere, and the bit
of her that's in all of us.

In loving memory of Leslie McLysaght,
who would have been so proud.

Oh My God, What a Complete Aisling

EMER McLYSAGHT
and SARAH BREEN

MICHAEL JOSEPH
an imprint of
PENGUIN BOOKS

MICHAEL JOSEPH

UK | USA | Canada | Ireland | Australia
India | New Zealand | South Africa

Michael Joseph is part of the Penguin Random House group of companies
whose addresses can be found at global.penguinrandomhouse.com

First published in Ireland by Gill Books, 2017
Published in Great Britain by Michael Joseph, 2018
001

Set in 14/16.5 pt Garamond MT Std
Typeset by Jouve (UK), Milton Keynes
Printed in Great Britain by Clays Ltd, St Ives plc

A CIP catalogue record for this book is available from the British Library

HARDBACK ISBN: 978–0–241–36172–6
OM PAPERBACK ISBN: 978–0–241–36173–3

www.greenpenguin.co.uk

MIX
Paper from
responsible sources
FSC® C018179

Penguin Random House is committed to a
sustainable future for our business, our readers
and our planet. This book is made from Forest
Stewardship Council® certified paper.

Prologue

'Your one Aisling is absolutely gas, isn't she?'

That's definitely not a local accent. But I know the voice – it's the brunette with the complicated updo sitting two up from me on Titanic – all the tables are named after Denise and Liam's favourite films, you see. Lovely idea, very personal. His cousin, I think she is. There are two of them – down from Dublin and very glamorous altogether. Shellac this, that and the other. Nice and chatty too, and not making beasts of themselves with the bread. The only thing worse than being at a zero craic table is when some brazen shnake takes a second bread roll when they think no one's looking. Well, I'm always looking. Eight Points in a bread roll and worth every single one. But you can't be getting into bread-basket politics with strangers at a wedding. I've no idea why this girl thinks I'm so gas though. We've only had the usual small talk about work and wasn't it great they got the weather. And there was the usual throwing of the fiver into the pint glass for the speeches, of course. You have to be vigilant and make sure everyone contributes or else you get stung with a massive round. It's only fair.

'Is she the one in the red fascinator who was saying she commutes up to Dublin from here for work? Seemed obsessed with the *Rose of Tralee*?'

That sounds like the blonde who was sitting beside John. Kerry, she said her name was. Wearing a lovely long, floaty number. Boho, I think you'd call it? Yes, I am the one in the red fascinator – twenty-five per cent off in Coast and it goes with everything. Three weddings in the last year alone and who knows how many ahead of me? And what's wrong with the *Rose of Tralee* anyway? It's so much more than a beauty pageant and I'd be only delighted to compete for the country. And all I did was mention that we'll never be Roses now, what with everyone getting married off. I'd never have *actually* gone for the Rose of Tralee, but I did feel a pang of regret turning twenty-eight on my last birthday knowing that they'd never have me now. Treble jig while reciting all the verses of 'Pangur Bán', that's what I always said my talent would be, with a removable long skirt revealing a shorter one underneath for the dancing.

'Yeah,' confirms Updo, rifling through her handbag. 'That's her. You're sitting beside her fella – he's a bit of a ride an' all.'

Well, she's got that much right, although she'd want to keep her eyes to herself. John is looking fierce well tonight in fairness, he's filling out his good suit in all the right places, like only a centre forward can. I'm a bit worried now, I shouldn't be earwigging. I'm half afraid of what I might hear if I don't cough or do something to let them know the walls have ears. Plus, I've already been in this cubicle ten minutes. I came in mostly to rest my feet. They're in ribbons and the dancing hasn't even really got going yet. I have a rule about keeping the shoes on until midnight at least and, if you ask me, Denise has missed a trick not having a little basket of flip-flops in here. That won't go unnoticed. I suppose I'll just soldier on in my kitten heels until it's time to fire them under the table, get on the dance floor and rock the boat. I can hear the strains of 'Sweet Caroline' coming through the wall. Things are obviously heating up out there.

Updo and Kerry have fallen silent for the time being. By the sound of bags being unzipped and plastic tubes and things hitting the sinks, they're fixing their faces. I'm willing them to hurry up, although the little rest is grand. I'm trying to count the number of drinks I've had but I keep losing track. I was doing so well too, alternating glasses of water and pinot greej at the dinner like I usually do, but then I got caught in a round and it all fell apart. Best-laid plans. I'll just sit here a little bit longer and wait for them to go. Take a little breather from my control tights before they do some real damage to my internal organs. John is outside in the thick of it anyway, I won't be missed for a while yet.

'I nearly broke my arse laughing when she thought she'd left the immersion on and dived under the table to get her phone,' Updo pipes up again. 'She nearly took the tablecloth with her – Usain Bolt couldn't catch her.'

'Hrrrnngghhh.' I make a cough-like rumbling in my throat. There. Surely they have to have heard that? It was good and loud. No offence intended to them but, sorry, who wouldn't almost have a heart attack at the thought of leaving the immersion on when I won't be home 'til tomorrow? The stress of it would have ruined my whole night. Better to call Daddy and double-check.

'She has me in stitches,' Kerry says. 'Loads of the girls in work are like her. Real sensible types, all from down the country. One of them wears her county jersey every casual Friday and then throws on a pair of earrings for going to the pub afterwards. She's the only one in the whole company trusted with the keys to the stationery cupboard.'

There's a bit of tittering now and I'm not sure why. Sure, a good pair of dangly earrings can jazz up any outfit. I have loads. Earrings, jersey, jeans and a pair of boots with a nice manageable heel. That outfit would take you from a match at Croke Park to Quinn's and even to Coppers afterwards if you're going Out Out. And who doesn't love a night in Coppers – some craic.

I clear my throat again but they're so deep into their contouring or whatever that they still haven't noticed.

'Oh, it's a definite type,' Kerry says. 'My brother has actually just started going out with one of them, a *complete* Aisling. He met her in Flannery's – she's a primary school teacher from Leitrim. Goes home every weekend to play camogie and has a lot of strong opinions about tea.'

I rack my brains. She sounds very familiar; I bet Majella knows her.

'Is she nice?' Updo asks, and I feel myself tense up. How could she not be nice? She's an athlete who works with children. It sounds like she'd give Mother Teresa a run for her money.

'Oh god, yeah, she's lovely,' Kerry says, to my relief. 'He's mad about her. She actually gave me one of those tokens for the supermarket trolley to hang on my keyring. It's dead handy. I don't know how I survived without it for so long.'

Trolley tokens ARE dead handy. I'd be lost without my Superquinn one. Trolley tokens don't grow on trees.

'One of the Aislings in work, I can't think of her real name, confessed the other day that she's been hanging all those passive-aggressive signs in the break room begging people to clean the microwave after heating up their soup,' Updo says. 'She does them in Comic Sans to pretend she's not that put out, but it's obvious she's slowly losing her mind. She also casually mentioned in the bathroom one day that she'd never dyed her hair. Like, ever. Not even as a teenager.'

There's a gasp now and I wonder how long Kerry has been a slave to the peroxide bottle. She probably doesn't even remember her natural colour, God love her. And I'm sure it's lovely. I feel for that poor girl in Updo's work – really, I do. The crowd in my office have no respect for the communal kitchen either. None at all. It's driving me to distraction but sure what can I do only keep replacing the sign above the dishwasher and hope that they'll stop living like animals one of these days?

'She also told me that she's just counting the minutes 'til her fella proposes so she can move back down home.' Updo is up to ninety now. This poor girl's ears must be burning over in Galway or wherever she's from. 'Apparently her da is giving them a plot of land as a wedding present so that she can build a massive gaff with the utility room of her dreams and a driveway the size of the Aviva Stadium.'

'Isn't it well for some?' Kerry says, zipping up her make-up bag, and off they clip-clop back out to the ballroom in their ridiculous heels.

Suddenly I'm alone again. I must admit, that last bit cut a bit close to the bone. The bit about proposing. Why do I drink wine at weddings? It makes me maudlin. Know the one that's one too many, Aisling. A few glasses of water when I get back out there. Be grand. Then I'll move on to the West Coast Coolers to keep myself ticking over. A couple of paracetamol before bed to ward off any hangover. Never fails me. The bathroom is mercifully quiet as I exit the cubicle, feet worse than ever after the bit of a sitdown.

You know, I'd kill for one of those utility rooms with a big worktop and a rail for John's shirts. To be honest, I'm starting to wonder if he's ever going to pop the feckin' question. Daddy has my site ready to go – road frontage, obviously. A good stretch too. When all our friends started getting engaged, I said nothing. When the wedding invites started coming in the post, I said nothing. I know the pregnancy announcements will be kicking off soon and there's still no sign of a ring for me. It's been on my mind for a while now but there's never been a good time to bring it up. Maybe tonight's the night? I probably shouldn't do it when I'm half pissed though . . .

'Aisling! AISLING! Are you in here? Denise is about to throw the bouquet!'

I

My eyelids are sealed shut, but I can tell from the brightness of the room that we've definitely over-slept. My mouth is dry, my head is thumping and I'm parched. None of this is surprising, considering we started drinking at two o'clock yesterday. That's the problem with early weddings – everyone is fluthered by teatime, even if you finish the night on West Coast Coolers like me (although there was that Jägerbomb at the end in the residents' bar . . .). And the dinner took bloody ages to be served – beeforsalmon, naturally. I went for the beef, but it was very tough and the mixed veg was absolute mush. The trio of desserts was faboo though.

When my Big Day finally arrives, whenever that might be, I've already decided I want the ceremony no earlier than three o'clock and we're definitely doing the speeches after the meal, not before. Of course Daddy won't be able to relax and enjoy his beefor-salmon but I couldn't have the girls as pissed as Denise's bridesmaids were yesterday. I caught Eimear Flanagan – I used to babysit her – with a fag in her hand puking in the leylandii hedge at nine o'clock.

Slowly, I open one eye, aware of John's considerable mass in the bed beside me. He's face-down, snoring softly, absolutely out for the count. Of course he would be, having spent a good two hours on his knees, sliding around the dancefloor to AC/DC and Kings of Leon with his tie around his head. Honestly, lads are so juvenile when they get together. If they're not trying to out-do each other buying rounds every fifteen minutes, they're making a show of themselves as soon as the band starts. It's even worse when the lads in question are all from Knocknamanagh Rangers' hurling team because, in fairness to them, they're very fit. They can carry on like that for hours and not even break a sweat. No wonder they're county champions.

Jesus, Denise looked gorgeous. She went very traditional – we're talking ivory A-line dress, beading, lace, floor-length veil and a train, the whole shebang. I wasn't gone on her hair, mind, but that's just because personally I would go for an updo if you're going to do strapless. Not that I would even do strapless, but I think you have to work with the dress and not against it, you know? She was stunning though.

The bridesmaids wore a sort of salmony-pink – again, wouldn't be my first choice, especially for a January wedding, your arms would be like corned beef – but they all looked well. Sinéad McGrath told me she lost nearly two stone on Slimming World in

three months and could eat as much pasta and potatoes as she liked. It just sounds too good to be
true – but she hasn't looked that slim since our Debs
and I must admit I felt a pang of jealousy when I saw
her slinking around the bar. But I'm very loyal to
Weight Watchers and my leader Maura, having been
going on and off for six years. I told Sinéad not to
lose any more – being too skinny ages you in the
face. And lads prefer a bit of meat on the bones –
John is always saying it to me when I'm writing
down the Points in my Curly Wurly (3) while he's
having his Snickers (12). Still, I'm trying to lose just
another few pounds before the summer.

Suddenly the clock on my phone catches my eye
and I sit bolt upright. That can't be right, can it? 10.52,
it beams back at me. I think back to the conversation
I had with the lovely girl on reception who checked
us in yesterday: 'The pool is closed for refurbish-
ment. Breakfast ends at 11 a.m., even on Sunday. It
will be very busy from about ten so come down early.
The sausages won an award.' Luiza, I think it was?
Or Leticia? Something like that. Even though the
Ard Rí Hotel is a good thirty-five-minute drive the
far side of Knocknamanagh, it does benefit from
the town's thriving Brazilian community.

I grab the phone, beads of cold sweat gathering
on the back of my neck. 10.53. Jesus Christ, we're going
to miss the hotel breakfast. It's a continental buffet

as well as hot food *a là carte*, Luisa slash Letitia told me. I can hear her voice now: 'Yes, madam, breakfast is definitely included in the price.' We got the room in a Pigsback deal. Sure it ended up costing less than a taxi to drop John home to Knocknamanagh and then me on to Ballygobbard. John's mammy always has me in the spare room if I stay in their house and I'd rather sleep in my own bed, to be honest. Mammy's boiled eggs are nicer.

'John,' I whisper, my voice shaking. 'I think we're going to miss the hotel breakfast.'

As quick as Clark Kent nipping into a phonebox, twirling and suddenly transforming into Superman, John's out of the bed, stumbling in the half-darkness, rapidly releasing himself from the many surplus sheets knotted around his ankles. I'm shocked at how limber he is. Only six hours ago, he was singing 'Mr Brightside' with his eyes closed in the residents' bar and looking back now I'm fairly certain he was crying. Baby Chief Gittons, the best full back in the country, was on the acoustic guitar. John loves The Killers. Everyone was a bit emotional, myself included.

'It's included in the price, isn't it?' he asks, his voice husky. 'The breakfast?'

'It is,' I say, prying my legs out from under the seventeen blankets and feeling for my jeans.

10.55. I hit the floor, crawling around on my hands

and knees until I locate my good overnight bag –
Orla Kiely, fifty per cent off in the Kilkenny Shop
because there was a stain on one side but I swear to
God you can't see it, even in broad daylight. I grab
my clothes and stumble into the *en suite* – two sinks,
nice touch – where John is simultaneously brushing his teeth, rubbing a cloth across his face and
attempting to hold in a puke. I catch sight of my
reflection – mother of God, I didn't even take off
my make-up last night, that's highly unusual – and
wince. Brown mascara is muddied under my blue-
green eyes and there are traces of Heather Shimmer
still clinging to the corners of my mouth. The layer
of foundation I applied twenty-four hours ago is
long gone and my freckles are well and truly back
out to play. My hair looks like a crow's nest. Róisín
Flood did my usual wedding updo in Scissor Sisters
yesterday, but you pay for it the next morning trying
to find the three hundred clips you know well she
put into it. They'll be finding them in this hotel
room for a week. I've no idea where my dress is – I
got it in TK Maxx, only delighted to get a twelve to
fit me rather than the usual fourteen – but I somehow managed to get into my pyjamas last night. I've
an awful fear my holdy-in knickers are lying around
on the floor somewhere. I know John wouldn't care
but even after all these years together, it's nice to
hold onto some bit of mystery. Scrubbing at my face

with a baby wipe – they're exactly the same as the make-up remover ones, only cheaper – I pray that I won't bump into anyone I know downstairs. They've probably all been and gone, I think. Sure you'd want to be mad to miss a hotel breakfast.

10.59. In a cloud of Lynx Africa (John) and Clinique Happy (me), we slip out of the room and leg it to the lift, which, and this is proof that God exists, is apparently waiting for us. Forty-five seconds later, we walk into the dining room, which, to my horror and disgust, is absolutely heaving.

It's 11.25 a.m. and people are still arriving down to breakfast, heading sheepishly towards the buffet like they have all the time in the world. The staff, apparently used to this kind of carry-on, are still happily taking orders, and towering plates of bacon, sausages, eggs and beans keep being paraded past me as my stomach starts to flip. I'm not feeling great. Of course I had the works – fresh fruit and yoghurt, croissant, made-to-order omelette, *pain au chocolat*, full Irish, about three litres of orange juice in those little thimbles that you get in hotels, although the glasses in the Ard Rí are quite generous – because we'd already paid for it. But it's starting to turn on me. The smoked salmon was probably a bad choice. I catch Sinéad McGrath's eye across the room – she's tucking into a stack of pancakes like someone who's never heard of a Syn – and give her a wave. Her own wedding is less than a year away. She'd want to lob a few Speed foods onto that plate or she'll regret those calories later. No sign of Kerry and Updo.

Beside me, John is horsing into the contents of his second trip to the buffet. He's always happiest when he's eating, and he looks so cute that I can't stop myself reaching out and squeezing his hand affectionately. His dark brown hair is sticking up here and there but he's pulling it off. You can get away with a lot when you're tall and wear a day's worth of stubble as well as he does. His plain white T-shirt is inside out, I've just noticed – the big gom. *And* his hungover eyes are puffy. Cute as anything though. He looks up from his sausage-sandwich as I touch him and raises his eyebrows quizzically.

'Nothing,' I say, coyly. 'I was just thinking – imagine, this could be us in a couple of years.'

He raises his eyebrows even higher.

'Here, in a nice hotel, the day after a wedding,' I clarify, looking at him straight in the eye. 'Except it could be *our* wedding,' I add, glancing across at the door where the bride, clearly a bit worse for wear, is making an entrance wearing a blue and yellow Knocknamanagh Rangers jersey with 'Mrs Kelly' printed on the back above Liam's number, 8. A present from the bridesmaids, Sinéad told me at the bar last night. They gave it to her at the hen. I wasn't there myself, due to being at my great-aunt Breda's ninetieth birthday.

I feel a little sting of jealousy watching everyone crowd around Denise. John and I have actually been going out eight months longer than she and Liam, and they got engaged two years ago. Meanwhile, we're not even living together. It's not that I'm not happy with how things are going – I am; it's just that I always thought they'd be going a bit quicker after being together for seven years. Sure we were at those three weddings last year alone – all Rangers lads – so it's not like we'd be blazing a trail or anything.

'Maybe more than a "couple",' John guffaws, looking back at his sausage, knocking me out of my trance. I hold out my cup for a tea top-up. Barry's, of course.

'What do you mean, more than a couple?' I ask, trying to keep my tone breezy.

'Well, it's not exactly on the horizon for us, is it? I'm twenty-nine and you're only twenty-eight. You'd be a child-bride by today's standards,' he adds with a hollow laugh, spraying toast crumbs onto the white linen tablecloth.

'Denise is twenty-seven,' I reply quietly. 'She didn't do Transition Year. She thought it was only a doss and that it would get her out of the routine of studying – she actually never shut up about it . . .'

I let the words trail off and look down at my plate

full of croissant crumbs so he won't see my eyes fill with tears. I can't cry here, in a room full of girls I went to school with and lads from the hurling team. I'd never live it down. And I don't want to get into a disagreement about potentially getting married in the dining room of the bloody Ard Rí Hotel. I haven't even showered.

'Come on – check out is at half twelve and I want to have a wash before we go. The toiletries are Crabtree & Evelyn, I'm not missing that,' I say, standing up and throwing my napkin on the chair a little harder than I mean to.

At 12.31, we're pulling out of the driveway, the atmosphere between us in the car a little warmer than in the dining room, but there's still a strange tension, hanging around like a ferocious smell.

I arrive home to find Daddy asleep in front of *The Sunday Game*, a fluffy ginger ball curled up on his lap. Technically the cat is Paul's, but since my younger brother's departure for Australia four months ago, Daddy and Tiger have forged a weird sort of bond, borne out of a fondness for the fire and a desire to avoid Mammy's incessant questions. He wakes up as I reach for the remote, even though I haven't made a sound.

'Don't change that, the second half is just after starting,' he grumbles, pushing himself up in the chair and fixing his glasses. 'How did That Bloody Cat get in?'

He shakes a startled Tiger onto the floor and she stalks out, glaring at me like it's my fault – which, technically, it is.

'The match is in extra time with less than a minute to go,' I point out, nodding at the telly. 'You were out for the count. And isn't it funny how That Bloody Cat is always sneaking in when me and Mammy are out? She must have a key.'

He pretends not to have heard me. The lambs are coming early this year and he was probably up half the night. He should be in bed, not sleeping awkwardly in an armchair. He's getting a bit old now for that carry-on and he's just not able for it any more. The tufts of hair around his temples and ears have greyed an awful lot and his skin, usually permatanned from a life spent outdoors, is a bit waxy and pale. Mammy will go through him for carrying in half a bale of hay on his brown Work Trousers and bobbly old Work Jumper. (All of his Work Jumpers start life as Good Christmas Jumpers, becoming Work Jumpers after they've served sufficient years at the top, in a kind of comforting cycle of clothes.)

'How was the wedding? Mammy said Denise was a stunner. And the Knock lads did a guard of honour at the church for Liam? They stole that idea from us, you know,' he tuts.

There's nothing Daddy loves more than bringing up the 'legendary' (his words) rivalry between Ballygobbard, where we're from, and Knocknamanagh, our nearest town, six miles away via winding backroads. On the face of it, they're both sleepy little villages, nearly identical to the untrained eye. We have the Scouts' den. But they've got the library. We were very excited to get a Chinese takeaway in 2001 but were upstaged just a short while later when a gang of Brazilians moved to Knocknamanagh and opened a nursing home.

You get the picture. They both have one main street and plenty of pubs. The hurling teams play each other in almost every county final, with the competition frequently spilling off the pitch and into everyday life. As a result, Daddy sees myself and John as a sort of modern-day Romeo and Juliet but with fewer suicides and more GAA dinner-dances. Back in Daddy's day, the Knocknamanagh gang started referring to Ballygobbard as Ballygobackwards and then BGB, which has sort of stuck with everyone, even us BGB residents. Knocknamagh gets away much more lightly as abbreviations go, with everyone simply going for 'Knock' – although they do get a bit of stick about often 'needing a miracle', like their more famous namesake with the airport and the visions of the Virgin Mary.

'Oh Daddy, will you give it a rest? I'm in bits here.'

'Right so. Did you have the beef? Was it a late one? I'll put the kettle on.'

'Yes and yes,' I say, kicking off my shoes and grabbing a cushion. 'Will you bring in some biscuits? She has loads of leftover Christmas ones hidden around the place.'

'Are there biscuits hidden somewhere? I wouldn't even know where to look – that's your mother's domain,' he says, heading for the kitchen to first check the USA biscuit tin that we were convinced was a sewing kit. Turns out Mammy had been using it as a kind of double-bluff in her quest to keep anything 'good' away from us. A groan of defeat means she knows we're on to her. She's so great at hiding treats that I found a packet of Viscounts from 2012 in the food processor two weeks ago. Joke's on her because we ate them anyway.

I flick through the channels. There's nothing on, as usual, so I check to see if there are any episodes of *Home and Away* recorded to catch up on. Bingo, there are – so I flick one on and settle back.

'Ah, Aisling, I've already seen this one,' Daddy says, arriving in with a tray laden down with impressive Christmas Biscuits. 'They were in with the cat food. Slide over the coffee table with your foot there. Now, don't actually move – God forbid you might expend a bit of energy.'

'Ha ha,' I say, reaching for an iced ring (4 Points, but

to hell with it after the breakfast I just had) as he fills my favourite mug, a present from Majella the year I went to the Gaeltacht in remote Donegal to brush up on my Irish verbs, and she was grounded. It's a Forever Friends one. We were mad into Forever Friends.

For a dyed-in-the-wool farmer, Daddy is low-key obsessed with soaps, especially the Australian ones. I think part of him longs for a bit of escapism. He doesn't get much glamour moving sheep and cattle around all day.

'You're very quiet, Ais,' he says, eyes firmly on the telly. 'Was there a fly in your cornflakes?'

As if anyone in their right mind would have cornflakes at a hotel breakfast buffet.

'John's driving me mad.' The words fall out of my mouth accidentally. 'He was a bit of a dose this morning.'

'Hanging, was he? Knock lads are dreadful for holding their drink, I've told you that plenty of times.'

'That, and he sort of said that ourselves getting married any time in the near-future was a bit of a far-fetched idea.'

Daddy puts down his cup and reaches for a pink wafer. 'Far-fetched? After going out for seven years? Sure, Denise and Liam got engaged two years ago and they met well after you two.'

'I know, that's what I said,' I half-shout.

'Do you want me to have a word? He's seen the rifle,' Daddy smiles, and I know there's about two per cent truth in it.

'Jesus, Daddy, that's all I need – a literal shotgun wedding.'

At least it would be a wedding though.

2

Getting out of the bed and into the car in time to make it to the office in Dublin by 9 a.m. every morning is a struggle after the excesses of the wedding and with the January cold snap slowing everything down. Daddy's been up at the crack of dawn most mornings, pouring warm water on my windscreen to ward off the bit of overnight frost.

When I arrive into work on Friday morning, I'm fully ready for the weekend. It's sixty-five minutes door-to-door from BGB to PensionsPlus in Ballsbridge, if the traffic is with you. My ears are glued to AA RoadWatch every morning. The office itself is nothing to write home about, but we get to control the heat and there's free tea and biscuits, so I can't complain. I love the buzz of working in town and it's dead handy for getting a few bits on my lunch break. We're blessed with a city-centre car park under the office and they're very fair in giving preference to people with the longer commutes. I've laminated a sign for my space, just in case.

At the moment, I'm up to my eyes in client scheme

files – no rest for the wicked in pensions adminis-
tration. I've a load to get through this morning, and
have the PC fired up by 8.59 a.m., ready to fly through
them. I think I'll be having my mid-morning cup of
tea a bit earlier than usual – more like a very-start-
of-the-morning cup of tea. I have two Café Noir
siphoned off from Mammy's stash under the tea
towels in the hot press that I've been thinking about
since I left BGB. I almost ate them in the car with a
fierce hunger on me (I only had one Weetabix this
morning), but sure I knew I'd only end up having
more biscuits with my tea and there's all my Points
for the day nearly gone, so I resisted. I nearly collapsed when I found out last week I was miscalculating
the Points in a purple Snack and I've been trying to
be Very Good ever since.

I've one eye on my phone, waiting for Majella
to make contact. I suspect that she ended up in
McGowan's last night with her housemates. I just
know she won't have resisted the lure of Thursday-
night pints, even with a class of twenty-nine to face
first thing this morning. She swore blind to me that
she was only going out, not Out Out. It's an important distinction. Out is a couple of pints of Coors
Light in The Big Tree or The Foggy Dew, last bus
home, maybe a bag of chips if the hunger is at you.
Out Out is roaring along to 'Jump Around' at 1 a.m.,
spilling vodka and Diet Coke down your work shirt.

Majella loves going Out Out. Even better, she loves codding people into going Out Out. It's not even that she's as mad for mickey as her reputation might suggest ('Majella Moran's Mad For Mickey' has been scrawled along the wall in Ballygobbard handball alley since Fifth Year. To this day, I think it was Angela Clohessy, absolutely sickened when Tadgh Carolan lobbed the gob on Majella in the Vortex, our local nightclub). No, Maj just loves a session. Every person still on that dancefloor at 2 a.m. bellowing 'almost heaven, West Virginia' is a little victory for her. 'Sure you're out now,' she cajoles. 'You might as well leather it home.'

So even though she was swearing blind on the phone to me yesterday afternoon that 'Ah no, Ais, we're only going out for a few after work. Not Out Out. Sure we've work in the morning', I'd be nearly disappointed if she wasn't face-down in garlic-and-cheese chips at 4 a.m. I just hope she made it to work on time.

By 9.43 a.m., I've waited long enough for my Café Noir, so I push myself away from the desk to put the kettle on. I may add a few exclamation marks to the sign I've put above the dishwasher asking people to put their mugs into it while I'm at it. The company is spread over three floors, but the main kitchen is on the middle floor – my floor – so we've to put up with all the filth. By Friday, the sink is always overflowing with cups and all the spoons have mysteriously disappeared. On my way to the kitchen, I note the three mugs making maggots on Donna's desk beside mine. There all week, I'd say. What did her last slave di . . . Oh? Unknown number? Who's this now?

'Ais. I'm *dying*.'

It's Majella. She's lost the phone again. She's already done two pukes in the tiny school toilet, but thank God, Tracey went and bought a bag of hangover cures in Spar and she's managed to keep down the sausage roll and a packet of Burger Bites she had in the staffroom.

'I've the fear of *God* in me. I think I told the vice-principal Seán Delahunt that I fancy him and I don't fancy him at all. He smells like old towels.'

'Where did you lose the phone, Maj?' I ask, flicking on the kettle, rattling mugs in the press. Here's two not even washed. I swear half the people in this office would sooner butter toast with a stapler than have to clean a thing up after themselves. I have my suspicions someone's been throwing forks in the bin rather than washing them – only three forks left in the whole kitchen. I'll have to go get more.

'Flannery's, I think. Or the taxi. I tried ringing it but it's off. Sure look, it's only a phone.'

I'm not exactly annoyed that Majella's lost another

phone. But I'm not *not* annoyed either. She's my best friend and has been my best friend since we both got mountain bikes for Christmas when we were ten and cycled the high roads and byroads of BGB, avoiding its resident badgers. Apparently they'll take the leg off you if you're not careful. Everyone knows Cowsy Cullen puts sticks in his wellies to act as decoys if a badger goes for his ankles. He says if they hear the sticks break, they'll think they've shattered your bones and leave you be. Now, Cowsy Cullen is not all there, God love him, but I'd rather put a stick in my welly than lose a leg to a badger. Wouldn't you be mortified?

We used to always be begging Mammy for picnics to take with us on the bikes. We'd have her heartbroken looking for digestives sandwiched together with butter and jam on crackers in lunch boxes. One time she produced two bottles of Orangina and I swear I still remember it like it was yesterday. Orangina was mad dear – dearer than Cornettos. Clíona Sutton had it every day on holidays in France when she was eleven and God forbid she might let you forget it. The Suttons had one of those trailers that turned into a tent and they went abroad with it every summer. Well, we went to the Killarney Ryan Hotel once and it had a pool, so shove it up your hole, Clíona, to be quite honest.

Mammy says that Majella 'marches to the beat of her own drum', which is her diplomatic way of saying she wishes Majella would calm down a bit and stop acting the clod. She loves Majella obviously, but she's fond of the odd 'I hope she gets the weather she's expecting' dig at Maj's rig-outs. She's also convinced it was Majella who started the Sun-In craze when we were in Transition Year and was sure I was going to be lured to the dark side and end up turning my ash-blond hair a sickly orange. But sure I would have been mad to give up my lovely natural colour. A hair-dresser once called it 'brown' and Mammy nearly went through her, schooling her on 'natural high-lights' and telling her how golden it goes in the sun.

My hair has stayed the same shade since day one, while Majella's has been every colour of the rain-bow. She's currently trying to achieve the perfect hue of purpley-red and regularly shows up with any-thing ranging from burgundy to ginger, scalp and all. Over Christmas, she accidentally managed to dye it almost exactly the same colour as her annual festive jumper from Penneys: a deep pillar-box red. She didn't give a shite. This year's jumper was 'Jingle My Bells'. Not a patch on last year's 'Prosecco-Ho-Ho-Ho', if you ask me.

'Jesus, Maj, you're some hames. That's the third phone in six months.'

I try to keep the note of passive-aggressive

annoyance out of my voice, but I can't help sounding a tiny bit harsh. There's something about Majella's hamesiness that I . . . envy? She's always had a bit of that don't-care attitude about her and it's definitely made her more glowy, like a back-door light that the moths can't stay away from, hopping themselves off it like dopes. She's been single for two years now, but it's definitely not because she can't get a boyfriend. You should see her in Flannery's on a Thursday night – beating the lads away with a stick.

'I'll get a sim card at lunchtime and sure someone always has some old brick hanging around. Be grand. C'mere, are you driving home this evening? Will you pick me up at the Red Cow?'

I often give Majella and sometimes John a lift down home on a Friday. During the week, Majella lives in Phibsboro but she works only half an hour away in Inchicore, so it's handy for her to hop on the Luas to meet me. Although with the number of trams coming and going, AND the traffic, it's a bit of a nightmare. John's place is in Drumcondra and he works on the northside, but he sometimes comes out to Ballsbridge for the lift. I used to live in town too until Daddy took a turn in the calving shed two years ago. I still haven't managed to move back up. 'I'm grand,' he insisted. But he wasn't. 'I'm grand,' he insists now, when I catch him sleeping through his beloved matches. I watch him like a hawk. On Fridays, I work my lunch so I can leave a bit early and get out of town to miss some of the traffic. That N7 would have your heart broken.

Majella retches again.

'Go on. I'll pick you up at half four. Take two Panadol and drink loads of water.'

The girls in here are always horsing all kinds of tablets into themselves. Nurofen this and Solpadeine that. Next thing, they'll be addicted and their mams will be crying to Joe Duffy on Radio One, saying they never saw it coming. Trying to cod Solpadeine out of a chemist isn't worth the hassle anyway. They act like you're trying to make off with the Shroud of Turin: 'Have you tried anything else? Have you taken it before? Do you know the rules of a five-decade rosary?' It's easier to get onto the Hill on All-Ireland Final Day. I always have a heap of Panadol in my drawer for doling out. Nurse Ais to the rescue.

The kettle finally boils and in swings Donna. A tut escapes from my gob before I can stop it. She's two days back from her honeymoon and I swear she has the phone set up to make as many bells and whistles as possible any time someone likes one of her seemingly infinite wedding photos on Facebook. She got your one who did Brian and Pippa's photos to do them. You know it would only be the best for Ireland's most glamorous celebrity couple. Donna and Martin are no more Brian and Pippa than my foot. She planned the whole wedding sitting right there beside me in the office. She had spreadsheets going all right, but they certainly weren't the type of spreadsheets the rest of us were working on. And no sooner is she back from the honeymoon than she's off planning a hen party for her cousin Suzanne. I heard her on the phone the other day organising a cocktail class and describing the *Fifty Shades* theme to the poor craythur on the other end. I mean, a hen isn't a hen without willy straws and L-plates, but I've read all three books out of pure interest and I wouldn't want Donna draping anal beads around *my* neck.

Ding. There goes Auntie Mary saying 'u look great donna + martin', under a picture of Donna and Martin looking wistfully at a man-made lake while their guests drink too much prosecco on empty stomachs, wondering what time the dinner's at.

Bing. There's Cousin Gráinne bleating 'you and hubby luk fab Dons. tanks for a fab day', under a scene of Donna and Martin cutting the cake – one chocolate-biscuit layer, one fruit-cake layer (because Donna's granny baked it and you can't have a wedding cake without fruit in it – we're not Protestants or animals). There are seventeen near-identical photos of the cake-cutting. Gráinne has liked every single one of them.

Ding. Bing. Buzz. Clang. Donna's phone's about to take off as she rips open a new packet of ginger-nuts, even though there's one already open on the table. Chuckling away at it like a goon, she fires her spoon

into the sink. The *sink*. And I know she's the one opening new milks when there are milks already open.

'Tea, is it, girls?'

Barry, our new team leader, arrives into the
kitchen. He's alarmingly tall – at least 6'2" – with
thick, dark hair and a good, tall forehead, which is
supposed to be a sign of intelligence. He was actually
one of those big quiet husbands you've seen on *Room
to Improve* – one of the ones with the stylish wives
and the mothers-in-law who just want a granny flat
and a bit of mass and have the heart crossways in
them about all the windows starchitect Dermot
Bannon is trying to put in. In his episode, Barry was
there in the background, silently agreeing to more
credit-union loans and those dear cushions from
Arnotts. The house was lovely when they finished,
to be fair, with the exposed concrete (although
would they not put a bit of emulsion on it?) and the
reclaimed utility poles, but Donna says the marriage
is in tatters after it. She whispers the word 'tatters',
for extra emphasis. She said she heard Barry might
be moving out on account of his wife having an
affair with one of the cameramen . . . if he can ever
find his suitcase in one of the many hidden – sorry,
'recessed' – wardrobes.

'The kettle's boiled there, Barry – plenty in it,' I say.

I'm just about to head back to my desk when the
glamorous Sadhbh from HR on the second floor

sails into the kitchen, nearly taking the tea out of my hand as we collide by the bin. Sadhbh. I'd say she has a harder time than me on holidays trying to tell people how to pronounce it although Sadhbh rhymes with hive and nothing rhymes with Aisling.

'Oh Jesus, sorry, Sadhbh, I'm an awful clown.'

Balls, there's tea on her top . . . if you could call it a top. It's one of those shapeless auld bin-bags from that place Cos, where everything is a different shade of off-white and looks a bit like a bib you'd wear in playschool. I went in there once by accident, looking for a new navy cardigan, and couldn't make head nor tail of it. Sadhbh's managing to pull off her bin-bag though. She looks nonplussed as she dabs at the tea with a bit of tissue.

'Oh, no worries at all,' she breezes. 'I was going too fast anyway – just wanted to see if there's any almond milk down here. I usually keep some at my desk but it's all gone.'

'None in here,' Donna bellows, her head inside the fridge. 'We've gingernuts though!'

'Ah no, you're grand,' Sadhbh politely declines. 'I'd go absolutely berserk if I ate all that sugar in one go – you know yourself.'

Imagine having the will power to not eat sugar. I was practically raised on gingernuts. Maybe Sadhbh was raised in one of those yurts? She's exotic enough with her beige clothes and her seemingly constant trips to places I've never heard of. And she seems lovely. Off back out she sails, in search of the elusive almond milk, her sack billowing behind her and what looks like a necklace made of . . . could it be? . . . spanners clinking gracefully around her neck.

The rest of the afternoon plods along handy enough. I eat my lunch at my desk, so I can head off that bit early. A bit of leftover ham and some Ryvita – 11 Points. Müller Light for dessert – 5 Points. I've left the car at the other end of the car park to get in a bit of a power-walk and I've the Skechers in a dead handy Brown Thomas's bag ready to go – I got it when I popped in before Christmas to get some Clinique for Mammy. Sure you'd nearly pay for the bag itself, it's so nice.

Before I head off for the weekend, I check my phone and cop a text from Mammy. We got her a smartphone for Christmas and she doesn't trust doing a thing on it if she's not connected to the wifi: 'Will that use up my texts now?', 'Does it cost me to text you that picture?', 'What am I after doing here now?' So for safety's sake, she does all her mobile business from inside the house, pressed up against the modem. She also didn't trust the girl in the phone shop when she told her that all of her contacts would magically appear on the new phone without her having to do anything, so she spent a whole evening copying them into her Important Notebook – Brigid Home, Brigid Mobile, Geraldine (Dead Husband), Daddy, Daddy (old), etc. Anyway, she's texting to say she has chops for dinner and Daddy was out with Paddy Reilly earlier looking at trailers, which is good.

Four o'clock and I'm out the door. Flat-out to the Red Cow to get Majella at the Luas and hit the road for BGB. John's having pints with the tag-rugby lads in work and will get the Timoney's bus down home later. It doesn't always go through Knock but Derek Timoney will make the journey if he recognises you from the team. Great lift for the parish and all that. I swing into the Luas car park and it doesn't take long to spot Majella hunched over on a bench.

'Oh Jesus,' she pants, lowering herself gingerly into the passenger seat. 'Drive before I puke again.'

3

Majella manages to hold in the pukes on the journey home, bolstered by a bottle of Lucozade Sport and intermittently sticking her head out the window to gasp in some fresh air.

'So how was Denise and Liam's wedding in the end? Any gossip? You've said very little about it. Did you get a good feed?'

Majella knows Liam and Denise well enough but seeing as she's not a Knock Rangers WAG, she was only invited to the afters, and she had another wedding anyway – one of the Mary Immaculate lot.

'Oh, it was grand. You know that Knock gang, mad for road. Actually, there was a bit of drama in the church when Liam's mam was way quicker than Denise's bringing up the gifts and Liam's mam was bulling that she was up there for ages waiting on her own with everyone looking at her. It was her own fault for flying up the aisle though. And Francie McMenamin was so ossified by midnight that he sat down and took a whole table of pints down with him. All over the girlfriend's Michael Kors bag.'

'Jesus,' Majella whistled through her teeth. 'I'd say there was war.'

'The dinner was grand and then there was a – wait till you hear this – a crisp sandwich buffet at half eleven. All laid out in baskets with Brennan's bread and everything. No expense spared.'

'Crisp sandwich buffet! I knew that Denise one had notions. Whatever happened to a few goujons and cocktail sausages?'

'I know. There were bags of Tayto everywhere. Good craic though. We were dying the next day – nearly missed the breakfast.'

'Mother of God!' Majella is stopped in her tracks. 'And the Ard Rí does a lovely breakfast – buffet *and* a menu, pancakes on the go and it nowhere near Lent, bigger than average orange-juice glasses. You made it down in time?'

'We did – there were a good few stragglers so we were grand. I . . . I was a bit pissed off though, Maj, to tell you the truth.'

'Oh? Why? Shite rashers?'

'No, John was being a bit of a gom about the wedding, and weddings in general. Basically saying we were nowhere near getting married and laughing at the very idea of it. I thought we were on the same page but I suppose I was wrong. To be honest, it ruined my whole breakfast, and you know how much I had been looking forward to it.'

'Ah, what was he at that for? The shitehawk!'

Majella and John get on like a house on fire, and sure they've known each other for as long as I've known John, so she's allowed to call him names when the time is right.

'I know.'

I almost tell her about overhearing those girls in the toilet but I don't really know how to explain it.

'Ah, hello! Good girl. I've the chops on. Have you any white washing?' Mammy is hot out the gates with the questions the minute I'm in the door. Like me, she's pear-shaped and sturdy of stature, and there's not a grey hair on her head. It's surprising, considering everything she puts up with. 'I'm putting on a white wash and I don't want you whinging to me that you've no pants next week after me asking you.'

'OK, Mammy, give me a second. Sure I can do my own washing – I'm twenty-eight!'

'I'm just saying, you might as well put them out when I'm doing a wash anyway because Evelyn Cusack said there'd be impressive drying tomorrow.'

'Mammy!' I roar, a little too loudly. Between the chat about John in the car and being treated like a teenager, I can feel the hot rebellious tears threatening to spill down my cheeks any second and it's only a matter of time before she starts laying into me about 'all the glasses' on my bedside locker (there are never more than two). 'I'll get them in a minute.'

'Will ye two cut it out!' Daddy shuffles in, slippers already on. 'She's only in the door, Marian. She'll do it. Give me those spuds and I'll mash them. Off out this evening, Ais?'

'No, Daddy, I'm in tonight. Out tomorrow night though, to the Vortex for Maeve Hennessey's birthday.'

We're getting a bit old now to be having nights out for every birthday in the gang, but Maeve's happens to fall on a Saturday so we might as well make the most of it. We didn't know her that well in school, but she's another Knock Rangers WAG, like me, and she's actually lovely, despite the rumour that dogged her for years – that she stole Carmel Kinsella's new fleece in Sixth Year. Carmel Kinsella will be out tonight as well, so whatever happened, they must have buried the hatchet.

I give Daddy a little smile. 'Will you give me a lift?'

'Oho, taxi driver to the rescue again, eh?' Daddy loves the 'taxi driver' joke so much that he didn't even mind when I got him the same 'Dad's Taxi' sticker for his car three Christmases in a row. He has two of them now in the window of the Mégane.

Mammy has slightly less time for the joking. 'Thelordsaveus, will you take off those clodhopper shoes when you come in tomorrow night, Aisling, and don't be waking us up with your crashing around? And put away those sheets I took out of the dryer, will you? Put them in right, now – I don't want them falling down and braining me in an avalanche every time I open the hot press.'

She's in an awful mood. What's going on at all at all?

'We had Paul on the Skype there a while ago,' Daddy mutters.

Oh, this could explain things.

'He has the passport lost again.'

This definitely explains things. Mammy (and Daddy, to be fair) still haven't recovered from not having Paul home for Christmas. Mammy's heart was broken looking at pictures of him on the beach at County Coogee with about 200 other Irish expats on Christmas Day: 'In that heat. He'll be scalded. And not a roast potato between them.' He said they even got mass. Sure there are so many of them out there he might as well have been at home.

He looked like he was having a ball, in fairness, the lot of them in their county jerseys, faces puce as boiled ham on the beach, eating the Tayto and Twirls Mammy has been sending over in regular batches. She sent her reading glasses in one of the care packages by accident, gathering them up with the teabags and the bourbon creams. Everyone was blamed for hiding them on her, even That Bloody Cat, until they showed up in

Sydney. Daddy laughed so hard he had to sit down (he sat on the cat – another injustice).

This is Paul's second lost passport, and almost certainly the reason for Mammy's fouler. 'Maybe I should go over to him,' she fretted the first time he called with the news. We talked her down that time and of course the passport showed up in some other loo-la's shorts pocket. Sure they're all living on top of each other over there. Things are bound to get mixed up.

'It'll turn up, Mammy – it has to be there somewhere,' I offer.

He doesn't seem too worried about it anyway. He changed his job on Facebook this morning to 'Works at: being a full-time mad bastard' and was tagged in twenty-four pictures today in an album called 'de craic lads'. Someone he knows has already been on *Bondi Rescue* for trying to surf on an ironing board. But I'll rinse him for worrying Mammy and Daddy like this. He's planning on doing some kind of road-trip across the country in a van with about seventeen other lads to go fruit-picking before heading back to wherever it is they film *Home and Away* to get a selfie with Alf Stewart.

'Two days they'll be driving.' Mammy is incredulous about the distance. 'There's no need for Australia to be that size in this day and age.'

Mammy has the chops on the table and Daddy has the potatoes mashed and the cat heftily nudged out the back door with a slippered foot. They're quite the pair, Mammy and Daddy. Fond of their walks up to the top of Reilly's Lane and back down again (although Paddy Reilly is in dispute with Terry Crowley over a right of way, so calling it Reilly's Lane could be dangerous in the political landscape of BGB these days). Fond of *Winning Streak* and Phil Collins and Big Tom and the Mainliners and knowing the difference between hips and haws and the fluctuations on petrol prices for the next four towns over. Best pals. Not without their rows, but best pals. Daddy often acts as a buffer between me and Mammy, especially now that Paul's not here to bounce off too.

'Don't fight with your mother, like a good girl,' he sometimes says to me.

'But . . .' I start.

'I know. But just don't fight with her. Because then she fights with me.'

And that's fair enough.

When I wake up the next morning, Mammy is already gone off to do her few hours in Tessie Daly's charity shop. She retired early from nursing (Mammy, not Tessie) to help around the farm but even then, she couldn't reconcile herself to spending so much time alone, so she volunteers in the shop and, of course, she's involved in the local Tidy Towns chapter. Ballygobbard has been 'commended' in the large village category the last three years and Mammy swears it's down to her commitment to hanging baskets.

She loved nursing and she was good at it too, sharp as a tack. But she seems happy enough with Tessie and the other women in the shop a few mornings a week, each of them trying to out-boss each other. I'd say they've hardly bought one cow or built one well in Africa in the past five years because nobody ever buys anything, but sure they keep ticking over all the same.

I've to spin down the town to get a card for Maeve's birthday. I've no present for her but there's been a kind of unofficial acceptance that it's madness at this stage to be buying presents for every birthday. I get Majella something every year, of course, and when the thirtieths start rolling around, we'll have to make more of an effort. But for the moment, the gang make do with cards and a few drinks. Except Sharon Conratty – she always makes a show of us, producing something wrapped from her bag, like a nice candle or a tasteful notebook. She's away in Lanzarote though so no fear of that tonight. The selection of cards in Filan's is minimal and I have my choice made in no time, so I knock into the charity shop, happening upon Dolores Reilly mid-rant.

'She *waltzes* up to me in Aldi and snares me putting the Swiss roll into the trolley.' The Aldi is Knocknamanagh's biggest claim to fame over Ballygobbard. It was the talk of the town for months after it opened. Daddy is now the proud owner of two leaf-blowers, a ski-suit and four plastic faux-oak barrels 'for the garden'. They're still in the shed.

I know immediately who they're talking about: Constance Swinford, the very height of Ballygobbard notions. She lives at Garbally Stud Farm and is rumoured to have once dated George from *Glenroe*. Or else she was once in *Glenroe* – one or the other.

'Starts congratulating me for "keeping the Christmas spirit going" and "not giving in to the healthy-eating pressures of the new year". You could barely *see* her for all the kale and what do you call those things . . . butternut turnips in her basket.'

Mammy and Dolores have a fair few queer vegetables they wouldn't trust now. Aubergines ('awful slimy'), asparagus ('sure they're just twigs') and especially sweet potatoes ('since when are potatoes sweet?').

'Just because she lives on horse nuts and air, it doesn't mean we all have to.' Dolores finally pauses for breath and turns to me. 'Well, Aisling, any news? How's John?'

'He's grand now, Dolores. We're off out tonight to the Vortex for Maeve Hennessey's birthday. Should be a bit of craic.'

Leaving the charity shop, I say a silent thanks that Dolores didn't drop her usual 'when are you giving us a day out?' and 'give me a look at that hand – any new additions?' spiel. I might not have been able for it today. John's complacency has been weighing heavily on me. I could nearly be moving back out of home now. Daddy has been doing well for ages and me and Mammy are going to go for each other if we have to live under the same roof for much longer. But there's no mention of us even moving in together, never mind getting married. I've never even thought of a life without John, of having to go back to square one and start all over again and waste all those years together.

I start to well up at the thought of it. Without my small hand in his big soft one. Without his proud face when I beat everyone in the room at Trivial Pursuit. Without our complete inability to stop laughing when either of us so much as mentions the time Leslie Cahill went on *Winning Streak* and fell backwards off the chair he was so star-struck. Without . . . Aisling and John.

The Vortex is situated fairly bang-on halfway between Knock and BGB. It's tacked onto the side of the Mountrath Hotel, although why anyone would ever stay in a hotel halfway between Knock and BGB is beyond me. Tourists being tricked into thinking they're staying in a countryside retreat 'within driving distance of Dublin', maybe? They get some land when they arrive at the Mountrath, I'd say. Every room is still holding onto carpets the seventies would only dream of. Itchy blankets and radiators pumping out heat summer and winter. Soup never deviating beyond vegetable or maybe leek and potato the very odd time. It was the scene of our infamous Presentation Girls' Debs of 2007, when Sandra Molloy and Cormac Culleton locked themselves in a toilet cubicle and Sister Anne had to take a mop over the wall to shoo them out. The scandal. It's *still* talked about. Sister Anne threatened Sandra Molloy with detention, even though she was already finished school. Sister Anne would somehow make you do it too. Terrifying.

The Vortex carries much the same decor as the hotel. The carpets are stickier, of course, and if the walls could talk, they'd tell the tale of many a local romance that began within its hallowed space, of girls doing laps of the dancefloor and lads sinking pints too fast.

We get in nice and early, thanks to the lift from Daddy, although Sinéad McGrath and Deirdre Ruane are there before us with a table nabbed. Maeve arrives shortly afterwards. She's overdone it a bit on the fake-tan, if you ask me, but it's her big night so I turn a blind eye. One birthday tradition we haven't done away with is the ceremonial drinking of the sambucas. Majella and Sinéad have made a trip each to the bar already, making a big show of carrying the tray back and landing it in front of Maeve, ordering her to 'knock it back' and joining in. I could do without sambuca, to tell you the truth, but it's the lesser of two evils. I overdid it on the tequilas on my twenty-second birthday and haven't been able to even think about them since.

I'm wondering is it time for another sambuca round when John and the lads arrive, pushing through people to reach us. He looks well. He's wearing the Knocknamanagh Out Out uniform of bootcut jeans, a good shirt ironed to within an inch of its life and brown shoes (piss-catchers, Majella calls them) better than most of his gang. He turns the odd head.

'There's the girls,' he calls, swinging into the seat beside me, slinging his arm around my shoulder and turning his brown eyes towards me.

'Well, lads?' Majella counters. 'Nice of you to join us.'

They'd been having a few drinks in Knock, no doubt. John's playful touching of my shoulders tells me that. There's no way he'd be at that in front of everyone without four pints inside him.

I wriggle out from under his arm and say 'bar?', looking from John to Majella. I've decided against the third round of sambucas. I'm not buying them for all the lads too – I'm not made of money!

'Will you get me a pint, love?' John smiles.

'Just a vodka, please, Ais,' calls Majella. 'I've enough Coke here for another one.'

Elbowing my way to the bar, I still struggle to get any closer than two people deep. Sure they'll get to me eventually. Casting my eye back towards where the gang are sitting, I spy Majella and John deep in conversation. Well, she's talking *at* him. What is she at?

My attention is turned back to the bar when some blow-in causes a scene trying to order a margarita. Jocksy Connolly behind the bar is looking fierce lost with a salt-shaker from the hotel dining room in his hand and your one telling him it goes *on* the glass. They did try to do a cocktail menu in the Vortex about six months ago but they ran out of orange juice after about twenty minutes and the wait-time at the bar became so immense that they had to scrap it.

Eventually, I push my way through to the front and shout out the order. Jocksy looks relieved that it's just a pint, two vodkas and a Diet Coke. No messing with salt and bits of weeds. *'Diet* Coke,' I roar at him, just to be sure. All those Points in a fat Coke. Madness.

'Ais!' Majella hisses to me as I arrive back at the table with the drinks. 'Come and do a lap with me.'

'Back in a minute,' I call to John as she drags me away.

'He's mad about you,' she says confidently.

'Ah, Maj, what are you after saying to him? We're not teenagers. I don't need you finding out if he wants to shift me.'

'No, but you were upset, so I asked him what his plans are. Don't worry. I didn't tell him what you told me.'

'Aaaand?' I look at her impatiently.

'He said he can't imagine life without you. He was actually worried that you wanted to finish things with him after the row, in fact.'

Despite my annoyance at her interfering, a warm feeling rushes over me. I know he's three sheets to the wind but the ball of anxiety I've been carrying around for the last while begins to unwind. Of course John is mad about me. Sure look at him there, in the middle of the gang. Good old John. He wouldn't be the best at talking about his feelings, but he's proven plenty of times over the last seven years that he's serious about me, about us. It's not even the big stuff, although he did take the hint and buy me the Michael Kors handbag I wanted last Christmas. No, there are plenty of little things too, like when I'd just started working at PensionsPlus and Valentine's Day fell on a Saturday and he had flowers, a nice big bouquet, delivered on the Friday. Or every time he likes and shares a competition on Facebook because I've liked and shared it. That doubles my chances of winning. And I'll never forget how he was there for me the time Daddy wasn't well. And did I mention that he's a fine thing? Because he is, shoulders and arms to beat the band. He's a keeper all right.

4

I stay in John's house most Tuesdays and Thursdays, and on the Tuesday after Maeve's birthday it's nearly seven o'clock by the time I get there, even though I left Ballsbridge at half five on the dot. I'd be quicker driving down home. I force myself to go over twice a week but I hate this bloody commute and all the sitting in bumper-to-bumper cross-city traffic it involves, even if I do have Ed Sheeran to keep me company. But if I didn't do it, we'd never have any time *alone* together. I'm a woman, I have needs – so off I go.

I pull on to John's street and of course there are no spaces. Why would there be? The people who actually live here have taken them all, and I can't argue with that. I drive around the block, my eyes on stalks for any little scrap of kerb to wedge my trusty Micra into. No luck. I go round again and say a prayer to Saint Anthony. Of course I haven't technically lost anything – I didn't have a space to begin with – but it can't hurt. Bingo! Like magic, I spot someone leaving a space about three doors down from No. 57 and make a beeline for it, studiously averting my gaze when I see the driver eyeballing the county colours I have hanging from my rear-view mirror with open disgust and mouthing something at me. It's dog-eat-dog here in Dublin 9, but it's a stone's throw from Croke Park so I know John will never move, even if his rent doubles. He gets too much mileage telling the lads at home they can stay on his floor for the All-Ireland, because hotels triple in price on match day, and everyone gets to go on a session in Quinn's afterwards.

I walk up to the door and knock, my usual overnight bag over my shoulder. I leave some underwear and a toothbrush in John's bedside locker but that's the extent of my footprint in No. 57. I feel like half the time I live out of a bag.

'It's open, Aisling,' shouts Piotr, before I can get a word out. Are they mad, leaving the door on the latch in Dublin? It's like they're trying to get robbed.

'How did you know it was me?' I retort. 'I could have been a cat burglar, here to take all your worldly goods and Polish vodka.'

'You knock on the door every Tuesday and Thursday at seven o'clock. You're more regular than the Angelus bells, Aisling, and that's saying something.'

I had a little crush on Piotr when he first moved in with John. He wouldn't be my usual type – he's blond, for a start – but there is something about him. He's very tall and enigmatic and a bit, I don't know, brooding. He's always on the phone home and even though I haven't an iota what he's actually saying, he sounds very charming. But my crush disappeared fairly sharpish when I found out what a mess he is. Even peering into his room through a crack in the door is enough to give anyone palpitations – wet towels and mouldy plates everywhere.

'I'll take that as a compliment,' I shout up the stairs, letting myself into the narrow hallway. He mutters something in Polish and retreats into his room.

I poke my head into the sitting room in search of John. No sign. Cillian, my first cousin and John's other housemate, is in there, a jumbo-sized meat feast pizza and a large tub of coleslaw on his lap, absolutely bet into *Nationwide*. Mary Kennedy, looking glam in a turquoise two-piece, is on a farm in west Kerry doing a piece on some kind of notiony sheep's cheese a crowd of English hipsters are making. It looks rank, all covered in mould, and I can just imagine the smell of it. It's clearly not affecting Cillian's appetite though, because he's horsing into the pizza and coleslaw and washing it down with a pint of milk. He gets his iron constitution from Mammy's side of the family. They are notoriously healthy.

If it wasn't for Cillian, John and I would probably never have met. OK, that's not strictly true – we only grew up six miles apart. But if Cillian hadn't brought him to my twenty-first, and convinced him to be kiss no. 17, we'd never have ended up shifting the heads off each other behind Maguire's that night and going steady shortly afterwards. It always makes me think of that film *Sliding Doors* with Gwyneth Paltrow and how some things are just meant to be.

'Hiya, Ais,' he says, his mouth full, not bothering to look up from the telly.

'Hiya. Where's John?' I ask, surveying the room, which is a pigsty as usual. The ashtray by the couch is overflowing – Piotr's work, he smokes hash – and there are empty Tuborg cans on the windowsill and half-drunk mugs of tea on just about every available surface. It smells like the lower shed back home, so I start to pick up the debris, as I always do. Sure if I don't, who will? And I don't particularly mind – if I don't get to my daily target of 12,000 steps, I'll only end up doing laps of the house later.

'I think he's in the kitchen doing an emergency wash-up,' is the reply.

Now Mary's talking to a woman – sorry, a *mumpreneur* – who is running a service where she turns women's placenta into pills after they have a baby. So then the new mother basically eats her own placenta, albeit in pill form, to get the iron and vita-mins and minerals and all the rest of it.

'The recession hit the family hard,' she's telling Mary, who's nodding away looking a bit peaky. 'The mortgage was slipping into arrears,' she's going, 'I had to do something.' So she started cooking up placentas and now they're going to Marbella in July and building on a conservatory. It's a feel-good story, to be fair, but that's one of the most disgusting things I've ever heard. I don't know where people get these ideas.

I gather up as many mugs as I can carry and, balancing the ashtray on top, head for the kitchen where John is slopping plates into grey dishwater and jamming them into the draining rack like his life depends on it. Which it sort of does, because if I've told him once, I've told him a thousand times – I hate coming to this house when it looks like a tip. It's not that it's just messy – it's filthy. The hob is greasy and splattered with food droppings, the bin stinks and the carpet makes me itchy just looking at it.

'Hi,' I sigh, wanting to convey my annoyance but not wanting to get into a row immediately.

'Hiya, love.' He leans across and takes the mugs, giving me a quick peck on the cheek.

To be fair to him, at least he's making an effort. OK, he doesn't exactly have the place spick and span but he's *trying* because he knows the dirt gives me the heebie-jeebies. The other two lads are the main problem – Piotr, with his moods, and Cillian, who still goes home every single weekend with a bag of laundry for Auntie Sheila. I genuinely don't think he could point out the washing machine in an appliance line-up and I strongly suspect he has scurvy. He must have – I've never seen him eat anything that hasn't come out of a square box marked Goodfellas. Unless there's vitamins in coleslaw? But I doubt it. Now, John's not much better, but at least he can throw on a steak and wash his own clothes.

The house itself is not bad – it's a little red-brick terraced thing. Small, but just the right amount of space for, say, two people. Definitely not three. And definitely not four.

'Will we go out for a drink and something to eat, Ais?'

Music to my ears. I know it's Tuesday, and a school night, so I shouldn't really be going out, but I've had an idea.

'I thought you'd never ask,' I beam. 'I want to talk to you about something anyway. In private,' I add, nodding towards the living room, where Mary Kennedy could be rolling around in a silage pit and Cillian would still be drooling. He has this weird thing for older women.

Twenty minutes and one quick hoover later, John and I are on our way to Fagan's. It's bitter out, the coldest January in three years, according to Daddy, but it means we have a good summer ahead of us, and I'm grateful to slip my hand into John's. It's a bit battered from his tag rugby training yesterday, but big and warm all the same. We look good together, I've been told. He's at least a head taller than me and you can tell he's into sport. The muscle definition is there. He makes me feel petite, even though I'm far from it, and I like that. We're always in much better form as soon as we leave the house and those other two. They're bad for my mental health and if my undying allegiance to Bressie has taught me anything, it's that your mental health is very very important.

We arrive at the pub, which ends up being jammed because of a bloody football match, and manage to find a table in the corner. The place is hopping but neither of us has much interest, although John can't help himself throwing an eye at the score every now and then. Chelsea or United or whoever everyone is into must be winning because the crowd is in good spirits and even though it's only an auld foreign game, the atmosphere rubs off on us and we end up spontaneously ordering pints, even though neither of us intended to drink. Emboldened by the roars and cheers, I decide to tackle John.

'Soooo,' I say, as the lounge girl plops down the glasses – Guinness for himself, Coors Light for me, and we order the grub. 'I've been thinking.'

'Oh. That's never a good sign,' John goes, with a sly smile to prove he's only messing.

'I know it's only the middle of January, and we're

both fairly broke after Christmas so I probably shouldn't even be suggesting this, but would you by any chance fancy going on a holiday? Like out foreign, for some "winter sun"?'

I do the quotation marks with my fingers and look at him hopefully. John isn't a great man for the sun. Truth be told, neither am I. The last time I was in Majorca, a girls' holiday with Majella and a few others, I got third-degree burns on the second day and had to stay indoors for the rest of the week. Even my toes were scalded. John doesn't fare much better, although he eventually goes brown, which is quite sexy. Until he takes off his T-shirt, obviously, and you realise it's just the forearms.

He takes a gulp from his pint and wipes away the Guinness from his upper lip with his thumb.

'Winter sun, Ais? It was far from winter sun you were reared. Next you'll be wanting to go skiing.'

My balance and general coordination are not up to much so I can't ever imagine hitting the slopes and not being airlifted off the mountain, but the girls in work are always talking about going skiing and it does sound like right craic. I couldn't imagine John in the gear, although he'd probably be great at it since there isn't a sport he doesn't excel at.

'It was just an idea. There are some good deals around this time of year if you go last-minute. Sharon Conratty is just back from Lanzarote, and Rachel in the office was telling me she got a week in Tenerife for €350 including airport taxes and transfers. And this is in a three-star self-catering apartment right on the beach, not some hellhole. Wouldn't it be nice to start off the year with the feel of the sun on your face?' I say, looking pointedly at the door where people are wrapping up in hats and scarves. 'I think we both deserve a bit of a break. And it would be nice to spend some time alone together, wouldn't it?'

The waitress arrives with our food and I realise I'm famished. John immediately gets to work on his steak sandwich while I dab my burger with a napkin because I read in STELLAR that you can mop up around 200 calories by getting rid of all that extra grease. I'll be good tomorrow too, and I've already decided I'm not drinking this weekend. And I'll go for three walks and maybe even a swim. I'll claw back those 27 Points no bother.

'You've twisted my arm,' John says abruptly.

'Really?' I'm surprised. He usually hates the hassle of organising a holiday (even though I do all the work), but he always enjoys it when he's there. I expected to have to cajole and needle him a little bit. I'm almost disappointed he was so easy to convince.

'Yeah, really,' he says, swigging from his pint. 'I'm wrecked. The shifts since Christmas have been intense.'

John's an engineer at one of those huge American

tech companies. He's been there for years, but I'm not exactly sure what he does and I'm in too deep now to ask. Something to do with microchips that requires a degree in engineering – that much I know. It's boring, he says, but the benefits are great and he gets a company phone. He used to work nine-to-five, the same as myself, but he's been covering for someone who's off having a nervous breakdown and the twelve-hour shifts have him wrecked, as well as interfering with his beloved training schedule – him and one of the other lads drive down to Knock and back every Wednesday to keep up with the team. Still, the extra money is good, and he might as well spend a bit of it on a holiday.

Beaming, I knock back my Coors Light, imagining the two of us sitting on a sun-drenched beach contemplating our future. In this particular fantasy, John is not having a conniption because I mention possibly getting married someday. No, he's mad into the idea. In fact, a small box has appeared on the sand between us. Is that what I think it is? I look over and he's down on one knee, taking my hand. My nails are perfect – a fresh French manicure, the height of sophistication.

'John, I thought you'd never . . .' I stammer.

'Can we get the bill, please?'

It's a good job he can't read minds.

5

I'm straight into holiday organising the next day and only I'm always so up to speed with my actual work, I'd have been snared by now looking at flights while I'm supposed to be processing new-client paperwork in the office. I mean, I burn like a gammon steak in anything over seventeen degrees but by God it's worth it, especially if I come home with a ring. And once the redness goes away and the peeling stops, sure don't you have a lovely bit of a glow for a week or two? What's the point of a holiday if at least three people don't comment on what a great colour you got when you come home and not a bit of it is Sally Hansen?

John and I have narrowed it down to Tenerife because it gets up to around twenty-one degrees in February and sure that's nearly too hot. Ideally we'd go somewhere mad exotic like Thailand but we can only take a week off so soon after Christmas and no doubt there'll be another few weddings before the year is out. One of the ones last year was in Bristol, God forgive me. Another had us camping. Camping, at a wedding, I ask you. It was a yurt, but if I'm paying anything over €100 to stay somewhere, it would want to have four solid walls. And anyway, John already went to that place Phi Phi a few years ago on a lads' trip and got sunstroke and the runs and was in bed for three days so he's gone off it for life. He says he had a fierce spicy dinner one of the nights and it nearly killed him. I'd say the three hours he was sprawled on a sunbed in a pair of GAA shorts without any factor 50 didn't help either.

I've fourteen tabs open on my work computer, each with a different computation of flight and hotel. I'm determined to get the best deal – the week after Valentine's Day is good and cheap. Our first holiday together, we stayed in an awful hole in Gran Canaria. There was a meter on the telly and a family of pigeons living on the balcony. Never again. Since then, we've steered clear of the package deals and stuck to city breaks and a ten-day stint in San Fran – safer options.

I'm firing options at John in emails every fifteen minutes but he's ignored the last three. 'I'm a bit busy, Ais,' he said after the first thirteen. 'Just book whatever one you want, pet.' But he's the one who'll lose the head when there's nowhere to watch the match or he's too warm and the air-conditioning turns out to be just a nice suggestion on the website.

I want us to stay somewhere nice – somewhere with free shower caps, sewing kits and brand-name shampoo. Majella stayed in a place in Singapore on the way to Oz before that had L'Occitane *in the bathrooms*. She took enough to last her a month and would have taken more only the suitcase was full of Monster Munch for her brother Shane.

Anyway, I'll just have to go for it and book somewhere because next the internet will do that thing where it knows you want to book flights and starts putting the price up on you. Designed by Michael O'Leary, no doubt.

Just then, an email lands into my inbox.

'Congratulations!!!!!!!' reads the subject line, and – I count them – seven exclamation marks.

Another baby maybe? Siobhán from Accounts was due last week, her second. Her first one was a monster, ranging in size from nine pounds to eleven, depending on who's telling the story, so all the women in the office have been talking about this impending birth with slight intakes of breath and furrowed brows as they whisper about the projected weight and impart their knowledge about how overdue she is, mutually bonding through supportive sentiments while involuntarily squeezing our legs together a tiny bit, so I expect the email to bring the news of a new little thumper into Siobhán's life . . . but no.

'He liked it, so he put a ring on it!!!!!!!!!' Nine exclamation marks.

'Congrats to Michael Brophy who popped the

63

question to his lovely lady, Janine, at the weekend in Monart.' The swanky feckers. Although I'll dock Michael Brophy marks for originality – that bloody hotel is the engagement capital of Ireland at this stage.

'Wishing them a lifetime of happiness together. Bubbles in the kitchen at 3 p.m.!!!!!!' Ah Jesus. Another one.

There's been a spate of engagement announcements in the office owing to the Christmas rush on question-popping. Lots of examining of fingers in the corridors and 'Have you a date picked?' being asked by the sinks in the toilets. Because I am keenly aware that John and I have been going out since the dawn of time without even a hint of a proposal, I feel each one like a little dig. I tell myself that I'm a woman of the world and I don't need a man or a wedding to fulfil me and I'm a great feminist like Beyoncé – although it was her singing about putting the ring on it, so maybe she needs to have a word with herself.

I check the time. Quarter to three. Right, I'm going to have this holiday booked before Michael Brophy's bubbles. Back to LastMinute.com, one more scan of Skyscanner, just double-check that place on Trip-Advisor. I make sure it's a real holiday website I'm booking on and not a Nigerian prince trying to scam me to use my card to buy flights to Tokyo . . . and it's done. I send the final confirmation on to John and then, with a sigh, push myself away from the desk.

One week in the Paradise Aqua booked: 'A short walk from the beach. Continental-style buffet-breakfast included. Two pools. Air-conditioning. Safe in room. Tea/coffee facilities.' No L'Occitane, I'd say, but it sounds lovely, and we've no need to bring the travel kettle. Mammy and Daddy had a nightmare in Malta last September – not a hint of a kettle in the hotel room, no tea before bed, only 'that auld shite' they had down in the bar. They were like antichrists over it. They had a nightmare with the bus on the way to the hotel too. After panicking every time the driver announced a stop, thinking it was theirs, they missed their hotel in the end because Daddy was convinced someone was after taking his suitcase out of the luggage compartment at the last drop-off. Turns out seventy per cent of the people on the bus had gotten the same black suitcases in a midweek deal in Aldi. There was chaos at airports up and down all the Costas for weeks as suspicious holiday-makers tried to make out if that was their GAA headband tied to the handle or someone else's.

In the kitchen, Donna is front and centre, clutching at Michael Brophy's arm and demanding to see photos of The Ring.

'Oh, and you picked it yourself – aren't you very brave?'

'Very brave, very brave,' go the murmurs around the kitchen, as if Michael had just wrestled a child from the mouth of a lion and barely broken a sweat. He is brave, of course. God only knows what kind of monstrosity John would pick out for me if left to his own devices. Surely he knows that a promise ring for fifty quid would be grand and then we could make a day of going to Field's to get the real thing. Michael seems to have coped OK with the task though; he has Donna's approval anyway.

'Oh, you went for the asscher cut,' she brays, nodding approvingly that it's 'gorgeous' while somehow imparting that it's nowhere near as good as hers.

'Jesus, I wouldn't have a clue.' Sadhbh has floated over to me in a mist of expensive perfume – probably your man Tom Ford they're always talking about on *Xposé* – and wearing something from the 'state of that' rack in Zara. I love the idea of Zara but it can be very dear and a lot of it has me gasping 'the state of that' before I can stop myself. But Sadhbh is managing to pull it off.

'How do people know the difference in those rings?' she asks. 'They all look exactly the same to me. Would you not want something a bit more unique if you're supposedly going to wear it for the rest of your life?'

I pretend that I haven't known about the different cuts of rings and the best cities to go on a weekend

66

mini-break to pick them out for the best part of a decade and succeed only in exhaling a long, drawn out 'yeahhhh' in response.

'Don't get me wrong – I like diamonds as much as the next girl, but I'd rather buy them for myself. Or even better, spend the money on a month on a desert island.' She could sound mocking, but she doesn't. She sounds genuinely baffled.

'That would probably be a smarter investment all right.' It's Barry, who obviously got the email too, even though he's only in the company a couple of months so wouldn't know Michael Brophy from Adam.

'It can't be that bad,' Sadhbh tinkles as she places her hand on his arm like she was born casually touching men's arms. You know the type – they come into the world peeping out from under hats like Princess Diana and just knowing what chia seeds were before anyone else. She probably didn't make her Communion or anything. I'd say she calls her mam by her first name and she definitely never worries about increasingly threatening letters from the Post Office about the TV licence (I wouldn't be able to sleep worrying about the ring on the doorbell). That sort of thing.

Now Barry looks as if he's said too much. The *Room to Improve* rumours must be true. The marriage is over.

Donna swings around by us, firing mugs of prosecco at people.

'You're next surely, Aisling,' she nudges Sadhbh

and Barry, winking and nodding. 'You and John will be nearly in the graveyard before you make it up the aisle at this rate.'

She careens off, inserting herself into the little groups around the kitchen, imparting her wedding know-how to anyone with ears, until her phone starts blaring 'Girls Just Wanna Have Fun' and she sneaks away to answer it.

Barry gives us a nod and then walks over to Michael to do that handshake and pat on the back thing that men somehow all know how to do.

'What's his name again? Brian? He's a bit of a ride!' Sadhbh murmurs conspiratorially. 'The girls in HR have been chatting about him.'

'Barry? He's actually my new team leader. He has a grand set of teeth on him, doesn't he? You better tell them upstairs he's married. Well, at least I think he is,' I tell her. 'Although I hear the wife has driven him stone-mad with demands about the house. There are rumours that she might have been into another man's cushions too, if you know what I mean.'

Tinkles of laughter again from Sadhbh. 'Oh Aisling, you're gas.'

6

Our flight is leaving in ten hours and I'm so stressed out I've started to wonder if going on holiday is worth it. I decided at the last minute that I desperately needed something to wear on the beach and spent the last forty-eight hours scouring the shops for a decent tankini and spent nearly €200 in Boots on travel-sized everything. If it's under 100 millilitres, I bought it.

We're only checking one suitcase, to save money. And of course we'll have John's Rangers holdall as our hand luggage for the heavy stuff, like his Niall Quinn and Muhammad Ali autobiographies and my Cathy Kellys. It was John's idea – he has strong feelings about Michael O'Leary and refuses to 'line his pockets' with our 'hard-earned cash'. I go along with it because, well, it's easier than listening to him launch into one of his earnest rants, but right now I'm cursing him because there's feck-all space for my Skechers and I'm determined to get my 12,000 steps in every day. I know I'm going to be indulging in ice-cream and the like and I'm adamant I'm not going to let this holiday derail my Weight Watchers journey. I couldn't let Maura down.

'John, I'm going to take out your T-shirts and try rolling instead of folding them,' I call down the stairs. 'It saves space – I saw it on Pinterest.'

He's below in the sitting room, sandwiched between Cillian and Piotr, watching *Westworld* or *The Walking Dead* or one of those horrific American shows that I can't stomach. So much violence.

'Fire away, Ais,' he shouts up, as I remove seven near-identical navy Jack and Jones T-shirts and try to defy the laws of physics in order to make them nearly disappear. He put in his stuff first and as I'm feeling around in the case, I'm half-trying to be careful, half-pawing for anything I shouldn't find. Like, for example, something that he knows I really want. Something I've been hoping to get for a while. Something to finally put on the ring finger of my left hand.

My own holiday wardrobe consists of the fabled tankini (Dunnes, TG), three maxi dresses (one Oasis, two Penneys), a pair of white linen trousers – so versatile, as long as you have an iron (Sasha, RIP), two pairs of khaki shorts (Penneys), three T-shirts (Dorothy Perkins), my trusty county jersey, a going Out Out dress (River Island – so dear), two pairs of flip-flops (one bejewelled – Barratt's, one plain – Penneys) . . . and my Skechers, if I have anything to do with it. I think it's what's called a capsule wardrobe? I got the idea from an interview with Alexa Chung I read in *U* magazine. She's very stylish – the girls in work are obsessed.

An hour later and the case is bursting at the seams, but I've managed to get the zip done and wedge in 200 teabags. Our sun-hats are hanging from the strap and we'll have to wear at least two outfits each on the plane, but Michael O'Leary won't be getting rich off us, which is the main thing. Will it fit into the metal yoke at check-in? Hopefully, but only time will tell.

I head downstairs, buoyed by this small victory, to find the lads a good few cans in and Piotr in particular looking glassy eyed. On the hash again, I suppose, which has the place stinking. Although I must admit he looks cool blowing those smoke rings – so effortless. I note John's close proximity to him and immediately start to panic about sniffer-dogs at the airport in the morning. It would actually be typical if he ended up in Mountjoy on drugs charges and ruined our special holiday. Well, hopefully it will be special . . .

'Is there any wine?' I ask, sitting down in the one armchair that doesn't quite face the telly. I'm suddenly feeling a burst of pre-holiday excitement so I'm willing to overlook the fact that my boyfriend can't be arsed asking one of the lads to swap places so we can cuddle up on the couch.

'There's some red open on the counter,' is Piotr's

unexpected reply. 'I needed it to make spaghetti Bolognese last night.'

I'm shocked. I've never witnessed Piotr cook anything other than questionable Polish dishes before, which seem to be largely based around cabbage and vinegar – or at least they smell like they are. And wine in spag bol? Very fancy altogether.

'Do you mind if I help myself to a little glass?' I ask.

'Knock yourself out,' he replies with a definite north Dublin twang. John gives me a weak smile and mouths 'it's nearly over' while gesturing at *Game of Thrones* or whatever it is I'm doing my best to avoid.

Out to the kitchen I go and, true to Piotr's word, the cab sauv is there. I pour myself a generous sup – payback for all the mugs I've washed in this house – and sit down at the little kitchen table, where I allow myself to indulge in a fantasy I've been trying to quash ever since we booked the holiday.

There we are, himself and myself, walking on the beach at sunset on our way to a romantic dinner – one of those ones where they bring the little table out on to the sand just for one lucky couple. I'm wearing the good going Out Out dress and the bejewelled flip-flops and feeling happy after a day of relaxing on the beach. We're a bit giddy, having stopped into our hotel bar for a cocktail on the way out. Of course John wouldn't be caught dead drinking anything other than pints back home, but he's different when he's on holiday. The more radioactive-looking the beverage, the better – more little umbrellas, please.

Anyway, we're laughing, holding hands, the smell of sand, salt and sun-cream thick in the air, when I turn around and realise he must have dropped something because he's suddenly on his knees looking up at me earnestly. But hang on, he hasn't dropped anything at all. In fact, he's produced something from his pocket! OMG, it's a ring and he's about to . . .

'Love, did you make us a little sambo for the plane?' I nearly jump out of my skin as he walks into the kitchen.

'Of course I did,' I say, looking down at the fresh French manicure I got on my lunch break. 'Michael O'Leary can go and shite if he thinks we're paying €8 for a soggy toastie.'

'Good woman. We better hit the hay now. Piotr is bringing us to the airport at 4 a.m. I told him I'd rather give him the €15 than the Aircoach.'

I'm trying to rise above it but the trolley-dolly at the check-in desk is clearly talking about us to her colleague in her native tongue, whatever it is – Czech or Russian or one of those. It's 4.30 a.m. and they're both wearing full faces of make-up: big eyebrows, contour, loads of sparkly eyeshadow, the works. It's the sort of make-up Majella wears going Out Out – like, Coppers on a Saturday night Out Out. I'm suddenly conscious of my lick of brown mascara, sweep of blusher and hairband, aka my normal day-time look.

'You pack this bag yourself?' the blonde with the massive bun asks John.

'Ha! I didn't, no,' he answers with a little laugh. 'That would be Aisling's domain. She wouldn't trust me with such an important job.'

I just smile and nod. I like looking after him – it makes me feel indispensable. And sure he enjoys it. What man wouldn't? I swear, I'm going to be the perfect girlfriend on this holiday.

I've just realised I forgot to pack my razor. Shite.

7

The first thing I notice when I step onto the tarmac in Tenerife Sur Airport is the general lack of oxygen. Jesus, there's not a breath. It's stifling.

I feel like I'm wading through lava as we make our way slowly towards the terminal, and it's not even noon yet. According to the air steward – or is it hostess? I can never remember which one they want to be called – today marks the start of an unseasonal heatwave that's expected to last the week. Everyone else on the plane seems delighted, clapping and rolling up their sleeves, wringing their hands with glee, but I can practically hear myself sizzling as I try my best to slink through the shadows until we get to the heavenly air-conditioning. I swear John's forearms are a good three shades browner by the time we get inside. He seems happy out and despite the sweat pooling in my bra, I can't shake the feeling that this holiday is going to change everything for us.

Since we saved a packet by sharing the check-in bag, I decided to splash out and book a private transfer to the Paradise Aqua in advance online. It's €35 each way but I figure it's worth it to get the trip off to a glamorous start. When we were in Rome four years ago, we spent about thirty per cent of the week trying to decipher the public-transport system and looking for wifi so we could peer at Google Maps. I'm not going to lie, it was tense. And of course John wouldn't hear of me asking for directions, even though the locals were shockingly good at English and so friendly I was sure they were all trying to rob us. Turns out they were a genuinely sound bunch of lads. No, the transfer was a much better idea.

'Oh, there we are,' I nudge John and point to a scruffy-looking but beaming teenager holding a sign that says 'Mr and Mrs Aisling'. 'Mister and Missus! God, they're gas here. What's the legal driving age in Spain, do you know?'

John strides over and nearly takes your man's arm off with a vigorous shake, all the while rejecting his multiple offers to carry our one miserable bag. I don't want to get off on the wrong foot, but I'm consider-ing asking him for a look at his driver's licence. On closer inspection, he can't be more than sixteen. Bloody internet! You do your best to save a few bob but you end up putting your life in danger in the process . . .

John appears to have no such misgivings and the two plough on ahead, making comfortable small talk about the weather – it's forecast to reach *thirty-five* degrees today! – while I scan the shops for a chemist. Out of the corner of my eye, I spy Los Boots and nip in to buy a packet of Bic disposable razors before either of them miss me. I couldn't be getting engaged with hairy legs on me.

The trip to the Paradise Aqua only takes twenty minutes but it seems to last a lifetime because John is determined to explain the intricacies of hurling to fresh-faced Pablo, who has dropped into the conversation that he's twenty-two. I snort. A likely story. I'm sweating quietly in the back of the 1998 Lada, watching the dingy commercial buildings around the airport slowly turn into suburbs and give way to high-rise hotels, bars, restaurants and eventually, the Paradise Aqua. Not a hint of coastline to be seen. John and Pablo, having clearly bonded, are swapping phone numbers as I try to ignore the alarm bells in my head. The exterior of the twelve-storey apartment block looks somewhat shabby – and I'm being generous there. The pale pink paint on the walls has started to peel and there are several feral-looking cats sunning themselves around a murky pond.

With a screech of rubber, Pablo pulls off roaring something that sounded suspiciously like 'fock the focking Kilkenny Cats'. And just like that, I've got John all to myself again and suddenly it doesn't matter that I'm getting institutional vibes from the Paradise Aqua or that there are bars on all the windows. What matters is that we're here, together, for a whole week.

Well, it turns out that whoever took the pictures for ParadiseAquaApartments.com was a cute hoor with a knack for Photoshop. When we eventually reach our unit (fourth floor, no lift – I'm puce by the time we get there, despite the fact I've been religiously doing 250 steps on my lunch break for the last month), it technically has everything it's supposed to have, apart from the double bed. In its place are two narrow singles covered in hairy blankets – you know the ones. On the plus side, the kettle is where it should be, as is the iron.

I'm like a bear with a sore head. My perfect romantic holiday requires a double bed. I ring down to reception ready to eat the face off whoever has the misfortune to pick up the phone, but the nice woman is so apologetic that I end up saying it doesn't matter at all. It turns out there's a convention in town – for oncologists. Well, who could begrudge them the double beds? Aren't they doing God's work, trying to cure cancer? And she assures me the beach is just behind the high-rise car parks directly in front of our balcony. Then, the clincher: she offers to send up a complimentary bottle of cava, to which John mouths 'now we're sucking diesel' and gives me the double thumbs-up. He sticks the kettle on while we wait for the cava and we sit on the balcony and flick through the local guidebooks while complaining about that rotten UHT milk and how unnatural it is. Holiday mode: activated.

After sinking the bottle of cava, a three-hour nap on top of the hairy blankets, a scout around the local shops for another bottle with lots of '*hola*'-ing and pointing at things, it's 7 p.m. when we finally head out for dinner and there's no denying it: I'm well on my way to being pissed. I think it's the combination of the unmerciful heat and the fact I haven't eaten anything since the ham sandwich and packet of Taytos on the plane. Oh, and the cava. The bubbles have gone straight to my head. I know for a fact that John will be gagging for a steak (well done, pepper sauce on the side), but I'm feeling more adventurous and weighing up the pros and cons of having something local, like fish. Well, that's the type of thing you're supposed to have when you're on holiday, isn't it? I couldn't stomach anything elaborate like paella though. With all those little octopuses looking back at me? Or is it octopi? Anyway, no thanks. And shellfish is too risky – Mammy is allergic and despite the lack of medical evidence, she has me convinced I must be too. Maybe fish and chips then? Sure we'll see.

'Hang on a second there, Ais – let me look at the menu here,' John says, pointing to what looks suspiciously like an Irish pub on the strip of restaurants and bars that line the seafront, which, it turns out, is a ten-minute walk from the apartment. Now, don't get me wrong, I love nipping into an Irish pub when I'm on holidays – sure you always meet someone you know – but on the first night? We were only in actual Ireland a few hours ago – I'm not exactly homesick yet. John seems so happy though . . .

'Steak? Check. This looks good, Ais. Nothing too spicy on here at all. Here, take a look,' he says, gently tugging at my hand.

'Guinness On Tap', it says in big block capitals and I know there's no going back now. But they're serving up chicken goujons and fish and chips, so what do I have to complain about? And there are loads of tables outside.

'Yeah, looks good,' I say, squeezing his hand. 'Fibber Magee's it is. Will we try and get a table on the patio so we can watch the sun set?'

'Anything for you, Ais,' he says, patting me on the arse as I take my seat and making a beeline for the bar.

To be fair to Fibber's, the grub is top-notch – massive portions and half the price you'd pay at home.

I text Mammy: 'The food is half the price u'd pay at home! Having gr8 time.'

She'll be delighted with that. We're drinking Blue Lagoons and having serious craic with our waitress, Ciara, who's here on a year out. It turns out she used to go out with a lad from Knocknamanagh and is on the local camogie team here. All fifteen of the players and both coaches work in Fibber's in some capacity, from waitresses to bouncers, she tells us. The pub sponsors the league too. It turns out we've found ourselves at the epicentre of the Irish GAA community in Tencrife. Isn't it always the way?

My phone goes and I steel myself for a barrage of questions from Mammy about the weather and the milk.

'Luvly Ais. Not 2 worry but daddy not feeling gr8. CareDoc here.'

The hairs on the back of my neck stand up and beads of sweat gather on my upper lip, even though the sun went down a good two hours ago and it's really not that hot any more. CareDoc is with Daddy?

The phone goes again and I stiffen.

'Did u find real milk or are u managing with the UHT?'

'What is wrong with Daddy???' I reply, watching John chatting away to Ciara at the bar, where he's already on first-name terms with most of the regulars. She's shaking up another two Blue Lagoons, going heavy on the vodka. Not that it matters – I'm sober now, my holiday buzz well faded as I imagine Daddy at home, pale, frightened, so far away.

'Was feeling dizzy. Doc gone now, just said to rest. Overdoing it – 12 lambs 2day!'

I exhale. Twelve lambs! No wonder he was dizzy. Sure who wouldn't be wrecked, supervising all that?

'Tell him to slow down n stop giving us frights,' I fire off, as John meanders back carrying the cocktails as well as a couple of Slippery Nipples. Jesus, he's gone mad.

'I will luv. Cloudy and showers here 2day. Hope ur weather is better.'

OK, that's put my mind at ease a little bit. I'm a daddy's girl. Always have been. I suspect Mammy might sometimes be a little bit jealous of our closeness, but sure doesn't she have her pet, Paul? I think about firing Daddy off a text but he's even more afraid of the phone than Mammy. He has his PIN Sellotaped to the back of it. Top-notch security. I relax again and one shot leads to another, which leads to a few more, which leads to me and John at a lock-in in Fibber's until 4.30 a.m.

'Can you believe that this time yesterday we were in Piotr's car on the way to the airport?' I say, slurring slightly, as we make our way back to the Paradise Aqua. John's good Ben Sherman shirt is tied around his waist and I'm carrying my flip-flops, which are giving me blisters even though they're completely flat. It's no wonder I can't wear anything higher than a kitten heel – my arches are fecked. 'We've only been on the island eleven hours but I feel like I've known Ciara and the girls all my life.'

'Sound women, seriously sound women,' John replies, sounding a tad emotional. Ciara and himself did some intense bonding over how underrated camogie is. It's a subject John is actually very passionate about. 'Will we walk along the beach for a bit, Ais?'

I hadn't even noticed but the sun is starting to come up and the sky, streaked with pink and purple, looks like something you'd get on a computer screensaver. It's gorgeous. The beach is deserted, save for a few figures running in the distance – I try to imagine what could be going on in their lives that would have them exercising on holidays. The sand feels cool underfoot, even though I can already feel the sun warming up. Temperatures are set to be record-breaking today, according to Ciara. Lordblessusandsaveus, we won't be able to leave the apartment.

I suddenly notice that John has stopped and is looking down at his pocket, fumbling for something. I freeze. Oh my God, it's happening. He's going to propose. All that fantasy-quashing and I was actually on to something. My eyes dart around in the hope of finding someone nearby who can take a picture of us, delirious with joy, to send home. You know the kind: me holding up my left hand, him looking like the cat who got the cream.

'John,' I blurt out. 'Oh my God.'

I can't help myself. But now that we're on the beach, watching the sun rise on day two, I'm suddenly a bag of nerves.

'Aisling . . .' I can hear his voice, but there's also a ringing in my ears that's in danger of drowning him out. This is going to be the speech now where he apologises for making me cry at Denise's wedding and admits that he's always known it was me – just like Ross said to Rachel in *Friends*.

'Let's take one of those selfies and stick it up on the old BookFace for the gang at home,' he says, pulling his phone from his pocket. 'Make 'em jealous.'

A selfie? John doesn't take selfies. In the whole time we've been friends on Facebook, I've only ever seen him post 'thanks for the birthday wishes' and share videos of police chases and links to 24 Of The World's Hardest Fails. What's going on? Oh Jesus, he's not proposing at all. And of course I'm locked, so I burst into tears. Well, I'm only human. He looks like he's been shot.

'What's wrong, Ais? I thought you'd love it. You could put it on your Instagram. I'll put my shirt on,' he trails off, looking confused.

I can feel all the frustration of the last month and

a half fizzing up inside me and I realise I can't keep a lid on it any more.

'What's wrong? What's *wrong*? *You're* what's wrong, you big gobshite,' I roar. The roaring feels good. Cathartic. 'I thought you were finally going to propose. Would it kill you to pop the question, John? How long do you think I'm going to hang around waiting?'

'Pop the question?' He looks even more perplexed now. 'Aisling, I'm happy with how things are between us. You know how much I love you, how I'd do anything to make you happy. But we're only young yet – we have loads of time ahead of us. I think we have loads of time. Aren't we grand as we are?' And he sort of shrugs.

'So you're genuinely happy living with Piotr and Cillian?' I'm screaming now and glad of the relative privacy of this public place at dawn. 'Do you know how much I spend every month on petrol? I'm not happy living in limbo any more, throwing my eyes up to heaven when Dolores fucking Reilly asks me when we're giving her a day out. I'm embarrassed. I want the bloody ring. Not even an expensive ring, any ring will do.' I say the last part quietly so hopefully he'll feel sorry for me instead of looking really, really angry.

'Since when were you so obsessed with getting engaged, Ais?' he asks, wrestling himself back into the stupid check shirt.

'Since always,' I fire back, not able to lie any more. 'I'm sick of seeing people we know getting engaged after eighteen months together while I'm still here on the shelf. I'm a laughing stock at home – I'm sure of it.'

Nobody hates confrontation more than John, and I already feel guilty for losing the head at him, but I'm done pretending. We stand on the beach, eyeballing each other as the sun makes its way above the horizon. I expect him to reach out to me, say something comforting, maybe even say he was actually planning on proposing later in the week – but the silence is deafening. Suddenly he takes off and, brushing past me, heads in the direction of the Paradise Aqua. He's bulling. I can't move.

'Is that it? Is that *it*?' I roar at his back as he strides down the beach, fists balled at his sides. No response.

I sink down into the sand and sit on my arse crying, wishing for a taco fries from Abrakebabra. After ten minutes, I feel myself start to burn and curse the day I ever suggested getting some winter sun.

8

I haven't called in sick since I thought I had meningitis that time last year. It was just a cold, but you can never be too sure with swollen glands. I keep a glass in my room to check for rashes. But this is bad. I'm back in BGB, wailing along to Adele's greatest hits, head full of snots, eyes like two honeydew melons. Bad. I'm swinging between denial and sobbing over what happened last night.

The taxi dropped us off at John's in Drumcondra after a frosty flight home and an even frostier car journey. When John went to bring the suitcase into the house, I kind of half-shouted, surprising myself, 'I'm going to drive on home.'

He looked stunned and sad and angry at the same time. I could see about forty questions and realisations flitting through his mind all at once.

'Ah, Ais, don't be like that. Sure haven't you work in the morning?'

'No, I'm going home.'

It was like something out of *Home and Away*. The drama. Everything was kind of buzzing and the words were out before I could stop them.

'And . . . and I think maybe this is it for us, John.'

My voice went then. Really, I'd been thinking about saying it since the awful row on our first night in Tenerife. We patched it up a bit the next day because we were there for a week and we were hardly going to sit there, looking at the pictures of wine bottles and grapes on the walls, not talking. But we were as prickly as briars most of the time – him at me for not taking enough euros out of the safe for the glass-bottomed boat/donkey sanctuary trip-combo, me at him for absolutely swinging out of my insect-repellent after him bringing none, even with me warning him that he'd get et. Even on the last night in Fibber Magee's, when John, overcome with emotion and Fat Frogs, roared 'You're the One That I Want' right at me at karaoke, pawing in my direction and leading the chorus of 'ooh ooh oohs' from Ciara and co., I couldn't shake the knot in my stomach.

The minute we got back to the airport in Tenerife, any holiday joy we did have went right out the window with the smoke from Pablo's fags as he joyfully roared '*Póg mo thóin!* Jimmy Barry Murphy!' at us, pulling up to departures. He made a great show of saying goodbye and making sure he had John's number right for when he comes to Dublin to visit. I suppose he'll fit right in now that he can say 'kiss my arse' in Irish. 'Viking splash!' he bellowed, as he left us standing outside the terminal. I'm already imagining him bombing around Dublin in those big yellow boots, shouting at other tourists.

I was silent as the grave as John wandered through duty-free, reminiscing on the pre-euro days when you'd have to spend your last few pesos in the airport on *Hola!* fridge magnets, decorative spoons and paella-recipe tea towels.

On the flight home, I was thinking about it – thinking about giving him a shock, about putting an end to all this carry-on, about showing him that I'm not going to wait around for ever.

I still can't believe I actually said it to him though, right there on the road outside his house. I felt like I was going to get sick. I turned on my heel, digging into my handbag for the car keys I'd put in the inside pocket (Piotr would have been to Poland and back in the Micra if I'd left them behind me).

'Ah, Ais . . .' he said feebly. 'This is crazy. What about your stuff?'

'It's all holiday stuff. I'll get them from you again.' I knew that if I didn't get out of there then, I'd never go. 'Don't bloody put it all in the washing machine together. My linen trousers will be ruined.'

I said it louder and angrier than I meant and got into the car, praying that it would start after sitting there for a week. Part of me was hoping that maybe it wouldn't, so I would have an excuse to stay and curl up beside John to watch an episode of something, forgetting all of this shite. But the car spluttered once and then sprang to life, putting an end to any cold feet I was having.

As I pulled away good and fast, the fat hot tears started spilling over, increasing as John disappeared in the rear-view mirror, standing in the driveway holding onto our one suitcase.

Poor auld Mammy got an awful land when I arrived back home. 'Jesus, I thought it was the guards and something was after happening.' Nobody calls to your house in BGB after 8 p.m. unless there's been a terrible accident or there's a calf coming. 'I thought you'd stay up in John's tonight. I wasn't expecting you until after work tomorrow evening . . . Ah, what's wrong, Aisling?'

I remember the panic in her voice, that very special panic reserved for a mother who's not used to seeing her grown daughter in floods of tears and assumes the worst.

'What's after happening?'

Mammy is downstairs on the phone to someone – Auntie Sheila, probably – whispering about 'she's not great' (probably me) and 'in bits' (definitely me) and 'the louser' (possibly John but possibly also the milkman who only brought Slimline milk – 2 Points – for me and no full-fat for them. Daddy has no time at all for that 'watery shite' but it's grand with the Weetabix, I think).

It's my second day off work. At home. In mourning. They don't know what to do with me at all. Daddy is doing better, diagnosed with just a chest infection, much to our relief. He floated nervously around the kitchen on Sunday night as I poured the tale of woe out to Mammy and she tutted and sighed and interjected with 'ah God' and 'my pet' every now and then, every kind little gesture pushing me into a fresh wave of sobs. I don't think either of them ever heard so much about my feelings in one go. Eventually Daddy came over and patted me gently on the shoulder.

'You'll stay at home tomorrow?' he asked, glancing at the clock. 'They'll manage without you.' You'd swear I ran the place.

It's nice to be at home during the day. Mammy left the heating on upstairs for me and Daddy shooed the cat into my room first thing, knowing she'd be up on the bed in no time. Mammy spent €20 on a cat bed about four years ago and I'd say Tiger got into it twice, preferring the armchair she's always slept in. We'll never hear the end of it.

Majella has been texting on the hour for an update on what state I'm in. I know the break-up has floored her. She exhaled a long 'fuuuuck' when I first told her on the phone, but she pulled it together fairly lively and has been full of support and inspirational quotes ever since. She wants me to come up and stay with her and go out. Out Out.

There's been no word from John. In a way, I'm not surprised. He's not the type to be getting into his feelings over text messages. But I did think he might get in touch, that he might try to smooth things over, might try to fix things. But nothing, no matter how much I stare at the phone. But do I even want to fix things? Can I stomach starting all over again? All those years wasted. A wave of self-pity and rage washes over me and I nearly pull a muscle hopping the phone off the floor just as Mammy knocks and walks in.

'Will you have any dinn ... Jesus, your good phone! *Aisling!*' She hasn't seen me in this state since the great Dropping to Pass Maths debacle of 2006.

'Ah, Mammy, will you just leave me alone!'

She opens her mouth to retort but thinks better of it, turning on her heel and closing the door gently. Her kindness in letting me behave like a right rip, if only for a few days, sets me off again. Although Mammy is dying for the Day Out and a chance to buy a special pastel number from Fascinators Boutique in Knock and Daddy would love to see me settled, I know really they just want me to be happy.

I suddenly consider for the first time in all my years on earth that they've been through all this before. They've had first kisses and first loves and break-ups and heartbreaks. Sure of course they had lives before I came along, dancing to local showbands and drinking glasses of Guinness. Then the crying comes in big heaving sobs as I imagine Daddy being heartbroken or Mammy in a heap – big gusts of 'ah ah ah ah' and my nose so blocked that my head might explode.

Fifteen minutes later and I'm all cried out, experiencing that strange sense of calm you get when you've roared it all out of you and you're nearly cracking with the dehydration. Everything will be grand. It's not the end of the world. People break up all the time. Think of how brilliant it will be not to have that constant sense of expectation hanging around my stomach. Maybe I'll go on Tinder!

Daddy knocks briskly on the door and pushes it open, as I take a deep breath and embrace my new-found sense of freedom and serenity.

'Are . . . are you all right there, pet?'

'Ah yeah, Daddy. Sure I'll survive.' I manage a watery smile.

'I just took your car out for a spin into town. It's due a service soon. Won't you make sure and book it, pet?'

'Yes, Daddy.' The double 'pet' usage is wavering my independent woman status. I feel so guilty for making him feel so sorry for me. For worrying about me. For minding me. I should be minding him.

'Oh, and I put a few bob of petrol in the tank.'

The crying didn't stop for forty-five minutes.

9

The next morning, I'm back on the road to Dublin. Three days off work and they come looking for a sick note and I'm not paying €60 to lie about a chest infection, heartbreak or no heartbreak. They even charge you now to get the repeat prescription for your Yasmin. 'Worth it though for the anti-babby pills,' Maj always says. 'Imagine having to tell Marian you were preggers. There would be war – wigs on the green.'

She has me convinced to go out with her tonight so I've a bag with me to stay in Phibsboro. I haven't stayed there in ages, because sure why would I when I could just go to John's? Instead of going over to Majella's, I packed bag after bag to stay in John's and wash Piotr's fifty-seven mugs and watch Cillian horsing another pizza while shouting out all the wrong answers to *University Challenge*.

'Freddie Mercury!' (It was Margaret Thatcher.)

'The Siege of Ennis!' (Battle of Hastings.)

Anyway, here I am, packing bags again, this time to sleep on Majella's couch like a student. I should be in my own house – *our* own house – cooking stir-fries with John and buying a Good Knife and never again finding my Patricia Scanlans ripped to bits by Piotr making his roaches.

I swallow the tears of anger and self-pity as I pull into my work car park. I've told them that I had a bad cold, so at least I'll probably get away with the puffy eyes. Although it does look bad calling in sick straight after you come back from holidays. I'll just have to style it out. I've two giant Toblerones to distract them anyway. I got Mammy to get them in Tesco's. Would you be well buying them in the airport? The price of them!

I don't want to go telling any of the girls in work what's after happening. The more people you tell, the more real it becomes. The thought of Donna's big shocked face gripping my arm and gasping, 'Ah no, what's after happening? Is he after cheating on you? Sure there's loads of lads out there – you'll be settled in no time'. No. I'll keep the head down.

I arrive up to the first floor to discover that, mercifully, she's out for the morning at the dentist. She cracked a molar yesterday eating a Milky Moo and apparently made such a scene that Des from Escalations had to bring her home. Hopefully the dentist will freeze her gob enough to keep her quiet for the rest of the week.

Majella has me all lined up for our Wednesday night on the tiles and is sending regular texts to make sure

I haven't tipped myself down the stairs. I make it through the morning, clicking through spreadsheets and occasionally going into the bathroom to look at our holiday pictures on my phone. John pointing at a sign that says '*LOCO!*' Me pointing at a sign that says '*LOCO!*' John and Pablo in front of Pablo's car. One just of Pablo that he insisted we take. A load of blurry ones of us with the Fibber's girls.

'Well, have you heard from him?' Majella asks when she rings on the dot of one.

'No.'

'Fuck him, Ais. Pull the socks up. Plenty more fish. I'll meet you at mine at six, yeah?'

Mammy gave me leftover spaghetti Bolognese for my lunch. Bolognese didn't make it to BGB until the mid-nineties and it's safe to say Mammy embraced Dolmio with open arms. So cosmopolitan and avant-garde! Daddy is still suspicious of pasta so she makes him a few spuds to go on the side. I'm under the usual strict instructions to bring the lunch box home. What kind of animal does she think I am at all? If anything, I'll bring *more* home. There's a whole press of them here that nobody seems to want to claim. Lunch boxes must grow on trees in their houses. I've my name on mine (lid *and* tub) to avoid confusion.

The kitchen is mercifully quiet until Sadhbh pads in, smiling away. She smells lovely, like rich ladies.

Swishy hair too, with that balayage carry-on in the ends.

'Hiya, Aisling,' she trills. 'Any craic? Were you away? You've a great colour on your face.'

Jackpot. That one day sitting out from under the umbrella paid off.

'Yeah, I was away there for a week in Tenerife. It was . . . grand.' No point telling her about the disastrous end to the trip.

'Any plans for the weekend?'

'Ah, I'll probably just see some of the gang down home.'

'Ah, lovely – where's ho . . . ?'

Suddenly I blurt out, not wanting her to think I'm a complete square, 'I'm going out tonight though, to McGowan's.'

'Oh, we're going there tonight too! Some of us from upstairs and some new team leaders from down here as well for a bonding-over-drinks thing. It's better than paintballing anyway. I've never been – is it good? It's one of the manager's locals and he swears by it. It would want to be a good spot – Phibsboro's a bit of a trek from Ballsbridge.'

'Ah, it's great craic. There's always a decent crowd, and a bit of dancing upstairs if the fancy takes you. And the DJ will play 'Caledonia' for you if you ask enough times. One time he let Majella plug in her iPod and play whatever we liked. You sometimes get the national anthem at the end of the night if it's been a particularly belting evening.'

Sadhbh looks amused at my enthusiasm. And also bemused. 'The national anthem? What?'

'You know, when the lights come on?' Was she raised in a cave? Sure the night isn't truly over until your big red face has been exposed for all to see in harsh fluorescent light, roaring about the soldiers who pledged their lives to Ireland, hands sticky with a dangerous vodka-and-Smirnoff Ice concoction.

'Well, this I *have* to see. See you later so, probably,' she waves and smiles off out of the room, just as I catch sight of her boots. They're *gold*. Sparkly gold boots. Honestly.

Majella got two bottles of wine in Centra. Dear ones. €11 each. 'We're worth it,' she said as she pulled them out of her handbag. She's poured us a pint of wine each to have with our chicken Kievs (feck the Points). She means business. Her housemates, Fionnuala and Mairead, are coming out with us too. They're also teachers and are well used to Tearful Thursdays trying to teach phonics and long division with hangovers, so they're up for it.

'We'll get these into us – go out, put our handbags down and have a dance. You'll dance that lad out of you, Ais.' She really does mean business.

Majella's house is only a few minutes from

McGowan's so as soon as it's a respectable time to show up and not be the only ones there (no earlier than 10 p.m. – early enough to get a good spot, but not so early you can hear your voice echoing around the pub walls), off Majella, Fionnuala and I march, wrapped up warm against the bitter February breeze. Mairead says she'll meet us there – she still has twelve religion essays to correct, all variations on how St. Patrick managed to get the snakes out of Ireland.

It's already busy when we arrive in McGowan's so we make the snap decision to head straight upstairs to the dancefloor to secure one of the tables nearby with our coats. The pint and a half of wine I guzzled with dinner is starting to hit me as I sway up to the bar to get us some drinks: 'Three vodkas and two Diet Cokes. *Diet* Cokes.'

Fionnuala and Majella are already on the dance-floor beside our coat-table, giving it loads to 'Hey Ya' and shaking it like a polaroid picture. I'm standing at the table, staring at them like a bit of a weirdo in a trance, people jostling and dancing against me. It's so weird to be out without John, to be in Dublin and not know where he is – to be so far removed from him and not allowed to know what he's doing.

'Aisling! Hiya!'

Sadhbh shouts her greetings as she spills past

with the gang from work, making a beeline for the one free remaining table in the corner.

'This is *gas*!' she calls back over her shoulder, as the DJ segues clumsily from OutKast into Rihanna. Majella and Fionnuala crash back over to the table, with Mairead in tow – she finally finished the essays – to refresh themselves and drag me onto the dancefloor, roaring at anyone who'll listen to make us feel like we're the only girls in the world.

We're soon joined by Sadhbh and a few other heads from the office – including Barry, who's looking well in his casual gear – and I nod at them and do little waves and mouth Majella, Fionnuala and Mairead's names at them, and by the time 'Gold Digger' comes on, we're all best pals, dropping it like it's hot and whatnot.

It's not until the strains of something oh-so-familiar reach me that I'm landed right back into reality, and I burst through people to make my way to the table, scrunching my eyes up to keep from crying. All around lads are stamping their feet in approval as 'Mr Jones' belts out of the speakers; John's favourite song in the world. He knows all the words, even the hard ones. He once made me promise that if he was hit by a car, I'd make sure they played it at his funeral (he was delirious with man-flu at the time and was also talking about leaving his county medals to charity and making sure his daddy looked after the dog).

Ah feck, Sadhbh has spotted me sitting down and is making her way over for a breather – how do I style this out without seeming like a complete drama llama?

'Jesus, I'm roasting. That's some workout . . . Oh, are you all right, Aisling?'

'Ah yeah, I'm grand – it's jus . . .'

Majella's in beside me in a flash, blustering about 'don't mind it' and 'it's only a song' and 'another drink' and 'she's grand. She's grand.' It took her a few seconds to make the connection between the song and my sudden departure but she's back on full Operation Mind Aisling mode.

'She's just a bit sad,' she mouths in a faux-whisper at Sadhbh, thinking she's being so discreet, 'over her boyfriend.'

Majella, you big mouth almighty!

'It's grand,' I roar at Sadhbh (the roaring necessitated by the frenzied Counting Crows singalong going on mere feet from us, pints going everywhere, one lad almost certainly crying, another lad on his knees, fists clenched). 'Me and my boyfriend broke up, and this song just made me a bit sad. That's all.'

'Ah, that's shit. I'm so sorry.' She looks genuinely sorry for me. 'Come out with me for a smoke and a chat.' She pulls me to my feet, heading first to the bar to order two Baby Guinnesses – coffee liquer with a Bailey's head – to keep us going.

Barry dances up beside us while I wait and she

orders. 'Hiya, Aisling, having fun?' Sure he doesn't know. He's just being nice. He has to be nice.

'Good craic all right.' I feel fairly woozy talking to him. He's saying something about the hangovers in work tomorrow and I'm just nodding and smiling, gazing at his big white teeth, swaying on my feet.

'Here!' Sadhbh shoves the shot into my hand and we knock them back. She pulls me away from Barry and the teeth. 'I'm telling you, he's a ride,' she says matter-of-factly.

The smoking area is crowded but Sadhbh pulls us into a corner with a big plant-pot to perch on, fending off 'howeyehs' from lads in their good shirts.

'Are you all right, you poor pet?' She's taking out a selection of things from her bag – cigarette papers, tobacco. Mother of God, she's going to start rolling joints there and then in broad dayli . . . er . . . night-light. My eyes automatically scan for CCTV cameras and visions of being 'done' for drugs swim before my eyes. She's shaping and pinching and licking and . . . oh no, wait a minute, it's just a cigarette she's rolling – one of those hipster cigarettes. My heart.

'Aisling? Are you all right?' she repeats.

And it all just falls out of me in one quick story. The years together and the frustrations about going nowhere and the holiday and the break-up and the not hearing from him. All in one big word puke. Told all together like that, he sounds like a monster, like an uncaring dope who eats a dozen Aislings for dinner and doesn't know what side his bread is buttered on. I feel like I'm betraying him.

'But like, he's not a bad guy. We were together seven years. We had a great laugh,' I start to pull it back, wanting to sell John a bit, and wanting to save myself from completely belittling the last seven years of my life.

'Of course he's not all bad, Aisling.' Sadhbh is doing just the right amount of nodding and arm clutching and tutting. 'You wouldn't have been with him if he was.' She's so right. What an oracle. 'But look how upset he has you. That's not right. Nothing is worth feeling that upset. You shouldn't have a knot in your stomach over someone who loves you,' she sighs deeply. 'Believe me.'

'You poor thing,' she repeats. 'You're doing great.'

I *am* doing great. Sure I could be in a heap down home still, listening to Daddy tut and sigh loudly at the news and Mammy giving out yards to Daddy for bringing in turf in his slippers, but here I am out, on a Wednesday! With a new pal, who is wearing what can only be described as a black dressing gown.

'You don't need him – look at you!'

She's right, of course. Who does he think he is, making me feel like this? I'm suddenly overcome with rage and power and wine and Baby Guinness. Fuck him.

'Fuck him,' I announce to Sadhbh, delighted with myself.

'Good girl,' she smiles. 'Come on, let's go.'

'Galway Girl' is in full swing when we head back upstairs to the dancefloor, people lepping around like their lives depend on it – and what a tune, to be fair. We rejoin Majella, Fionnuala and Mairead – and a selection of the work gang they've collared – back on the dancefloor and Sadhbh makes a big show of making eyes at Barry when he's not looking, nodding from me to him and generally making it clear that she thinks I should already be moving on from John. Is she mad? And John not cold in the ground.

Barry, meanwhile, is full as a tick and having the time of his life. I'm going hell for leather myself and I keep catching him looking at me and smiling. I swear I'm not imagining it. Every so often, he lamps his arm around my shoulders, shouting 'come on, Ais' in my ear, bringing me along with the frenzy of the music, which breaks into the opening chords of 'Sweet Child of Mine' – it's a miracle nobody has injured themselves.

Suddenly he puts his mouth close to my ear and shouts, 'I hear you're a bit down in the dumps. Come on and let me buy you a shot,' his breath hot against my neck.

Sadhbh! The rip. Feck it. Maybe he is a ride. Why wouldn't I let a ride buy me a shot? Barry finds a tiny clearing at the very end of the bar and manages to wedge the two of us into it, between the wall and a gang trying to fit eight of them into the one selfie. His hand is hovering ever so gently at the small of my back as he leans in to roar at the barman. He keeps it there as he turns back to me, grinning with the big white teeth.

'Jesus, it's great craic to get out like this on a school night. I haven't done it in yonks.' The wife. With all the windows and the dear cushions. She must have had him tied up, and not in a sexy way that I believe is all the fashion now.

'We'll all have some heads on us tomorrow – I hope you won't be giving out to us,' I shout back at him, as he leans in closer to hear me, hand moving infinitesimally up and down my back.

'Ah, sure,' he trails off as he leans in closer. Is he . . . I think he's going to lob the gob. Mother of . . . *Buzzzzz*.

I do a little yelp as my phone goes in my pocket, giving the two of us an awful bad fright. It's probably Majella looking for me, scandalised.

But as I step back from Barry and pull out the phone, an invisible hand clutches at my craw and gives me a belt in the stomach all at once. The name and message lighting up the screen. It's from John. Just the one word.

'Well?'

10

You don't know the meaning of the word 'agonising' until you've seen four girls tear apart what one solitary word could mean.

The 'Well?' text was enough to propel me away from Barry, nab Majella from the dancefloor where she was giving it socks to 'Wagon Wheel', and start gathering coats and bags. Once we'd crashed around Centra (twelve bags of Hula Hoops, a four-pack of demi baguettes, packet of ham, two litres of Diet Coke), we fell back into the house, wondering what it all could mean.

'Could he see me in the corner with Barry? Was he there?' I start getting a bit hysterical.

'Not at all. He was out and he was fluthered. Which is a good thing. Nothing like a drunk text to let someone know you're thinking about them,' Majella says, feeling a little more stable about the whole thing.

'Maybe he forgot you broke up?' Fionnuala is no help. She should really just go to bed before she falls off the chair and brains herself.

'What are you going to say back to him?' Mairead asks what everyone was thinking.

I'm dying to text him back. It felt so nice to see his name there on my phone, knowing that he was thinking about me, fluthered or not. I wanted to leg it out to wherever he was and get him to wrap me up inside his coat against the cold and go home together and forget anything had ever happened.

'You can't text him back now!' Majella barks. 'You have to wait until at least tomorrow. Give him the Seen, and leave him hanging.'

'Give him the what?' I'm glad Fionnuala asked so I don't have to.

'The Seen. He'll know you've seen his message because you opened it. Now he'll have to wait until you reply.'

'I don't know if John knows about the Seen. Sure he only graduated from his Nokia 3310 six months ago. He was like a bull getting rid of it.'

'Well, either way, don't text him back until tomorrow. You are out on the *lash*, you don't have time to be looking at phones and texting *eejits* back.' Majella waves her baguette wildly, lumps of Waifos flying out of it.

Seven hours later, I'm hunched at my desk, mouth as dry as Mammy's Christmas stuffing, which she forgets to take out of the oven every year without fail. I had to get a taxi to work – from Phibsboro all the way out over to Ballsbridge, the price of it – because I'm surely still over the limit. I can feel all the sweet and sticky drinks from last night glooping around in my veins and my teeth feel like each one has been knocked with a hammer. They're singing in my head. Beside me, Donna is slowly and deliberately eating porridge at her desk, scraping each mouthful off the spoon with her gnashers. She has an apple there ready to go and I swear it'll push me over the edge.

I managed to shnake into the office without seeing anyone who was out last night. My first thought when I woke up on Majella's couch this morning was the text from John. My second was the incident with Barry at the bar. What was I at at all? Who saw us? What will I say to him? The fear is prickling up over my scalp and down my arms like a shiver. Everyone is out to get me. Everyone hates me. Am I even wearing a skirt? I can't feel my ears. Could I ever feel them before? I'm never drinking again.

Plonk. A Cuisine de France bag lands onto the desk beside me, giving me such a fright that I jump backwards in the chair. Donna nearly sends the porridge flying.

Barry is standing beside me, looking a bit sheepish and smiling shyly.

'Thought you might need that. I know I do,' he says, gesturing to the croissant in the bag in front of me. 'Good night last night. Great craic. Where did you guys run off to?'

'Oh, eh, Majella was in a state so we had to take her home. It was good craic all right, good tunes all right . . . all right.' My face is puce. I can feel it. I'm babbling. How many times have I said 'all right'?

Thankfully he just smiles and nods and turns to go to his own desk.

'Thanks for the . . . yoke,' I call feebly after him. I can't even muster up the word 'croissant' – 12 Points in that. I steeled my resolve on the way in this morning and bought a Müller Light and a banana (in one of those fancy petrol stations – the price of the banana!) but the croissant is just so lovely and beige sitting there. I'll eat the fist off myself if I don't have a bit of it.

'Out last night, were ye?' Donna asks slyly, as she scrapes the bowl more times than is humanly necessary.

'Well, I was out with my friends. Barry and some heads from here were out on a work thing. We all ended up in the same place.'

'Very cosy,' she says cattily, pushing the bowl aside to allow the residue to harden into cement before she'd even think about putting it in the dishwasher.

I keep the head down and try to get on with some work. I've been looking at my phone every three minutes or so to check if the 'Well?' is still there, and to make sure nothing else has joined it. I'm only delighted I listened to Majella and didn't text him back last night. The longer I leave it, the more powerful I feel. I'm still clinging onto that lovely warm feeling that he was thinking about me, and wondering when would be the optimum time to text him back. Maybe I'll ring him instea . . . *Bing.* The phone goes, as I'm looking at it. I nearly get a bit sick in my mouth when John's name flashes up in a fresh message. I grab it and slide my finger across the screen.

'Sorry that was for someone else.'

I let out a little involuntary gasp and squeeze my lips tight together as soon as I do. No crying at your desk, Aisling. Only oddballs cry at their desks. The fucking prick. The absolute great big thundering fuck.

Disappointment and rage and sadness and more disappointment are coming over me in so many waves I can hardly cope and I'm squeezing the phone so tightly I could nearly shatter the screen – it's insured, of course, but the bloody rigmarole they make you go through to get it fixed. Luckily I'm a divil for keeping phones safe. Never lost one or broke one yet. The tears are definitely threatening to come and I'm pushing my hands against my cheeks like poor Emma Thompson in *Love, Actually* and even thinking about poor Emma and her sleeveen of a husband nearly has me in convulsions. I need to pull it together. I'll get some tea. Deep breaths and tea and no crying and it will all be OK.

'Ah, there you are!'

Sadhbh's in the kitchen. Of course. She's cutting a grapefruit open. Grapefruits are only to be consumed at a hotel breakfast when you've to try everything going, even if it tastes like poison.

'Are you dying? I'm dying. Trying to heal myself with fruit here.'

Fruit. For a hangover. I've heard it all now.

'Last night was great craic. I didn't see you leaving. Was it a late one?' She's not even going to put a bit of sugar on the grapefruit, the mad bitch.

'Ah, we left fairly lively once we decided to go. I actually got a text from John, my . . . my ex, and it kind of gave me a land so I dragged the girls out with me.' Sure she heard all about it last night. Might as well tell her.

'Oh God, what did he say? Did you text him back? . . . If you don't mind me asking, of course.'

I've my back to her, filling the kettle for my tea, so she can't see my eyes instantly starting to fill up with tears and the tip of my nose turning red as the threat to bawl hits me for at least the seventh time that morning.

'I didn't text him back, no . . .'

'Good woman!' Sadhbh interrupts, thinking I'm a strong independent woman like Beyoncé or Mary Robinson.

'. . . but sure it turns out he didn't mean to text me anyway. He sent me another text to tell me.'

I shuffle back down the counter with the kettle, not turning to face her.

'Oh. Oh. Well, balls to that anyway. Fuck him. You don't want him texting you anyway.'

She's right, I suppose. Well, like, she's not – but that's what I'll just have to keep saying to myself until it's actually true.

'Actually, I meant to say to you – I had an idea . . . Oh Aisling, are you all right?' I've finally given up my one-on-one with the kettle and turned around and she can see the big red eyes on me. 'It's very hard, you poor thing. What I was going to say was that I was thinking about what you were saying last night about wanting to move in with John and move back up to Dublin. I have a room going in my place, on the off-chance you were interested? My flatmate Holly is going to teach yoga in India. Elaine, my friend from college, is in the other room.'

Oh my God. Move in with Sadhbh. Start one of those new chapters you always see in inspirational quotes on Facebook. My own personal favourite is 'Dance Like Nobody's Watching'. A classic. I'm also partial to a cheeky 'Remember, Age Gets Better With Wine'. Maybe today is a 'New Beginnings Are Often Disguised As Painful Endings' kind of day.

'Do you know what, Sadhbh? That actually sounds brilliant. Is it far from Coppers?'

11

Spurred on by my flash decision to take Sadhbh up on her offer, I feel alive with spontaneity. I'm going to ring that eejit and give him an earful – tell him not to be texting me, accident or no accident, and that I'm moving on already and he better not even think about me for one more second. My heart is thumping in my ears as I sweep the phone up off my desk and scroll through to John's name in my contacts before I lose my nerve.

'Hiya, Aisling,' Leanne from Payroll calls to me and I barely see her as I stride out in a blind panic, towards the lobby for a bit of privacy. I would go into the toilet but there's always someone loitering in there, brushing their hair or gawking at themselves in the mirror. Bad manners if you're trying to get in to do a . . . you know. Nobody wants to be doing their business with Ellen from Defined Benefits reapplying her eyebrows six feet away.

John will be at work but he may answer his bloody phone. I will not be ignored. I have something to sa . . . oh Jesus, what if he answers it? I suddenly catch a hold of myself and hope to God that he *doesn't.* This is madness. What am I doing, ringing him like a loo-la at quarter to ten on a Thursday morning?

Just as I'm about to pull the phone away from my ear and figure out how to somehow hack into Vodafone's computers to erase any trace that I was trying to ring him, he answers with a subdued 'Hello?'

I miss a beat, and then croak 'Hiya.'

Silence. And then an equally subdued 'Hiya' back.

Silence again. This isn't exactly the fierce independent woman rant I was planning on. I'm stuck for words. It's lovely to hear his voice.

He speaks again. 'Eh, yeah, sorry for texting you last night. I presume that's why you're ringing me. I was out with the lads and I meant to text Cillian, not you. I was just looking for him. So it wasn't for you at all. You can just delete it. It was nothing. I didn't mean to upset you.'

Just. Delete. It.

It. Was. Nothing.

Does this clown think I've been sitting looking at my phone for the past ten hours, pondering over his almighty text? Tying myself in knots wondering what it all means and what's the hidden message? OK, so that's exactly what I've been doing – but he's not allowed to think that. The cheek of him. My rage returns. I'm not upset. I am WOMAN.

'Oh, that?' I'm trying to sound calm and flippant.

Breezy. 'No, I wasn't ringing about that.' I can barely hear myself think I'm so up to ninety. 'I was actually ringing to see about collecting my stuff from your house. I need that suitcase. I'm moving in with Sadhbh from work up in Dublin.'

Silence again on the other end of the line.

'Yeah, so I just need to call over or meet you or something,' I continue blabbering.

'You're moving up to Dublin?' He sounds weird. Annoyed. He sounds annoyed! The cheek of him.

'Yes, I am.' I'm ice-cold now.

'That was quick.'

'Well, I've been waiting for long enough.' It was out before I could stop it. And here comes more. 'I was out with Sadhbh last night and we had great craic. A gang from work. Barry was there too. You know Barry, my new team leader? He asked me out actually, so I better just tell you now before you hear it from anyone else.'

I'm sweating and pacing and it's all falling out of me so quickly I can't stop it. I just want to hurt him and make him feel bad. I'm telling lies about being asked out to make him feel bad. I'm a desperate human being altogether – but at the same time it feels good. Like that time Gemma Coveney was a bitch to me in school and the next day she fell down the steps practising for the musical and broke her arm. We were doing *Seven Brides for Seven Brothers* that year, which was an odd choice for an all-girls school, but sure we were well used to playing lads at that stage and Sister Joan in the Home Ec department was a whizz at fake beards. Gemma lost her spot as one of the brides and had to paint scenery one-handed. I tried to feel sorry for her but I was delighted.

There's no sound from John, just some angry breathing. I can tell he's trying to gather himself, so I jump in again before he has a chance. 'So when can I come and get my stuff?'

'Sure come this evening and get it over and done with so.'

'Grand so, I will. I'll be there around seven.'

He hangs up straight away. I feel like getting sick. I don't really know what I wanted to get out of the call but now I just feel like puking. There's no going back – we're officially over.

Because I left the car at Majella's in Phibsboro, I have to take two buses after work to retrieve it. I still feel sick on the second one, and it isn't helped by some hound beside me having a feed of Rancheros. The heating is on, every window is dripping with condensation, and there's not one but two babies grizzling away behind me. I've never felt more miserable. I check my handbag for the sixth time for the car keys. Imagine the head on me if I'd left them in work.

Finally the bus lurches to a stop on Majella's road, strong enough to nearly launch me through the windscreen, but I thank the driver getting off anyway. I'm not an animal.

Majella's gone spinning after work. She fancies a lad in the class – he's French and she thinks he's fierce exotic altogether. She's been trying out all her best Leaving Cert stuff on him, asking if he's from the '*banlieue*' and if he knows where the '*gare*' is. I head straight to the Micra – no clamp, of course, because Fionnuala gave me a temporary parking-permit yoke. I've never been clamped, and I have no sympathy for those who have been. Why risk it? I think it should actually cost more than €80 to remove, but you can't really say that, can you?

I'm a bit nervous getting into the car because my tax is two days out on my disc. I've renewed it, of course, but the new disc is down home in BGB. What if I'm stopped? I'll just have to explain what's happened and hope they don't take the car away or give me a heap of penalty points or something. Imagine the shame. So as I hit the road from Majella's towards Drumcondra, my nerves are not only like a bag of wild cats over seeing John, I also feel like a fugitive from the law.

I only have to do two circuits before I get a parking spot on John's street, about five houses down from his. After checking that they haven't installed parking meters since the last time I was here (they can be very shnakey about that, putting them in overnight and catching you out), I steel myself to knock on the door.

'It's open, Aisling.' That's Piotr. How did he know I was coming? They're not all sitting in there waiting for me, are they? Like the Spanish Inquisition, except with giant pizzas and cartons of Supermilk?

'Oh hiya, Piotr.' I'm hesitant, but take a deep breath and walk in, trying not to turn my nose up at the barely-clean socks drying on the radiator in the hall and nearly creasing myself on the bike poking out from under the stairs. I shuffle meekly into the sitting room and look around for John. No sign. Maybe he's upstairs. 'Is . . . is John here?'

Piotr sticks his head out from the kitchen where he's doing something pungent with pork, his blond hair sticking up at an angle from his head where he's obviously run a wet hand through it. 'He's not.'

Oh. Don't tell me he's going to make me sit here and wait for him, like an eejit.

'He won't be home until later. He asked me to make sure you got your case.'

Oh. He's not here on purpose. That doesn't feel good.

'Oh, OK. Thanks, Piotr. Sure I'll just get it off you so and I'll leave you be.' I can't see it in the sitting room. I don't want to go up to John's room and get it. That would be weird. What if there were some other girl's pants or something on the floor? I mean, John's hardly already bringing other girls home but I don't want to take my chances. He *is* what Majella would call a Coppers Catch.

'Sit down there a minute and I'll make you some tea.' Piotr sounds very kind. I always got the impression he hadn't much time for me. Maybe it was all the hard looking I did at his dirty dinner plates and my thoughts about his reliance on kitchen roll. But seriously, the way he goes through it. Pure reckless.

'Is Cillian here?' I haven't really spoken to my cousin since me and John split up, but sure he's more John's friend now than mine.

'No, he's out too. Just me,' Piotr says cheerfully, as he comes in and hands me a steaming cup.

I stop myself from examining it for mucky stains and smile gratefully. I'm not sure I've ever been alone with Piotr for any length of time before. Was he always this . . . good-looking?

'I miss you around here, Aisling,' he smiles gently. 'Nobody bashing around in the kitchen or remembering to buy the toilet roll.'

That makes me a bit sad. This lot will be all dead from E. coli by the end of the month without me here to mind them.

'Are you doing OK? John hasn't said much but he's been in a very bad mood.'

'Ah, you know yourself. These things happen.'

'I always thought you were too good for him anyway. For any of us.'

Why is he being so nice to me? And were his eyes always that twinkly? I'm starting to feel a bit weak and eager to get out of there, overcome by the pork fumes and the healthy glow from Piotr's sallow skin (despite all the joints and Tuborg).

'I better go. I've to drive all the way back down home and I was out until all hours last night.' I stand up, setting the mug down on the cluttered coffee table. 'Can I get the case off you?'

Piotr pushes past me to go out into the hall. Was he always that tall? He reaches past the bike and yanks out my case, still with its airport tags on from the holiday.

'Thanks a million, Piotr. I'll see you, er . . . soon. Tell . . . tell Cillian I was asking for him.' I don't want to bring up John's name. It's too weird. This whole situation has me in an awful fluster and I just want to be on the N7 crying to The Script.

Piotr and I pause at the door, unsure of how to say our final goodbyes. He suddenly comes at me with an embrace, leaning down from his great height with his big strong arms. The hug takes me by surprise and I lean awkwardly against his chest before shuffling backwards.

'Bye, Aisling. Don't be a stranger.'

I'm fuming on the drive home. How could John not have been there to do the symbolic handing over of the case? Seven years and he obviously just couldn't be arsed. What a monumental waste of my time he was.

I hear my phone buzzing in my bag so I find a safe place and pull over. It's a text. From him.

'Did u get the case ok?'

No apology. No nothing. What a prick.

'I did. And don't ever contact me again. It's over.'

I spell all the words out properly to make sure nothing gets lost in translation.

12

'Aisling! Oh Aisling, you'll never guess who's here! Come on down!' Mammy is shouting up the stairs in her telephone voice. It can only mean one thing and she can have her shite if she thinks I'm going down there. I'm not in the mood to face anyone, not least the person I was up against for Head Girl in 2006. I hear the kitchen presses being opened and closed at high speed – looking for the Good Biscuits, obviously – and the sound of the kettle being filled. I'd murder a cup of tea and a Penguin but God, I'm not sure I can face it.

I look around my childhood bedroom, with its single bed and glow-in-the-dark ceiling stars, and sigh. The place is upside-down but I'm determined to get as much stuff moved up to Dublin this weekend as I can in one go, rip the plaster off. Well, as much stuff as I can cram into the Micra at any rate. I'm taking the opportunity to downsize too. According to Sadhbh, who is mad into some Japanese book about being tidy and how having less stuff can change your life and make you, I don't know, feel more fulfilled, I should only bring things that 'spark joy'. Everything else needs to go straight into the bin or the charity shop. Mammy and Tessie are only delighted. Apparently this book is keeping them going at the moment and the donations are arriving by the truckload. Those dodgy door-to-door used-clothes collectors had their hearts broken for a long time but it seems now the general public is wise to the fact their old threadbare shirts and eighties dresses were no more going to charity than the man in the moon. Feckin' scammers, the lot of them.

I pick up an old hoodie of John's. It's a grey one, from the DCU GAA club. We were only going out a few months when he took it off and insisted I wear it at a barbecue for Cillian's birthday. It was June but only about eight degrees – typical Irish summer. He sat there for the rest of the night pretending not to shiver while I breathed in the smell of his Lynx and Brylcreem, practically getting high off it. I look at it again and throw it into the charity-shop pile, along with my three-quarter-length combats and a selection of O'Neills tracksuit bottoms I used to live in. This is sparking something, but I don't think it's joy.

My acute desire for tea suddenly overrides all my other needs and I decide I better show my face downstairs. If I don't, she'll probably start talking to Mammy about menstrual cups again and I can't face the questions afterwards.

'Aisling, I thought you were never going to emerge!'

It's Niamh From Across The Road, with her international accent of mystery. We were both born and raised here in BGB, and grew up about forty feet from each other. You'd think we'd be fairly similar then, wouldn't you? Ha!

Niamh Hatton is the human embodiment of notions. The Hattons are Protestants, for starters. Mammy's heart is broken trying to keep up with them – but you can't compete with Protestants, I'm always telling her. They pronounce 'scone' 'scon' and drive a Prius, for the love of God. There's not a peep out of the bloody thing unless it's going above thirty miles an hour. The amount of times Daddy has nearly come a cropper after walking out in front of it on the lane would put the heart sideways in you. Ridiculous vehicle. Unsafe.

Niamh jumps up and kisses me on both cheeks, despite being fully aware that I'm not a hugger. Country people are uncomfortable with physical affection – this is an absolute fact, but one she forgot as soon as she walked through the front arch of Trinity College. Her auburn hair is a few shades lighter than it was the last time I saw her but it's as thick and shiny as ever, bouncing away in a ponytail. When we were teenagers, and every one of us was determined to blend in or die trying, Niamh did her own thing. She was always so self-assured in school – she didn't mind standing out a bit. Some of the other girls thought she was stuck-up but the reality was she had more confidence in her little finger than the rest of the class combined. Sure she even turned vegan in Third Year, when Mr O'Sullivan tried to make us dissect an earthworm, and long before it was main-stream. Throughout the years, we've gone from best friends to mortal enemies but we've ended up with a fondness for each other – although neither of us can quite shake that competitive edge.

Today she's wearing a wide-legged jumpsuit that would one hundred per cent make me look like Worzel Gummidge, but of course she's pulling it off with typical Niamh From Across The Road aplomb. No doubt the cotton is fair-trade and it was hand-stitched by an indigenous tribe of fashion-savvy women in the Amazon basin. No 'thanks, Penneys' for Niamh. She works in some vague, makey-uppy role for a non-profit that seems to have offices in all corners of the world, hence the international accent and the non-stop Facebook updates from weav-ing classes in Tanzania and knitting circles in Peru.

Underneath all the pontificating and guilting and advocating for the less fortunate, she's actually sound as a pound, and mad for the rosé. But Jesus, she and Majella can't stand each other. Luckily she lives beyond in New York and only comes home a few times a year to make us all feel bad about ourselves.

'Have you lost weight? You're glowing, Ais – look at all your freckles!'

I steal a glance at Mammy, who is furiously re-arranging the biscuits and refusing to meet my eye. She's obviously already told her about me and John, the traitor. I've long felt that, compared to Niamh, I come up a bit, well, short – both physically and meta-phorically. Niamh always had her pick of the lads, was captain of the BGB camogie team and got 500 points in the Leaving. Not quite enough for Law or Medicine but enough that her mother still brings it up on a regular basis. I got 440. Mammy and Daddy were very proud. I fell down in French and my drop to Pass Maths still stresses Mammy out, but didn't I get a B in Biology despite the Krebs cycle not coming up? She could never hold down a rela-tionship though, and that's where I pulled into the lead. The one thing I had that she didn't was John – *had* being the operative word.

'Well, I was just in Tenerife,' I'm forced to admit, reaching for the teapot that Mammy reserves strictly for members of the Hatton family and possibly Phillip Schofield, were he ever to be thirsty and passing through. It's Royal Doulton, part of the set Auntie Noeleen got her and Daddy as a wedding present.

'Not sure if you've heard,' I throw a pointed look at Mammy, who's folding towels on top of the Aga, 'but I'm actually moving back up to the Big Smoke,' I say, desperate to change the subject.

'Really?' Niamh is surprised. She thought I was home now for good after the break-up, I just know it. She had me fully written off, destined to grow old and die alone under that Forever Friends duvet cover. 'Whereabouts are you going to be living? I heard that rent is, like, insane at the moment. Not like New York levels of insane but, you know, insane for Dublin.'

'In Portobello,' I reply. 'I'm moving in with a girl from work and her friend. Well, she works upstairs – we're more like work acquaintances than colleagues. Her name is Sadhbh. She's lactose intolerant.' I'm babbling but at least I have something to say that doesn't involve John.

'Wow, that's great news. I have some meetings in Dublin next week. We should have lunch!'

'I'm actually just in the middle of packing, Niamh, so I have to leg it,' I say standing up and grabbing a fistful of Chocolate Kimberleys. Mammy is staring at me open-mouthed at my rudeness, but I know Niamh is on the brink of asking about John and I don't trust myself not to start keening away again.

'Lunch in town next week it is,' I call over my shoulder as I head out of the kitchen and back upstairs to finish what I started.

As I continue mercilessly adding anything I

haven't worn in the past six months to the charity-shop pile, I can't shake the feeling of . . . relief. At least I think it's relief. There's a definite lightness to me – maybe that's because I've felt like I've been drowning for the last few days and now I'm starting to get some perspective. I mean, look at Niamh there. She's never settled down and it hasn't done her any harm. She probably has a lad in every port, and more power to her if she does. Maybe I was wrong all along – maybe having a boyfriend didn't give me the upper hand. Maybe Niamh, with her carefree, no-strings life, had it all along. Head Girl 2006 strikes again.

I always thought that John and I would end up married. Sure everyone did. There was never any question in my mind. But was that because it was right for us or because it was what everyone else was doing? I just assumed it would happen like dominoes – John would propose. My parents would give us a site as a wedding present and on it we'd build a five-bedroom house (a McMansion, Niamh would call it) with a walk-in wardrobe and the massive utility room for me and a man-cave for him. I'd be pregnant within a year and that would be it. It's what happens around here, what all the gang we hang around with are doing.

But did I ever even want that life, really? We probably never stopped to think about other options. And now I've pushed him away and we'll never know.

13

With my trusty Micra heaving under the weight of all my worldly belongings, I pull up outside Sadhbh's apartment block in Portobello on Sunday evening just as it's getting dark. She neglected to tell me I'd need a zapper to access the underground car park but on-street parking is free today so I find a spot close enough and reverse in. Like everyone I know, I learned to drive aged twelve in a tractor and it's a skill that has stood to me. Feeling equal parts excited and nervous, I hop out, clutching the bottle of champagne Mammy sent up as a housewarming present. I know for a fact Úna Hatton gave it to her for her sixtieth last year but I didn't let on. Oh, she was straight down to Maguire's to price it and on discovering it cost €50, immediately put it away for a 'special occasion', winking at me conspiratorially. Looks like there won't be an engagement announcement from me anytime soon and as for Paul? Mr Bondi Beach with three blondes in Cavan jerseys in his Facebook profile? Good luck with that, Mammy.

So here I am, walking around with a bottle of Moët in my Michael Kors like I'm on *Made in Chelsea* or something. It was far from Moët I was raised, let me tell you.

I ring the doorbell.

'Hello?'

'Er, hi, Sadhbh. It's me, Aisling. From work. I couldn't get into the car park?' I hope I don't sound bitchy now, but I have to call a spade a spade.

There's a squeal. 'Aisling, we've been waiting for you! Welcome home!'

Ah, she's so lovely, in fairness to her – and she doesn't have to be. She's one of those girls who's so effortlessly glam you just assume she's a thundering bitch. The door buzzes open – she wasn't exaggerating when she said all mod-cons – and I step into the lobby, which has a lovely marble floor and smells like a five-star hotel. I've been known to nip into The Merrion for a go of their toilets and the free hand lotion. The apartment is on the sixth floor so I tip on into the lift and hit '6'.

I look at myself in the mirror and take a deep breath, fighting the mild waves of anxiety that I feel rising. Why is the lighting in lifts the same as the thing they use in the supermarket to keep meat looking fresh? I look like a chicken thigh that's about to turn, all pale and puckered and sad. But this is good, I remind myself. This is a fresh start. This is exactly what I need, and sure I haven't lived in Dublin in so long now. Not since me and Majella and her cousin had that house in Inchicore after college. I brought the landlord to the small claims court over the mould in the bathroom. Daddy was fierce proud. Anyway, no good can come of staying at home in BGB. 'If you stay at home, you'll die alone with a two-bar heater and a descendant of That Bloody Cat ready to eat the face off you as soon as you croak,' were Majella's exact words.

I've announced my big move to the world by posting inspirational quotes on Facebook: 'The Comeback Is Always Stronger Than The Setback', 'Don't Call It A Dream, Call It A Plan', 'If Opportunity Doesn't Knock, Build A Door'. Not getting as many likes as I expected, but I'm trying to stay positive in the face of . . . everything.

The first thing I notice when the lift doors open is that there's only one door on the sixth floor. Jesusmaryandjoseph, the apartment must be massive, I'm thinking, racking my brains trying to remember if Sadhbh ever let slip that she lives in an MTV *Cribs*-style penthouse.

Before I have a chance to stick my key in the door, it's flung open and there's Sadhbh and another girl who I can only assume is Elaine. She's a tiny waif of a thing with a white-blond bob and a blunt fringe, wearing one of those billowing black sacks that Sadhbh is so fond of and a pair of – no, they couldn't be – orthopaedic sandals. Her lipstick is bright pink and I immediately feel like a big lump in my faded black leggings and good Vero Moda tunic with the butterflies, which looked quite cool when I put it on at home. I thrust forward the Michael Kors to prove I'm no stranger to fashion myself, even if I don't look it right at this very moment.

After much squealing and air-kissing – yes, I was forced to do it and sure lookit nobody died – my new flatmates usher me inside and I produce the champagne and wait for them to ooh and aah over it.

'Oh my God, you're such a dote, Ais,' Sadhbh says nonchalantly, leading me down a long corridor. 'We actually just opened a cold bottle, so I'll stick this in the freezer to chill.'

We're still walking, by the way. It's becoming more and more apparent that this is not your average Dublin apartment with a plywood kitchen, rising damp and rat-filled basement. On the walls are black-and-white photographs of people I don't recognise – possibly drug addicts from the cut of them – and paintings that look like they were done by a three-year-old with a shaky hand. Modern art. Would you be well.

After walking down a corridor the length of the garden at home, we eventually get to the L-shaped kitchen/living room/dining room, which is the size of a football pitch and has one of those American fridges and an island and a chandelier over the table.

'Lads, I cannot believe this place,' I blurt out, taking in the view of the roof garden outside the floor-to-ceiling windows and noting the state-of-the-art television I'll get to watch *Fair City* on. Somebody pinch me. Although I notice there's no clothesline and wonder how blasé these girls are about tumble-dryer use, because I'm not one bit blasé about it at all – the cost of it. I decide against bringing it up right now; I don't want to get off on the wrong foot. 'Are you sure my rent is only €650? Did I miss a zero somewhere? I'm not sharing a room with eight students, am I?'

Elaine bursts out laughing. 'You weren't making it up,' she says to Sadhbh, nodding in my direction. 'She's wild.'

Wild? Is that good? If I was to guess, I would say it has negative connotations, especially in the farming community – but according to Majella, things that are 'sick' are actually cool now so who knows? Elaine pours the champers and we all clink glasses, delighted with ourselves. Am I sharing a room with several other people though? Nobody answered me.

'Do you want to see your room, Aisling? Where's all your shit?' Elaine goes.

'I'd love to!' I say. 'And all my, er, shit is downstairs in my car. Actually, I better slow down on this,' I add, putting the glass down on the marble worktop that is surely worth more than said vehicle.

'Oh, you have a car – amazing,' says Elaine.

'If I didn't drive, I'd have to stay at home and listen to Mammy complaining about Filan's selling damp turf,' I reply. 'I'd crack up after a week.'

She's off again, in stitches, and I start to relax as

Sadhbh turns up the music on her phone, which seems to be connected to speakers in every room. It's very loud, especially for a Sunday. Then again, we don't really have any neighbours, unless you count downstairs.

Off to the bedroom we go and I'm not disappointed: the bed is massive, king-sized at a guess, and there's a big wardrobe as well as an *en suite* that looks like a massive shower with a toilet and a sink in it. I'm wondering if this is some kind of design flaw and my face must give me away because Elaine goes, 'It's a wet room.'

I stare back at her blankly.

'It looks like it's one big shower?' I can't help myself.

She stares into the room for a minute.

'I suppose it is,' she eventually admits. 'Don't leave anything on the floor and you'll be good.'

I'll take her word for it.

Four hours later, I've started to put my stamp on the place – I'll be knackered in work tomorrow but it's worth it to get settled in. The girls had all sorts of mad stuff in the fridge – tamari and miso paste and coriander and the like – but I managed to make space for my Low-Low cheddar slices, Müller Lights and Kerrygold (I refuse to compromise on butter, to hell with the Points). I've wrestled queen-sized sheets onto the king-sized bed, using moves that would put

Conor McGregor himself to shame in the ring, and am tucked up with my trusty hot water bottle. Although considering my new luxury digs, I'm seriously thinking about upgrading to an electric blanket. Could I handle the responsibility though?

All my clothes are unpacked and taking up about a third of the wardrobe space. Looking at them now, none of them spark joy. Not one little bit. The 'Live, Love, Laugh' decal I painstakingly peeled off my bedroom wall at home suddenly looks a bit naff too. I've kept the black sacks I transported them up in to line the household bins at a later date and stuck the cardboard boxes into the recycling bin downstairs. For some reason, both Sadhbh and Elaine thought all this was gas. They were still milling into the champagne at 11 p.m. and talking about potentially going out. On a school night!

'I think it was a full week before I'd fully unpacked,' Sadhbh said, and my skin started to itch at the thought of it. Tidy room, tidy mind, that's my motto. Also: tidy desk, tidy mind. If my mind isn't tidy, I just can't relax. And if there's one thing I need right now, it's to be relaxed.

I give the room a quick once-over again. I know I should be thrilled to be here, in this lovely apartment, with two lovely new flatmates, but of course I'm still thinking of John in that kip in Drumcondra with the dripping taps that used to lull me to sleep.

14

By Friday, I'm wrecked. Between settling into the new apartment and what Sadhbh described as a 'monumental fuck-up' in work, John has barely crossed my mind, which is, all in all, A Good Thing. Because Sadhbh's in HR, she always knows everything before anyone else. She was the first to know when Carl from Sales was sacked for stealing €450 worth of Sharpies over the course of five months. In fact, I think it was her that sacked him. Nobody could figure out where they were going and there's nothing more precious than a good Sharpie.

But the latest big scandal, which Sadhbh told me all about on Monday before everyone else found out, is that €56 million, instead of €5.6 million, has been transferred to a Dutch bank account and has since basically disappeared off the face of the earth. The shit is about to seriously hit the fan. Now, I don't want to name names . . . but Donna has been very distracted lately, too busy trying to choose a picture to put on her wedding thank-you cards. At one point, she had the whole department voting on it. She eventually whittled the twenty-four contenders down to the final two pics – one of her lying on her side, laughing maniacally, being held up by the lads in the bridal party, and the other, a shot of herself and the hubby, kissing in front of their local pub, the one where they first shifted. As if we had nothing better to do! I voted for the pub one. It was a better shot of the dress, which was gorgeous altogether. Well, it would want to be – she went to New York to buy it, in that shop on *Say Yes to the Dress*. But Randy wasn't even there – I'd have been asking for my money back. She was livid.

Anyway, we're being audited. Several of the London bigwigs, the ones who wear suits they had specially made for them and buy their shiny pointy shoes in Italy, are being drafted in to follow the paper-trail and try to resolve the issue. What if they find out about all the time I spent booking that bloody holiday? Or that afternoon I was tied up disputing a mysterious €4.50 on my mobile bill? It turned out to be a competition I forgot I'd entered to win a year's supply of Herbal Essences. I didn't even win.

On Tuesday, I met Niamh From Across The Road for lunch in a place suggested by Elaine's friend Ruby, who's basically a permanent fixture in the apartment. Not that I'm complaining, mind, because she's mad into *Fair City* too and it's nice to have an ally when it comes to the remote. The restaurant was vegan, obviously, very new and it had a DJ. Yes, at lunchtime on a Tuesday. Dublin has truly lost the run of itself. I could tell Niamh was impressed, because she stuck a picture of her tomato and avocado ceviche with a corn tostada and herb salad straight up on Instagram. I ate what can best be described as a slice of €8 toast covered in grass and raw mushrooms. Never again.

Then, on Wednesday, the PensionsPlus fax machine broke and I discovered that, in a company that employs 236 staff in Ireland and another 1,200-odd in the UK, I was the only one who could work it in the first place. Imagine not being able to work a fax machine! All right, I know email is quicker and more convenient and maybe faxing is a bit of a waste of paper in this day and age, but surely knowing how to send one is an important life-skill.

I was never so relieved to leave work as I was today. Nobody said anything to me personally about the decimal-point mess, but we're all eyeballing each other and I can't shake this guilty feeling. The same thing happens to me every time I see a Garda. Truth be told, I skived off about a half an hour early, even after factoring in my flexi-time. Blind eyes were turned. But in spite of my skiving, Dublin traffic is against me and it's gone five by the time I pull into the Red Cow to pick up Majella. She's bulling, I can tell, because tonight is the Knock Rangers GAA dinner dance and she needs to be in her dress and sitting at the bar in Dick's by 7 p.m. This will be the first year in the last seven that I'm missing it and I feel a lump forming in my throat when I imagine the craic.

'Well, hello, stranger,' she booms, as she gets into the Micra, jamming her tattered wheelie bag into the passenger-seat footwell and tapping on the dashboard – the universal sign for get a move on. We haven't spoken all week, which is unusual for us, but it's been mental in work and both Sadhbh and Elaine, plus various pals, have been in nearly every evening so the chats at home have been off the charts. There are only so many hours in the day. 'How's life in hipster central?'

'Oh Maj, I can't wait for you to see the flat.' I know it will annoy her but I can't keep the excitement out of my voice. 'Well, it's obviously an apartment, not a flat, being the penthouse and that.'

A silver BMW pulls out in front of me and Majella gives your man the finger while I dole out a few good bips. I hate Friday evening traffic. I'm half-thinking of doing something mad and staying up in Dublin next weekend. I know better than to mention that now though, but going home for the weekend is just what we do. Sure what would you do with yourself rattling around in Dublin of a Saturday? Mammy and Daddy like to see me, too. It's home. I turn my attention back to Maj.

'It's absolutely faboo. We even have a wine cooler. With wine in it! I don't know where it even comes from but there's hardly ever a spare hole. And I don't know myself being able to walk to work – it's so much easier to get my steps in.'

'Switswoo. An upgrade from home anyway. And what are the girls like to live with? Saoirse and the other one? She seemed all right that night in McGowan's.'

She knows right well her name is Sadhbh but Maj's nose is easily shoved out of joint if she suspects any-one is moving in on her turf. Irene Treacy will testify to that. Maj spread a rumour that Irene had been caught shoplifting a push-up bra in Shaw's Almost Nationwide in Transition Year when Irene and I were paired up for our mini-company project. Oh, she says she heard it from someone and only passed it on by accident but the whole class all knew it was because me and Irene were spending every waking minute in each other's pockets, trying to get our personalised stationery business off the ground. Majealous, the girls started calling her.

'It's Sadhbh, and she's lovely. You'd actually get on great with her, Maj. She's very down-to-earth, although she doesn't look it. And Elaine, the friend, is gas altogether – and a vegan. She works in some kind of start-up social-media place with free food – as much as you like – and sleep-pods and standing desks and a basketball hoop in reception. That's when she actually goes into the office – she usually works from home on her company laptop. Oh, and she knows Colette Green. Like, personally knows her. She just casually mentioned it last night.'

Majella is obsessed with Colette Green, so I know this will sting. We both are; she's the best-known fashion and beauty blogger in the country, with something like 200 pairs of nude shoes and all the fanciest handbags. Everything in her house is marble and rose-gold. We were both going to go to an afternoon-tea yoke she was running down in Killarney last year but the tickets were €100 each, which was a bit rich for our blood – even if the goodie bags are supposedly worth twice that.

Majella's silence is deafening, but I swear I can hear her heart pounding in her chest. I shouldn't have mentioned Colette. I decide I'd better change the subject. 'So what are you wearing tonight?'

'A bandage dress I got off Fionnuala. It's black, can't go wrong. She's worn it to six weddings. It won't be the same without you though, Ais. Are you sure you won't come? You can pull a seat up at our table. John will be over with the team anyway.'

Hearing his name jolts me out of the trance-like state the stop-start of the traffic had lulled me into. They complain about it, of course, but John and the lads love getting dressed up in their rented tuxes for the annual dinner dance. After a few cans in Dick's, it's straight onto the minibus and into the Ard Rí Hotel for the presentation of prizes for the year's big achievers followed by 'dancing 'til late' aka 2 a.m. and then back to Dick's again for the inevitable lock-in and dancing on tables.

'Do you know if he's bringing anyone?'

'Ais, are you mad? You're only broken up two weeks. I haven't heard, but I seriously doubt it. Everyone is hoping you'll get back together.'

I snort, involuntarily. 'That's not going to happen.'

'How can you be so sure? You miss him, don't you?'

'Of course I miss him. We were together for seven years. I'm actually sickened thinking of you all out together tonight . . .'

'Jesus, Ais, I'm sorry . . .'

'It's hardly your fault, Maj. And I've had a good first week living back up in Dublin, so my perspective on the whole situation is changing. Maybe building a house at home with seven bathrooms is not the be-all and end-all.'

'I'm not following you, bird?'

'I'm just saying that, I don't know, maybe I'd be better off putting down roots up in Dublin for the minute, rather than going up and down to BGB like a yo-yo every weekend and not feeling properly at home anywhere. I'm even thinking about moving my vote, truth be told.'

There's a gasp. Majella knows well that the only way you get potholes fixed at home is by voting for a certain local councillor. It's pushing seven o'clock so I decide I better distract her and lighten the mood.

'By the way, you'll never guess who might have bankrupted PensionsPlus,' I say, glancing sideways at her.

'*Who?*' she roars, desperate for any smidgen of gossip, as always. Telephone. Telegraph. Tell Majella.

'Donna, of course,' I say, whacking the steering wheel. 'Someone's after making the stupidest mistake anyone could ever possibly make – a decimal point in the wrong place – and millions of euro gone just like that.'

'Go 'way.' Majella is agog.

'I know! And we don't actually know for sure who it is, but Barry called her in for a meeting today and has been looking stressed and flying in and out of conference rooms so I think it must be someone on our team. Whoever it is will have some fight on their hands not to be let go, because whoever got the money into their account has done a legger with loads of it. Sure it could bring down the whole company.'

'Fuck me, Ais. Thank God it wasn't you.'

It couldn't have been me, could it? I have been fierce preoccupied with John and all the carry-on, but I'd never make a mistake like that, would I? Surely it was Donna.

'No, sure it couldn't have been me. I'd know.' I would know, wouldn't I? I'd have caught it right away, wouldn't I? I'm gazing at the road ahead of me, suddenly gripped by a tiny sick feeling. I've seen *Orange is the New Black*. I wouldn't last a minute in jail and the jumpsuits on my hips would be a crime in themselves.

Majella hasn't even noticed. 'Poor Barry having to sort all that out. He's a bit of a cool customer, isn't he?'

'Yeah, I suppose he is. What did you make of him the other night?'

'I wouldn't kick him out of bed for eating Taytos. What was the wife doing cheating on a man with teeth that good? She'll regret that.'

'I don't know if I was hallucinating or what, Maj, but I swear he was going in for the shift at the end of the night in McGowan's.'

'You're not interested in seeing anyone else at the moment though, are you, Ais? I mean, I know you've been testing the waters a bit, and fair dues to you, but you and John . . .'

'Me and John are most definitely over, Majella,' I say, taking the exit a little sharper than I mean to as she adds a twelfth coat of mascara and sprays a good dose of dry shampoo into her hair. Sometimes I wonder how Majella would get through the week without dry shampoo. It wouldn't be pretty.

The clock in my car (never wrong – I always immediately change it for Daylight Savings Time.

I forgot once about two years ago and couldn't sleep thinking about it, so I was up at 2 a.m. setting it, reciting, 'spring forward, fall back.') reads 7.26 p.m. as I indicate left down Main Street, Knocknamanagh. What a waste of a Friday evening, sitting in Dublin traffic and then coming down here to . . . nothing. Well, Mammy and Daddy aren't nothing, I know, but I'm not even going out with the gang this weekend. What's the point?

The car is still moving when I roll up to Dick's and Majella hops out, nearly taking off my good door with her wheelie bag in the process. My eyes are on stalks looking for John but also hoping to avoid him. I wave her off as she legs it into the toilets to change into her dress and heels and head out with the crowd who, up until two weeks ago, I would have called my best friends. Now I couldn't bear to see any of them – it would hurt too much. I turn the Micra west and head for BGB, the decimal point and the millions of euro nagging at me. At least home, Daddy will have the fire lit, a pot of tea brewing and the Good Biscuits ready. That's something, I suppose.

15

The house is mad quiet when I pull in. Usually Daddy would be up, flinging on the hall light and twitching curtains to see who it was coming in the driveway, and at the front door before I'm out of the car to check if I'm in for the night and to close the gate behind me. Nobody is more up to speed on local break-ins and home security than Daddy. If there's a lawnmower taken or a set of car keys lifted within a ten-mile radius, Daddy knows about it. He's the king of alarm codes and garage-door locks and is always telling us about the importance of minding a house when there's a funeral on. Funerals are prime house-robbing opportunities down the country. Sure don't gangs read RIP.ie and come down the N7, knowing full well that the family and all the neighbours will be gone for hours? Not Daddy though – he'll park himself in the tragic house's sitting room like a well-trained Alsatian until the grievers return. And if he can't do it, he'll organise someone else to do it. Isn't that what good neighbours are for?

Maybe he's not home this evening . . . although the

car *is* there. Maybe they got a lift down to Maguire's for a few drinks (a pint or maybe a brandy for Daddy, peeeno greeejo for Mammy, or a Baileys if she's feeling particularly swish). They don't go often to the pub, preferring to stay in to give out about the *Late Late* on a Friday and enter any and all competitions for cars and holidays, but perhaps tonight was a pub night and they forgot to text me.

I let myself in the back door, cursing to high heaven as I fall over a discarded bale of briquettes left right in the middle of the floor. 'For *fuck's* sake,' I rage, the gouging of my shin on their sharp brown edges bringing my misery close to the final straw. The racket propels Mammy out from the sitting room. So she *is* here.

'Is that you, Aisling?' She sounds odd – worried and yet relieved at the same time.

'What kind of place is that to leave briquettes, Mammy? For God's sake!'

I'm really hoping she didn't hear my 'for fuck's sake' a minute ago. Cursing in front of Mammy and Daddy is something I'm simply conditioned not to do, although I've heard some amount of blinding and damning out of the pair of them over the years – most recently when the cat got at the ham on Christmas Day. She went from That Bloody Cat to That Feckin' Cat for several days. Still, cursing in front of them feels so wrong.

'Oh, Daddy dropped them there on his way in, I think. He . . . Ah, Aisling, he wasn't feeling well at all.'

I'm horrified to see her face start to crumble. My heart sinks to my feet and I feel all cold and hot at the same time.

'Is he all right?' I bark. 'Is he all right, Mammy?'

'He is, he is. I just got an awful fright, that's all.' She takes a deep breath, already pulling herself back from full-on breakdown and heading for the kettle.

'What happened?'

'He went out to get the briquettes from the garage about an hour ago and next thing I knew, he was crashing back in the back door. Kind of . . . staggering.'

'And where is he now?'

'In, sitting down. He's grand now. He said he just went funny for a minute. He's annoyed I'm fussing about it, but he's not right.'

'Do you think . . . ?'

'Ah, I don't know, Aisling. But it all feels very familiar. I was going to ring to get the CareDoc out but he said not to be worrying and that he'd be grand after sitting down.'

We've been here before. We've seen this before. We know Daddy isn't invincible.

'Sure I'll go in and see him so.'

Mammy nods and sinks into one of the kitchen

chairs, looking more shook than I've seen her in a while. More shook than the night before Paul was leaving for his travels and Lorraine Keaveney called in and told her about a programme she'd seen about Australian spiders who move into your shoes and bite the toes off you when you put them on. Kill you stone-dead in three seconds, they do. Mammy went out and got two cans of fly-spray and tried to convince Paul to bring them with him. He hid them in his bedside locker but told her he was taking them, to stop her worrying.

As I go to leave the kitchen, she calls after me, 'See if you can get him to go to the doctor in the morning, Aisling. He might listen to you.'

Where does she think she is? Dublin? There's no doctors open in Ballygobbard on a Saturday. 'It'll have to be CareDoc again though, surely?'

'No, Dr Maher is open on a Saturday morning now. He gets loads of business from people thinking they're dying from the night before.'

Well, this is the most cosmopolitan thing that has happened to BGB in quite some time, equal only to when Filan's finally got an ATM. It lasted four days before it was empty and nobody ever came back to fill it up, but my God they were a golden four days.

When I go into the sitting room, Daddy is propped up in his chair, feet on the good pouffe (things must be really bad), eyes closed.

'Hiya, Daddy.'

His eyes open slowly but he doesn't move. 'Hiya, pet.'

'Well, how are you feeling?' I ask him matter-of-factly. Matter-of-fact is the way to go when you're trying to avoid an air of 'fussing'. Like I said, we've been here before. 'Mammy said you dropped the briquettes like a big eejit.'

'Ah, I just felt a bit wobbly. Sure I'm grand now sitting down.'

'Oh good, good. What are you watching?'

'Ah, some old rubbish.'

Sure he wasn't watching anything at all. His eyes were closed, and they're closed again now. He's wrecked. I'll give it a few minutes before I launch my offensive about going to the doctor.

'The new place is going well anyway, Daddy. It's huge and I have my own bathroom, including a shower.' Daddy installed a hand-basin in my bedroom when I was twelve and I thought I was the poshest thing going, so I knew he'd appreciate the entire bathroom to myself. 'The girls are very nice. Fierce for leaving lights on though.'

His eyes fly open. 'They can't be at that now, Aisling. Aren't you paying the bills too?'

'Don't worry, Daddy, I'll train them. I'll stick up a few notes. That'll soon sort them right out.'

'Good girl.'

'Mammy was telling me Dr Maher is opening on a Saturday now. He must be saving for a new coat.'

Daddy chuckles. Dr Maher is . . . well, he's mad. Stone-mad. He's known for striding around the town in a bright-green raincoat. He's been wearing it for years. You can see him coming a mile off. When he's not firing into the shop or mass in the green coat, he's in his surgery at the side of his house in the middle of Ballygobbard. He has no receptionist, and he makes no appointments. You just go along and hope to God there aren't too many other people in a bad way that day, so you won't be waiting hours. The waiting room is just his utility room, and the three chairs – you may stand if there are more patients than there are chairs – share the space with an ancient washing machine and an old turf-basket full of decrepit *National Geographic*s and an *RTÉ Guide* from 1992.

Mammy once brought Paul in to Dr Maher for a tetanus shot after he creased himself on his bike and Dr Maher came out into the waiting room, stuck the needle in his arm right there and sent him on his way. He told me once that I had the biggest tonsils he'd ever seen, pushing himself away from me in horror like they were going to attack him, tongue-depressor flapping in the air. I got them out when I was twelve but Mammy still talks about them. 'The biggest tonsils he'd ever seen', you'll hear her proclaim proudly if anyone even mentions a sore throat in her vicinity. Still, Mammy and Daddy are fiercely loyal to Dr Maher and even when the swish new health centre with the lifts opened in Knocknamanagh, they refused to have their heads turned.

'Will you come with me to see him tomorrow, Daddy?' I seize my chance. 'Just to be on the safe side.'

'Right so.' His eyes are closed again. That was surprisingly easy. I always did have him wrapped around my little finger.

Daddy was up and ready for me this morning, looking a good bit better but still unsteady on his feet. He didn't protest at all when I said I'd drive instead of him. Daddy would always be the one to drive everywhere, except when I was a learner and we nearly killed each other around the back-roads of BGB, fighting about biting points and ten to two and whether or not having the radio on was appropriate for someone who still hadn't mastered the three-point turn. Sure I was only allowed onto the roads after two months of doing figure-eights in Daddy's tractor around the hay-bales in the Far Field. It feels weird to have him back in the passenger seat. Mammy waved us off, wringing a tea towel in her hands. I don't think she could face coming with us.

We've got a chair each in the waiting room. Daddy

isn't saying much, letting me knock on the surgery door when we arrive to let Dr Maher know we're here. I can see John Towelly Doyle in there already, shirt buttons undone. He's John Towelly Doyle to distinguish him from the other John Doyle in the town, John Badbridge Doyle, so called because he lives at the Bad Bridge up the road (it really is a bad bridge – they had to re-route the St Patrick's Day parade last year when the Zumba with Maggie float got stuck on it for two hours). The origin of Towelly's nickname has been lost in the ether, but it has stuck.

You'd get away with nothing in this town. Dr Maher has seen that I'm here with Daddy and just nods at me and tells me I can nip around to the kitchen to make tea if I want. We've been coming here as long as I can remember. He knows us all inside out. Well, I don't go to him for my anti-babby pills. Would you be able for the mortification of him asking about your cycle and having a go at your chest? I'd be dead from shame.

There's only one person ahead of us – Geraldine. She owns the local boutique, called Geraldine's. It's where everyone in BGB goes to get their first bra, and she insists on measuring you with great attention to detail (she has a bra-measuring certificate proudly displayed above the Triumphs). I nod a quick hello but she's engrossed in a piece in *RSVP* about where Anne Doyle, Ireland's most glamorous newsreader, gets her highlights done, probably taking notes. Geraldine is also very glamorous, with her year-round tan. Mad for the sunbeds, although she'd never admit it.

Daddy seems happy to sit quietly and wait. I'm studying my phone for any sign of movement from Majella. I texted her last night before bed and then again this morning, looking for news of the dinner dance and nothing back from her, the auld shite. 'She's probably lost the phone again,' I think bitterly, before reminding myself that it's not her fault I wasn't there last night. I want to hear about what John was up to, but at the same time I don't want to know anythi . . . oh, out comes Towelly Doyle clutching a prescription. His lungs must be at him again. Geraldine stands up to head in and I notice she's limping. She must have fallen off the stool again while reaching for the Sloggies on the top shelf. You'd think she'd just move them at this stage. The same thing happened just before Christmas and Constance Swinford was drafted in to mind the shop after Geraldine was carted off in the ambulance. Sure Constance hadn't a clue how to work the till. Mammy found her breathing into a paper bag under the counter after half an hour.

'Won't be long for us now, Daddy,' I smile at him. He's so quiet.

'Yep, thank God.' He has on a good jumper and a cap. Medium Good Clothes, I'd call them, for going to the doctor and maybe the odd mass or going visiting – not up to the standard of the Good Christmas Jumper or the coat that comes out for funerals, but he's made an effort.

Geraldine is in there no length – I'd say she'll have to go to the General for an X-ray.

Dr Maher pops out of the surgery. 'All right, Seamus, in you come.'

I look hesitantly at Daddy. Should I go too? I've been in with him before for various appointments, of course, but it's been a while.

Dr Maher answers for me. 'You're coming in too, Aisling?' It's a question but mostly a command, an acknowledgement that maybe we'll need a second pair of eyes and ears in the room. Another adult. I'm the adult.

Dr Maher's surgery is straight out of the eighties – as in he definitely hasn't changed it since the eighties. Brown carpet. Wood chip on the walls, but not in the fashionable way I read about in the 'Hot or Not' bit in one of Sadhbh's *Style* magazines. His wood chip was there the first time around. A certificate proclaiming that he is in fact a doctor, and not a madman who wandered in off the street in a green coat, hangs on the wall.

Daddy and I are seated opposite him across his desk. Miraculously he invested in a computer about five years ago, although I strongly suspect he uses it only to display the flying-through-space screensaver.

'Well, what has you here?' He directs the question to Daddy, but includes me as he swings his gaze to meet mine.

I wait for Daddy to speak, and when he doesn't, I talk instead. I tell him Daddy wasn't feeling well last night. I tell him about the staggering. About the tiredness.

'And you're very quiet, aren't you, Daddy?' I ask him. He nods. 'I suppose I am.'

Dr Maher listens to his heart, takes his blood pressure the old-fashioned way and puts him through a series of tests, asking him to push against his arms, follow his pen this way and then that way with his eyes, walk in a straight line. I feel like he's only doing it half out of procedure, because I know what's coming.

'I think we'll send you for a scan, to be on the safe side. I'll get it set up right away.' Again, he directs it mostly at me, the 'right away' not lost on me. 'And no driving for the time being, Seamus, OK?'

Daddy doesn't even protest. I feel my heart sinking to my feet and the pins and needles feeling of 'this is happening to someone else' take over me. Daddy seems content enough to get back into the car and head home though, saying little except 'Good to get a scan done anyway', to which I matter-of-factly reply, 'Ah yeah, sure it's only a scan.'

Mammy's out to the front door the second we pull into the driveway. She ushers Daddy in, telling him there's tea made in the kitchen and an apple tart straight from the oven.

'Well, what did he say?' she asked me in a low voice when Daddy's out of earshot.

'He has to go for a scan. Very soon.'

Her face falls. We both know what that means. 'Oh no, Aisling, not again. He must think it's back.'

'I know, Mammy.' I'm struggling to hold back the tears. 'Fuck it anyway.'

16

Yes, we've been here before. Mammy and me. And Daddy. And Paul. All of us. Two years ago, I came home on a Friday night to find too many lights on in the house. No lights on – something's wrong. Too many lights on – something's definitely wrong. The place was lit up like a Christmas tree and there's no way Mammy would allow it unless she was going mad looking for something, room to room like an antichrist – the *RTÉ Guide*, the house phone (the day cordless was invented was the day Mammy's blood pressure started to rise), That Bloody Cat. All potential culprits.

But not only were all the lights on, there was a strange car in the driveway. I didn't recognise it as one of the neighbours' cars. I have them all memorised so I can prepare myself for the level of interrogation I can expect when I encounter them. If it's Veronica Murphy, I'm grand – I can slide in the back door and make it out of the kitchen fairly unscathed as she and Mammy go to town on whatever local councillor has let them down regarding hedge trimming this week. If it's Mick Cusack, I may creep in the front door or I'd be stuck hovering for an hour while he quizzed me about work and John and how I was a 'grand big girl now, all the same'. But it wasn't Veronica Murphy or Mick Cusack's car. It was a doctor's car. Daddy had collapsed in the calving shed.

He had a brain tumour, a dark evil shadow invading his memory and his personality and his balance. He had chemotherapy. He had radiation. He had so many doctors and so many appointments. He took pills and pills and more pills. He vomited. His hair fell out. He couldn't work. Some days, he couldn't move. But he made it through. They said he was responding well. They seemed positive. They had high hopes. And after nine months, he was told he was in the clear. For now. It could come back, they said. But for now, he was in the clear.

I moved home when Daddy got sick. I went from digs in college to THAT flat with Majella and her cousin Áine in Inchicore and was absolutely loving it. John was in a place in Stoneybatter with Cillian, another Cillian and a John-Paul. It was dead handy. I had designs on me and John taking over his Stoneybatter house as our own in no time at all. But my Dublin living was cut short. Daddy got sick and I moved home.

And now we're back here again. The recent scan confirmed that yes, the tumour was back and slightly more aggressive than before. We've fallen back into the oh-so-familiar routine of appointments and treatments and temperatures and watching, watching, watching. Always watching. There's talk of Paul maybe coming home. He wants to, but Dr Timmons, Daddy's consultant, says there's no need for anything drastic just yet. Paul Skypes us all the time and I teach Mammy how to use FaceTime on her phone, although it's usually her feet or a bit of the ceiling Paul can see. He sends me separate messages asking how Daddy really is and I tell him the truth. It's like last time, except we're a bit more used to it.

Work were great the last time and they're great again, giving me days off here and there when I need them. The investigation into the €56 million and the Dutch bank account is ongoing and the place is *alive* with talk of it. Between Head Office in London and the crowd in Holland, it's taking ages to get to the bottom of it. And it doesn't help that we only have one Dutch speaker here. God help Lotte, is all I'll say. I hope she gets a bonus.

We're all in and out of meetings about it, but I've missed a lot of them, what with being back home to help Mammy with the farm or taking Daddy to appointments up in James's. Everyone assumes it was Donna's mess-up. It happened on her watch. I haven't even had time to worry about it being someone else, although that niggling feeling still grabs me sometimes. Barry and his boss have been trying to catch me for a one-to-one about it, probably because I work closely with her, but they're not pushing too hard. They know what's going on with me.

I'm in a bit of a daze most days, but not that much of a daze that my eyes and ears aren't on stalks whenever there's any chat about it. I bring the news about it home to Elaine the odd time I do stay up in Dublin. She's absolutely bet into the whole saga and always pumping me and Sadhbh for info. Will Donna get the sack? Who'll take the fall? Sadhbh gently slags me about Barry from time to time too, but truth be told, he's the least of my worries right now – a work colleague and nothing more. He's asked me gently in the kitchen a few times if I'm all right, but that's about it.

I'm never in the Portobello apartment. I don't want to give it up so soon after moving in because I don't want to leave Sadhbh and Elaine in the lurch – and because I just don't want to give it up. Mammy told me to hang on to it for the time being and Elaine even knocked a good bit off the rent while I'm not there. Her dad owns it and they're loaded, so she said he wouldn't mind for a few months. I've met her dad once, when he called up to say hello one of the few times I was there recently, and I strongly suspect he might be some kind of gangster. He was wearing far too much jewellery and I'm almost certain he had two phones. I must keep a close eye on the papers and whatever they're calling *Garda Patrol* these days. He might pop up in a reconstruction.

When I *am* there, I feel a bit like a visitor. Sadhbh and Elaine treat me like I'm wrapped in cotton wool, pulling bottles of wine out of the cooler yoke like there's a fairy replacing them every night. One of the nights I do stay up, I drink too much wine and end up crying to them, initially about Daddy and then mostly about John. Why hasn't he been in touch? How could he be so cruel? Sadhbh gently asks if I would think about contacting him. Wasn't he there for the first time Daddy was sick? Would he not want to know and help? But I have enough on my plate. If he wants to get in touch, he knows where I am.

Another night, in early May, a rare Friday I stay up because Daddy is going through a good patch, Elaine has Ruby over and I invite a highly suspicious and on-guard Majella for drinks. The Grand Apartment Tour does nothing to lower her wariness – she keeps pointing out its notiony aspects, like my wet room and Sadhbh's precious juicer, which cost more than my Micra. But to her credit, she gives Pictionary a shot and the craic really gets going after a few drinks, when she warms up and forgets that she's meant to be calling Sadhbh 'Saoirse' or 'Sorcha'. Soon they're even on the same team – 'It's a baby! No, it's the Eiffel Tower. Eh, eh, *One Flew Over the Cuckoo's Nest*!' – and we end up staying in and having a great time, drinking first wine and then gin and tonics. Making gin and tonics in your own house is very swish, and we even have lumps of cucumber in them. I'm not sold on the cucumber, to be honest with you. It belongs in a salad with two slices of ham and a hard-boiled egg and maybe a scallion.

When we finally decide to call it a night at 3 a.m., Sadhbh offers to order Maj a taxi and we both nearly get sick. A taxi? From Portobello to Phibsboro? Is she well?

'She's staying with me tonight, if that's OK?'

'Of course!' shouts Elaine, swaying on her feet clutching her sixth G&T. 'We'll have a full house so, with Ruby staying too. I'll get the bagels in the morning.'

'I thought Ruby only lived up the road,' whispers Majella as we head into my room.

'She does,' I whisper back. 'But she stays here all the time. They're great pals.'

For four months, Daddy is up and down. I feel like I'm in limbo. Nothing is more important than getting him to his appointments, filling his prescriptions, making sure he feels OK, finding space in the fridge for the many shepherd's pies and pasta bakes dropped in by neighbours, trying not to kill Mammy with all her fussing, and then feeling guilty for even thinking about wanting to kill her. Majella is the best, sitting in and talking to Daddy for hours about the local teams when he's feeling up to it, sitting in the kitchen and talking to Mammy for hours about the local everything else when I'm feeling not that up to it. When I have the occasional cry, she pats my shoulder and says, 'It'll be grand' and 'Will we go for a drink?' We take ourselves down to Maguire's the odd time, but I steer clear of the Vortex or anywhere I might run into John. I haven't heard from him, not one peep. Of course he'd know what was going on from Cillian and because everyone knows everything. You wouldn't be able to have a cold in Ballygobbard and Paddy The Kettle Walsh (not to be confused with Paddy Kettley Doyle, Towelly Doyle's brother) up in Rathborris would know about it.

One June night in Maguire's, when I've had five Coors Light and am well into my second vodka and Diet Coke, I bring it up to Majella.

'I think . . . I think it's bad that John hasn't been in touch about Daddy, Maj. I think it's really bad. Nothing at all.'

Majella purses her lips and says nothing.

'Do you not think he might have rang me or something?'

'Look, I'm sure John knows what's going on. But you told him to leave you alone. You broke up. He probably thinks you don't want to hear a thing from him. Sure didn't you more or less tell him you were moving on? Maybe he's mov . . .' She stops.

'Maybe he what, Maj?'

'Nothing. But I'm sure it's not because he doesn't care. But he's not your boyfriend any more.'

She has a point. It doesn't mean I don't miss him though. All the drinks I've had combined with the nostalgia I'm feeling for John's big dry hands and strong arms mean that my eyes start to fill with tears.

Majella recognises the warning signs and changes the subject. 'Let's slag people we went to school with. There's Anna Malone over there in the snug. She's gone back to do teaching in St Pat's and has already changed her name to Irish on Facebook. Nothing screams "Pat's" like changing your name to Irish on Facebook. Smug cow. Sure Pat's is no better than Mary I.'

Majella is fierce loyal to her few years in Limerick. And she's right, I do feel a bit better already.

'And Imelda Kearney's after getting done with a pyramid scheme. She has a spare room full of weight-loss drinks and turbo-vitamins and nobody will touch off them. The dope.'

It's July before we know it. Almost two years to the day since this craic with Daddy first started, and the three of us, Mammy, Daddy and me, are sitting in a sterile hospital corridor waiting to meet with

Dr Timmons, the consultant. She has the results of the latest scan. She asked us all to be there.

My nerves are in ribbons. Daddy is weirdly calm. Some of the medication he's on makes him a bit spaced out. Mammy is up and down like a fiddler's elbow, getting water, checking to make sure Dr Timmons hasn't somehow made it out of her office past us without us seeing her, even though we couldn't have missed her, texting Auntie Sheila that there's 'no news yet', and then double-checking to see if the message has sent. Sure isn't she miles away from her internet down home? The chances of her phone even *working* are slim to none.

Suddenly the door opens and Dr Timmons smiles out at us.

'Come in, come in.' She's like Amal Clooney. Her hair is so shiny and her coat is so white and she smells like Brown Thomas's. She's always so warm and lovely, addressing Daddy in such a kind way that makes me want to burst into tears. When she delivered the bad news that it was back, back in March, she was the same. Imagine how many awful things she has to tell people every day.

'Now, Seamus, you're here for the scan results. You're all here for the scan results,' she smiles again, including me and Mammy in her radiant beam. I almost feel blessed. 'We have good news.'

My ears are roaring. I can't hear anything she's

saying apart from the odd word: 'significant shrinkage', 'responding well', 'few more treatments'.

She's handing pieces of paper over to Mammy and instructing her about a few more appointments. Mammy has tears in her eyes and is babbling: 'Thank you, Dr Timmons. Ah, thank you. You're great. Ah, Dr Timmons, it's great.'

Daddy is smiling away like an eejit. 'That's grand now. Grand altogether. Thanks, doctor.'

He's already up and putting the good coat on (Funeral Coat and Medium Good Jumper are out today), mad to get out of there. We sail out of the office and down the white halls and out towards the car park, repeating 'great news' and 'of course it was working' and 'text Paul there'. Mammy doesn't even bat an eyelid when the machine tells us we owe €9.40 for two hours. Coins are raining out of her purse. It's like Christmas. Daddy's coming back to us. Our lives are coming back to us.

17

With Daddy on the mend, Mammy assures me it's high time I moved back up to Portobello properly: 'You're a great help, love, but you're putting fierce miles on the Micra. And sure you're paying for the room, you might as well use it.'

Truth be told, it's good to slip back into Dublin life. And on a sunny Tuesday at the end of July, a week after I move back up, Sadhbh and I are walking into work when she tells me that today is the day the shit is really about to hit the fan – all confidential, of course. She says the whole company is on tenterhooks over it, especially her gang above in HR who have a pool going. Seems highly unprofessional to me, but I say nothing. Elaine is still heavily invested in Donna's future, and always wants to hear the latest goss from PensionsPlus when we get in every evening. This is what happens when you work from home as often as she does.

I'm dying to hit the shops and pick up a few new work bits for summer, but on mornings when I'm not in the mood to think up an outfit, I'm glad of my unofficial weekday uniform of a shumper (a jumper with a handy shirt collar sewn in) and bootcut black trousers. From what I can gather from the snippets that come through the walls, Sadhbh and Elaine seem to spend hours in the morning deciding what to wear depending on their mood/the weather/what various celebrities and 'bloggers' I've never heard of wore yesterday. You'd be exhausted listening to the pair of them and sure regardless of whether Mercury is in retrograde or not, they usually end up in various oversized garments that I just can't make head nor tail of, designed by people with names I can't pronounce. But each to their own. They can get away with it, swanning around Dublin, but I'd love to see the faces now if I rocked up to Maguire's wearing one of those swingy sheer dresses Elaine is partial to and which cost about a month's rent, even though you have to wear a whole other dress underneath. My face must have given me away the other morning when I bumped into her wearing one in the hallway, because she took one look at me and burst out laughing, saying something about me being a 'riot'. Even though we're chalk and cheese, not least in how we dress, we're getting on like a house on fire and I'm delighted Sadhbh brought us together.

When we arrive at the office, Sadhbh makes a beeline for the lift while I head straight for the stairs, determined to get my steps in for the day after all the driving I've been doing. I'm just through the door when I feel a gentle hand on my shoulder and swing around. It's Barry, looking understandably stressed – but wearing it well, I must say. The doors close and we both know we're going to be alone for the next minute or two.

'Aisling, thank God it's you and not one of the London lot,' he says, flashing the pearly-whites. 'I couldn't face seeing them first thing, not after having to take them all out for dinner last night.'

'What did you have?' I ask automatically, my brain poised and ready to calculate the Points. 'Sorry, I meant where did you go? And God, poor you.'

'I pulled out the big guns and took them to Shanahan's on the Green for steaks,' he says with a faint smile. 'Hoping a bit of arse-licking would work in Donna's favour. Not sure it has though.'

'Shite. When will we find out?'

'There's a conference call with Head Office in London at eleven so we should know either way. I have to have another painful meeting with middle-management beforehand though.'

He leans in slightly and touches my upper arm. 'Ais, don't say anything to Donna about Shanahan's, will you? It's no big deal, but I didn't use the company credit card and I don't want her to find out and think I'm pulling out all the stops. I need her to know the Ireland management team believes her and is behind her.'

'I won't say a word,' I go, miming pulling the zip across my lips, throwing away the key and immediately wishing the ground would swallow me up. My cheeks are burning. Why have I suddenly started acting like such a gobshite around him? Is it because I fancy him? It's been so long since I've looked at another lad seriously in that way that I genuinely can't tell.

Donna is already at her desk when I sit down and slip off my runners.

'Morning,' I wave, before copping the shiny silver handcuffs on her desk and immediately searching the surrounding cubicles with my eyes, convinced there must be a SWAT team lurking somewhere, about to make an absolute scene arresting her for misuse of a decimal point. Actually, hang on – do we even have SWAT teams in Ireland? But the office is still half-empty and she's putting on her make-up defiantly.

'Er . . .' I say, gesturing at the handcuffs, 'are you handing yourself in?'

'Very funny, Aisling. They're for Suzanne's hen,' she says, shoving them into her top drawer haughtily. I can see what looks like a whip already in there – this could be embarrassing if she's frogmarched out by security with everything she owns and a random pot-plant poking out of a box. Well, it's what they do in films, isn't it?

I lower my voice. 'How are you holding up?'

'Grand,' she says, swivelling a bit closer in her chair. 'I should find out either way this morning. Thank Jesus, I've hardly done a bit of work since last week.' She takes a deep breath. 'I'm so scared, Ais. Not just about losing my job, but about becoming unemployable. I've worked here for nine years now – if I'm let go for gross negligence, I won't be able to put it in my CV and my last job was sweeping up hair in Curl Up And Dye. No more career in finance for me.'

Jesus, when she puts it like that . . .

'I think you'll be fine,' I blurt out, desperate to stay positive. 'I just bumped into Barry in the lift. He's really determined to get you off the hook. He even took the Head Office crowd to Shanahan's last night – with his own money.'

She raises her eyebrows and lets out a low whistle. Despite never having been, we both know Shanahan's charges upwards of €40 for a steak. €40! You'd buy half a heifer for that in the butcher's down home. Barry is not messing around; he's not going to let them fire her. The €9 whipped potatoes with butter and chives will surely have seen to that.

I offer her what I hope is a reassuring smile and fire up my PC. 9.01 a.m. I better get stuck in – I still have loads to catch up on after being off so much.

*

It's Sadhbh who eventually breaks the news to me, just before lunch, in an email: 'Fuckit, Donna is toast. They offered her a massive pay-off and she took it. I'm up €20 though.'

I can't actually believe it. A deep sigh escapes my mouth. I hadn't realised I had been so tense. In the back of my mind I was worried that they might have pointed the finger at me. It was waking me up in the dead of night sometimes, like those dreams where you feel like you've fallen off a cliff or what have you. Sure it could have been one of us on the team. Though I must admit I'm also slightly relieved. It was in the back of my mind that maybe it could have been me. Sure it could have been anyone on the team. But they've pinned it on poor Donna. I always knew she was sloppy – her desk is testament to that – but I'd never known her to let it seep into her work. And she swore to me that she distinctly remembered double- and triple-checking those figures before the transfer was signed off. But this is coming from the same girl who had 'kind retards' in her email signature for three months before a client copped it, so I wouldn't put anything past her. Plus, she did have all the wedding-photo stuff on her mind.

She'd been called up to the second floor about an hour previously, so I stare at her desk, with its multiple half-drunk mugs of tea. The same mugs that would have sent me into a rage a week ago are now making me a bit weepy. She wasn't really a bad desk neighbour . . . although the constant reminder that 'girls just wanna have fun' drove me absolutely berserk and I once had to lodge a formal complaint to HR about how loud her apple-eating was. Even though she ignored my frequent Post-its asking her what her last maid died of, she was kind – and she always bought the fancy tissues, the ones infused with balsam. I'm suddenly acutely aware of how much I'll miss her. Better the devil you know and all that.

Another email pops into my inbox and I feel a familiar heat rising in my cheeks as soon as I see Barry's name. My cheeks have always been a barometer of how I actually feel before my head has fully figured it out. Before I was sure I fancied John, I'd go almost purple any time his name was mentioned. And coming from a household where hurling is a hot topic meant it was mentioned 'on the reg', as Elaine would say. No wonder Daddy knew I was mad about him before I did.

'Hi Aisling,' it reads. 'As Client Services team leader, I wanted to personally let you know that Donna has left the company, effective immediately. I don't suppose you fancy going for a drink after work?'

A drink? Does he mean just us or the whole team? Either way I've got nothing to wear. What if it's a date? I check the clock on my PC. 12.46 p.m. I could nip out and buy myself a new top at lunchtime. I had my coat buttoned up when I saw him this morning – he'd never know.

Then I catch myself. He's married! Well, technically . . . I can't believe I'm actually considering going for a drink with my married boss. Who am I, Majella? Not that Majella's ever gone out with a married man . . . that she knows of. Feck it, what have I got to lose? If everything I've heard about the wife is true, the marriage is over. And, completely Sadhbh's fault now, but I've started to think that he's a bit of a lash. He has better teeth than Tom Cruise and I've sent two sneaky pics of him to Majella already. But most importantly, I think he sort of fancies me and I like how that feels. It's good for the ego, I won't lie.

'God, that's awful,' I type, not letting on that the cat had already been well and truly let out of the bag. 'Will we go to Doheny's?'

After double-checking that my VALUE club card is in my wallet, I head out for a quick lunch break trip to Dunnes. I'm not even past the frankly extortionate fancy bit at the front when my phone goes. It's Barry. Texting me!

'Hey, I actually can't make it this evening. Pulled into meetings. Want to meet on Saturday in town instead? Grogan's at 7?'

Oh my Jesus. It is a date. A proper Saturday night date. Maybe I'll go all-out and splash a chunk of change in Savida.

18

It's been so long since I've gotten ready for a date that I sort of forget how it's done. It's 4.22 p.m., so that gives me less than two and a half hours to have a wash, shave my legs bald, decide what to wear and do my make-up. Christ almighty, that's not enough time at all, I think, beads of sweat pooling on my upper lip. Why didn't I start this charade hours ago? OK, deep breaths. It's just Barry. Barry From Work.

The late-afternoon sun is streaming in the bedroom window, which is nice, in theory, but not when I'm trying to keep my body temperature down. I check my phone to see if there's anything from Donna. I texted her yesterday afternoon to offer my condolences and to suggest meeting up for lunch next week. I hope she doesn't think that going out with Barry is a bit shnakey but sure didn't he do everything he could to help her? Oh God. Barry. The date. I'm really doing it. I'm staring forlornly into my wardrobe – I already hate the two tops I got yesterday – when there's a soft knock at the door.

'Come in, I'm decent,' I shout and Sadhbh pokes her head in.

'So tonight's the big night, right?' she asks, brandishing a large glass of rosé and pushing it towards me. 'I thought you could do with something to steady your nerves.'

'You pet, Sadhbh,' I say, taking a sip and mentally reminding myself to go easy on the lady petrol. 'What am I going to wear? I have nothing.' I gesture at the half-empty wardrobe and flop down on the bed. 'I'm not sure I can go through with this.'

'You're not having second thoughts, are you?'

'I'm totally having second thoughts. It's not just Barry – it's the whole dating thing. And a bit about Barry. I'm not sure I'm ready for all the leg-shaving and pretending I care about how many sisters he has and all that.'

'It's only some drinks,' Sadhbh cajoles with her little tinkly laugh, handing me up the rosé again. 'You have to get back on the horse, Ais. You've had a tough time of it lately – you need a good night out and a bit of attention.'

I can't argue with her there. And the more I think about Barry, the more I think I fancy him. It's not just that he's easy on the eye – he's so bloody nice too. And he was really sound to Donna, even after she made such a balls of things. But now that there's an actual date on the cards, John is on my mind more than I'd like to admit, even to myself.

Sadhbh is right though – I'm never going to move

on if I don't take the first step. I glance at the 'Live, Love, Laugh' decal above my bed. It's time to practice what I preach. Life is too short to spend sitting around mooning over someone I've been broken up with for nearly five months. I take another slug of wine and I feel it going straight to my cheeks.

'Oh,' Sadhbh asks, 'did you ever find out what the actual real story is with his marriage? He's not actually still with the wife, is he?'

'No, they're definitely separated,' I reassure her. 'So Donna heard anyway. He'd hardly be so blatant about going out on dates if they weren't.'

'That's what I heard too, off Ann-Marie from Retention. Maybe you should get it from the horse's mouth too though, just to be sure.'

'Right so. What am I going to wear?' I say, fanning myself.

'That depends,' says Sadhbh. 'Where are you going?'

'We're meeting at Grogan's – I've never been there before.' I really hope it's not one of those notiony places that serves cocktails in jam jars. The last time I was out in town, Majella made us go to a bar that was so up its own hole it didn't even have a name. How they expect people to find it is beyond me – although it was packed, to be fair.

'Ah, Grogan's! It looks like such an old-man pub, but it attracts a mixed crowd – Elaine and Ruby are always there. Everyone sits or stands outside, especially on a night like this, so you can go quite casual. Do you fancy trying a pair of my mom jeans? You could wear them with that little grey top you got in Penneys. Maybe add some statement earrings?'

I knew this day would come, I think, draining the glass to buy myself some time. The mom jeans. Sadhbh is mad for them. I can't actually bring myself to say the word 'mom' out loud so they're mam jeans to me, thank you very much. They look like something Tessie Daly would reject from the charity shop on the grounds that no one in their right mind would ever buy them, even for 50 cent. And people in BGB would buy anything for 50 cent. Elaine tried to explain them to me once, but I still don't get it. Why would anyone wear jeans so high-waisted and unflattering that they make you look a size bigger than you are? One of the many style tips I picked up from Weight Watchers Maura is that dark denim with a bootcut leg is the way to go if you're trying to look slimmer.

'Yeah, er, maybe I'll try them. I'd say they'll be too small for me though . . .' I say, half-heartedly. Sadhbh has some figure. I suspect she's a size ten, max, although I can't really be sure considering she's usually buried under layers of fabric. It's madness, really.

'Not at all! I have a pair with frayed cuffs that will

look gorge with that new top. You go hop in the shower and I'll leave them here for you.'

'OK, sound,' I concede and drag myself up.

In the bathroom, the wine starts to take effect and I decide to fully seize the day. Out comes the Kérastase shampoo and conditioner John's parents got me last Christmas that I've been saving for a special occasion. I never thought the occasion would be a night out with another man but sure here we are, I think as I lather up. Next, I go hell for leather with the Bics until I'm bald as a coot pretty much everywhere.

After applying a generous layer of the Clinique Happy body lotion that came free with the perfume, I start getting dressed. The mam jeans are staring back at me from the bed where Sadhbh has laid them out with that grey strappy top and a pair of big red earrings I'm sure she must have got in a lucky bag. There's another glass of ice-cold rosé dripping condensation on my bedside locker and I wonder, what did I ever do to deserve her? And whether she's ever heard of a coaster?

I'll have to just suck it up and wear the mam jeans. I couldn't bear to see her disappointed little face if I didn't. I down the glass in one. Feck it.

Twenty minutes later, I'm standing in front of the full-length hall mirror looking totally normal on top, save for the earrings, and like Kelly Kapowski's mother from the waist down. The mam jeans have done exactly what they say on the tin: managed to make me look like a middle-aged mother of three. Stupid godforsaken trend.

'Are you sure about the jeans, Sadhbh? Really? I feel a bit self-conscious. And step back from the vino – if I have any more, you'll have to stretcher me to the pub.'

'Aisling, your look is so on point. With the Penneys top, it's the perfect high–low mix and you're one hundred per cent pulling it off. Now, what are you doing for make-up?'

High–low mix? I have no idea what she's on about, and I've just spent twenty minutes doing my make-up but I say nothing. Maybe there is such a thing as too natural. Although I thought the foundation and bit of mascara looked fine.

'Do you want me to do your eyeliner? I think a little flick would just finish off the whole look. And, here, I'll just fill in your brows. Make them a bit stronger.'

I'll make no bones about it – liquid eyeliner scares me, so I've never tried it. I got tricked into buying one in Boots once – it was to get the triple points – but I never worked up the courage to actually use it. Too much room for error. No, no thank you.

'Yes, please.' The words have tumbled out of my mouth before I can stop them. Go big or go home. Isn't that what Majella is always saying?

19

It's after seven when I leave the apartment so I know I'm going to be at least twenty minutes late. Me! Chronically Early Aisling. Aisling who once showed up the day before a job interview. But I don't care. I had another teeny-weeny glass of vino while Sadhbh was doing my eyebrows – she nearly passed out when I confessed I've never had them 'done'. I have a wizard of a yoke from QVC, a tweezers with a little torch attached. I know brow bars are all the rage now, but honestly I think you'd have to be mad to pay someone €20 to pluck out a few hairs that will be back in a week anyway.

My inhibitions are out the window and I'm feeling very sure of myself all of a sudden. I text Barry: 'Running a few mins late'. And before I can stop myself, I've added an 'x' and pressed send. The butterflies in my stomach start to wake up as I cross the canal.

It feels good to be going on a date, truth be told. It feels good to be in Dublin on a Saturday night, weaving my way through the thronged footpaths, listening to snippets of conversations here and

there, dodging tourists carrying Carroll's bags looking for the Guinness Storehouse.

The sun is starting to drop but there's still plenty
of heat in it and I slip on my sunglasses – Penneys,
€3 – as I turn onto Castle Market, where it looks
like the whole entire city has decided Grogan's is the
place to be this evening. Outside, the pub is heaving,
the crowd spilling out on to the footpath and even
the road in places. My watch says 7.22 – fashionably
late at last.

I check my phone. No reply from Barry but I'm
assuming he's sitting outside somewhere. The crowd
isn't giving an inch, but I manage to throw a few
elbows and break through the perimeter. I'm sidling
past a gang of hipsters sloshing around €7 pints of
craft beer and wearing backwards baseball caps
when the crowd parts like the Red Sea and I see
him, Barry From Work, tucked away at a corner
table in a tiny patch of sunlight, with a jacket flung
protectively over the stool in front of him. He's
obviously been in the sun because his teeth are blind-
ingly white against his tanned face and he's got a
five o'clock shadow that stirs something deep inside
me. By now, the rosé has started to wear off and I
feel the inhibitions creeping skywards again, acutely
aware of the mam jeans and grateful for the sunglasses. Then he spots me and jumps up waving.

'Ais!' he roars, gesturing at the seat, and I fight

through a group of Germans gathered around a single pint of Guinness to get to him.

'You made it,' he says, nearly taking my retinas out with a grin, while moving his jacket so I can sit down. 'You look great, by the way,' and he leans in for a hug. Unfortunately, he's taken me by surprise and my arms seize up so I sort of just press my body against his, wondering if it's possible to die of embarrassment.

'What are you drinking? West Coast Cooler or Coors Light or something like that, isn't it?' he says.

'I'll have a West Coast Cooler, yeah. Thanks. And a glass of ice – a pint glass, please, if they have it.'

'No problem, back in a second.' And just like that, the crowd swallows him up.

If they have ice? Of course they have ice, it's a bloody pub, Aisling. Christ, I *am* rusty at this dating thing. I check my phone to look busy.

7.01 p.m. Majella. 'Well, howz it goin?'

7.14 p.m. Also Majella. 'I'll take dat as a gud sign ;)'

7.22 p.m. Aubergine emoji.

It's now 7.25 p.m. 'Jus got here. Goin ok. Wearing Sadhbh's mam jeans tho,' I fire off.

7.26 p.m. 'Iv heard it all now', and the crying laughing emoji x3.

After the initial awkwardness has passed, Barry and myself fall into easy conversation and I finally stop sweating. He manages to grab the attention of a very efficient lounge girl and one very hefty tip later, the drinks start coming and don't stop. It's the mark of a good man, Daddy always says, to make sure your glass never goes empty – that and always standing a round. One of my pet peeves is people who come out to the pub and 'aren't drinking', and then stand there all night adding €4.50 pints of Lucozade to a round without ever putting a hand in the pocket. I often find a quick nod and a 'well for some' gets the message across. I'm not made of money. Or Lucozade.

'So how are things, er, at home?' he eventually asks, once we've oohed and aahed over the weather for a good half an hour and talked about how Irish people are all probably suffering from SAD on some level but don't the few fine days we get in July make living on the island just about bearable?

'Not too bad, thanks. He's – Daddy's – in good form. I'm feeling a bit guilty for staying up though. I'd normally go home at the weekend, you know.'

'So you stayed up just for me? I'm flattered,' he says with a smile and I'm glad of my sunglasses. I wonder what toothpaste he uses. No Irish person has a right to have teeth that spectacular.

'Don't go getting a big head – I had some other stuff to do this weekend too.' He probably knows I'm lying but I like where this is going. Banter, isn't that it? Suddenly something catches in the light and I realise that he's still wearing the wedding ring.

'Nice jewellery,' I say, lifting up his hand. Even though it's getting properly dusky now, I see him go red and I immediately feel guilty.

'Oh that. Yeah,' he says, holding it up like Beyoncé doing 'Single Ladies', the song that Majella will rise from the dead to dance to. 'Not that it means anything. Well, it didn't to her anyway.' He laughs.

'Oh God, I'm sorry Barry. I shouldn't have brought it up.'

'Nah, don't worry about it,' he says. 'It's been over for nearly a year. Longer actually, although she didn't let me in on the secret. I'll take it off one of these days, I swear.'

For the first time all night, I notice the glasses in front of us are empty. Your one's shift must be over and it's definitely my round at this stage.

'Another one?' I ask him, doing the international hand gesture for 'drink?' and standing up, slightly unsteady on my feet. 'Don't go letting anyone take my seat now,' I add, in a way that I hope seems flirty. When I look back, he's got his phone out and I wonder if his pals are texting him, wondering how it's going too.

The crowd in Grogan's has changed from the late-afternoon, post-shopping gang to the Out Out crew. It's wall-to-wall girls in break-your-neck heels and lads wearing their best shirts. I feel under-dressed in the mam jeans, but I don't feel as out of place as I thought I would. Before I go to the bar I make a beeline for the ladies' to smooth back my hair – bit of water, be grand – and make sure my eyeliner isn't down my face. But true to Sadhbh's word, it hasn't moved a millimetre and would it be big-headed to say that I think it actually suits me? I must remember to take a snap to send Mammy.

The queue for the bar is about four people deep and after ten minutes, I've just about given up hope when I hear my name.

'Aisling! Out in Dublin on a Saturday night – I never thought I'd see the day.'

The eight-foot tall, sixteen-stone, backpack-wearing American in front of me steps abruptly to the left and there behind the bar is Piotr. As in John's housemate Piotr.

'Jesus, it's yourself,' I say, caught on the hop. 'What the hell are you doing here? And also, while I have you, a West Coast Cooler and a pint of Guinness, please.' The American is giving me daggers so I shift my body slightly sideways to keep him out of my eyeline.

'I've been doing a couple of shifts here every weekend since the start of summer,' Piotr replies, pulling the pint. 'Who's this for? I know it's not John's.'

'I'm on a date, actually. He's out the back there. Lad in the grey T-shirt on his phone.'

The American is about to blow a gasket but Piotr is up on his tippy-toes peering out the back door of the pub, desperate for a look.

'Good for you, Aisling. Have you been together long?' He plonks the pint in front of me, followed by the West Coast Cooler and a pint glass of ice.

'God, no, we're not, I mean, we're not together together,' I say, handing over €10 and praying for change. 'It's very casual.' I lower my tone and lean in. 'This is actually our first date.'

Something flickers across Piotr's face, but I can't quite tell what. He breaths in. 'Fair play. I always thought John took you for granted, coming around and cleaning up after him – and the rest of us.' Piotr has a habit of just saying whatever he's thinking – he used to be always at it in the house. He once told everyone the reason Cillian's attracted to older women is because he drinks so much milk – something to do with all the extra hormones. He gets away with it because of his exotic accent and impressive shoulders. Still, I'm a bit taken aback at his conviction about the state of me and John's relationship. Who knew he cared this much?

The American turns on his heel and walks out muttering something about TripAdvisor while I'm still wondering if I heard Piotr right. Did John take me for granted? That makes me look a bit of a fool, doesn't it?

'Anyway,' Piotr continues, handing over a miserable 50 cent as I pick up the drinks. 'I'm delighted to see you've moved on too. And you're looking well.'

I walk back to Barry with the drinks, only one word ringing in my ears: 'too'.

20

'Is everything all right? You look like you've seen a ghost.' By the time I get back to the table, all the confidence I'd built up over the course of the evening, thanks to Sadhbh and her precision eyeliner and to Barry and the way he kept touching my leg as he was talking to me, has dissolved and I feel like an imposter in jeans that I have no business wearing. John has moved on. Moved on 'too'. John's with someone else.

'What? Oh, yeah, sorry, Barry,' I stammer, lowering myself slowly onto the stool. 'I'm not feeling great.' I push the bottle of West Coast Cooler into the middle of the table for dramatic effect. 'One too many of those. I think I need some fresh air.'

'We're outside, Aisling,' he laughs, taking a gulp of his pint.

'We are. Of course we are. But everyone is smoking – I can't catch my breath. I have to go.' I look at my watch – 11.40 – a respectable time to call it a night.

'Cool.' He looks momentarily awkward and then peeps out at me from under slightly devilish eyebrows. 'Will we go back to your place for a nightcap so?'

'What? No. I mean, not tonight. I have to go on my own. I'm sick, like.'

He looks crestfallen and I immediately feel a bit guilty. It must have been the flirting – he thought we were going to go off and do the deed. No one waits until the third date now – Majella told me several times over the past week. And she'd certainly know. But I'm a little bit annoyed that he just assumed we were going to jump into the sack after one date.

'Oh right, sorry, I must have gotten the wrong end of the stick. Sorry, Ais. I know you're a good girl,' he smiles.

'Honestly, Barry, I'm really not feeling well. I was actually three sheets to the wind when I got here. It's the weather – the girls won't stop buying rosé and making me drink it.'

His smile widens and he just shakes his head, taking out his phone and doing some elaborate scrolling.

'No problem, Ais. Some of the lads are over in Whelan's so I'll head over there. Will you be all right getting a taxi? I don't want to miss them.'

'Oh. OK.'

'See you Monday. Feel better soon.'

And with a quick peck on the cheek, he's gone, just like that, weaving his way out of the terrace and off into the night. I decide to pop to the ladies' to make sure he has a good head-start. Can't risk him seeing me in the chipper down the road, because that's absolutely where I'm headed now to eat my feelings. Thirty-two Points in a bag of chipper chips – but at this very moment in time, I couldn't give a shite.

I'm just about to leave when someone taps me on the shoulder and I swing around. It's Piotr looking . . . concerned.

'Aisling, are you all right? I saw your man leave alone and wanted to check.'

When Irish people say 'your man', it's clear that we just mean 'that man', but in Piotr's Polish accent, northside twang notwithstanding, it sounds like he's calling Barry my man. He's not my man. I don't think.

'I'm fine! Fine!' I reply, trying to mask the manic tone that's creeping into my voice. 'Just fancied an early night is all. And maybe some garlic-and-cheese chips.'

He looks at me quizzically.

'And an onion ring or two,' I admit.

'Was it something I said at the bar? I thought I saw your eye twitch. I know that's never a good sign.'

How much exactly does Piotr think he knows about me?

'Speaking of which, should you not be back there pulling pints, Piotr? You'll get yourself fired,' I say, trying desperately to change the subject.

'Ah, it's OK, my shift finished at eleven. Do you . . . fancy one for the street?'

'For the road,' I correct him absent-mindedly, and look around. The terrace has fairly cleared out, everyone off to the nearby clubs to dance to dintz-dintz-dintz music with no words and get off their heads and shift each other no doubt. Barry is long gone and the chipper is open until four.

'Sure go on,' I say, sitting down again. 'Vodka and Coke. Diet.'

And he's gone like a flash. I check my phone to look busy. Nothing from Barry. Nothing from anyone. It's Saturday night at half eleven – Majella is probably lining up tequilas in the Vortex and Sadhbh and Elaine are at Elaine's office, where there appears to be an endless supply of free hipster beer. Everyone is out, busy, living their lives. Meanwhile, I can't finish one date. I shiver, all the warmth of the July night now gone.

'Here you are now.' Piotr is back with the drinks, two vodkas and Diet Cokes – doubles, sitting across from me in the seat that must be still warm from Barry's arse.

As he's pouring in the mixers, I catch myself looking at how well his T-shirt hangs on him – like he was born to wear T-shirts and he grew the arms to match. His eyes are the kind of blue that wouldn't look out of place on a husky – and that strong jawline. He's always seemed a cranky fecker though, rolling his precious joints and never tidying his mess up, so I wonder why he's being so nice to me all of a sudden.

'So he's moved on, has he?' I take a gulp of my drink – definitely a double – and will Piotr to say that it was all a misunderstanding and that John is actually at home staring at pictures of me, weeping into his tea.

'Oh, I thought you would already know?' God love him, he looks horrified.

'How would I know?'

'I thought everyone where you're from knew everything about each other.' He sounds defensive and slightly mocking.

'She's from down home?' My skin starts to prickle. I know her, I must know her. Who could it be?

'Ciara? No, I don't think so. But I just thought you'd know.'

'Well, I didn't.' I'm grand. Totally fine. Ciara. Right. 'And have they been going out long?' I'm hoping I sound nonchalant and that he hasn't noticed I'm gripping my glass so tightly that my knuckles have turned white.

'They're not going out, Aisling,' he says gently. 'I bumped into her in the house one Sunday morning but she hasn't been back since as far as I know, and he hasn't really mentioned her.'

She's been in the house. In John's room. In his bed. I nearly swallow the straw in fright. I'll never understand how lads can live the way they do, not knowing anything about each other and not really caring at the same time. I'm imagining if some ridey lad – I'm assuming this Ciara is a ride, the biggest ride in the world, turbo ride – came wandering out of Elaine's bedroom one weekend and I never mentioned it, just went on about my business, not acknowledging the relationship blossoming under my very nose. How do they do it?

The staff of Grogan's are pottering around the terrace, bringing stools and chairs back indoors and sweeping the ground, but no one says a word to us and we carry on drinking.

'And you didn't ask?'

'I didn't ask. It's none of my business.'

I scoff. I just can't contain myself. 'But it's common decency! To take an interest in your friend's life. His love-life.' I wince involuntarily at that bit. 'Have you and John fallen out or something?'

'No,' he says, and I notice he's making shite of a beer mat. 'John's love-life has nothing to do with me.'

'Well, my love-life is going great,' I practically shout, draining the vodka. 'Me and Barry – that was him in the grey T-shirt – are going strong. He's a new team leader in work. A man on the up. Yeah, everything is great, absolutely great.'

Piotr flashes me a wry smile. 'Right. Got it, Aisling. I'll pass it on.'

'Pass what on?' I say, feigning confusion. 'About me and Barry? To John? Oh, I don't think he'd care. Bye now, Piotr.'

And with that I stand up, and turn on my heel. The last thing I need is for him to see me cry.

I consider jumping straight into a taxi, but come to my senses and listen instead to my stomach: I'm getting chips. I've earned them tonight.

2 I

I wake up with a jolt, forgetting for a second where I am, eyes practically glued together with the remnants of last night's tears and eyeliner. There's the remains of a tub of garlic-and-cheese chips on the bedside locker beside me, along with an empty can of Diet Coke. I give it a shake to see if there's even a drop left to soothe my hungover head, but I obviously horsed it all into me last night. The whole scenario with Barry and Piotr, and Piotr telling me about John, comes flooding back.

Me stumbling away from the pub, rather than stalking with dignity, with Piotr gently calling, 'Ah, Aisling, come back' after me.

Me getting the chips – a stellar decision at the time, but now cloaked in guilt and shame. There was a battered sausage too.

Me getting into a taxi to take me home and the driver barking, 'No eating in the car!' before the door was even closed. Of course I wasn't going to eat them in the car. Did he think I was raised in a pigsty? No need to be so rude.

Me staring out the window as he zipped up

Camden Street towards home, trying not to cry. There's no crying in football! Isn't that what Majella is always saying? Something like that anyway.

I exited the taxi, flinging a tenner at the enormous turnip in the driver's seat and not even waiting for my €1.10 back. I made it into the building and blessed the heavens that there was a lift waiting for me. I prayed for the doors to close swiftly as I spotted some revellers clutching bottles and crates of beer headed towards the apartment block from the street. I was not in the mood to be sharing the lift with happy partygoers. Probably going to spend the night off their heads on bang-bangs or yippers or whatever keeps them up until 11 a.m. the next morning talking shite. I heard some of Majella's neighbours one time I stayed over, talking absolute nonsense in their back garden at six in the morning about giant squirrels. You wouldn't catch me at that.

The apartment was mercifully quiet as I staggered inside, clutching my sweaty parcel of food. I toyed with the idea of sitting on the couch or at the kitchen island to eat my chips but didn't want to be happened upon by Sadhbh or Elaine coming home, so I plonked the styrofoam carton on a plate and brought them to bed with me, alternating forkfuls and heaving sobs. And so now I find myself with the mid-morning sun streaming in my curtains, hoovering the last few flat drops out of a can of Coke and finding the fork in the bed beside me. A new low. Weight Watchers Maura would be so disappointed.

I had been having a dream that John, Piotr and Barry all worked together in Supermac's, and that they were all fighting to serve me my chicken fillet burger, but throwing it at me rather than handing it to me nicely across the counter. It was a nightmare, to tell you the truth. I'm sweating from it.

I can hear Sadhbh and Elaine (and Ruby, of course) bashing around in the kitchen, making breakfast. The telly is on, some kind of nice, comforting cooking show that the BBC are so good at on weekend mornings and that I still can't get used to, even though the channels came to our house in BGB in 2002. I'll go out to them. They might not ask me about the date. I'll slink out and get under a blanket and listen to them chatter and everything will be fine.

'Ah, here she comes! Well, how was it? Do I need to make extra breakfast?' Sadhbh stage-whispers at me as I pad out of my room.

'Ha ha, no. Sure amn't I a lady? Home on my own with a bag of chips.'

I'm on the couch and under the safety of a blanket in a flash. On the telly, a footballer and one of The Saturdays – not Úna – seem to be having trouble chopping carrots while a presenter, who appears to be wearing a jumper *and* a jacket even though he's inside in a fake BBC kitchen, asks them about their favourite types of pasta. Is there more than one type of pasta? Lasagne sheets, I suppose.

'Well, was it any use?' Sadhbh presses. 'Was Barry a gentleman?'

'He was, yeah. I was a bit wrecked and headed home, and he went on to meet some friends but it was lovely.' I sound very forced but I just want them to stop asking me questions about the date . . . although I really want to tell them this new John revelation. And somehow add in that I ended the night having a drink with a different man than the one I started with. They might be sick to the back-teeth of me talking about John at this stage though. It's been months. Time to move on.

I turn my attention back to the telly for the time being, too despondent to even try to stop Elaine from taking a brillo-pad to my new non-stick frying pan. I got it on special in the Arnott's sale but it was still €27. I haven't even used it yet for fear of wrecking it and there she is practically sanding it clean. I'll never get a decent fried egg out of it now. I turn a blind eye too to Sadhbh firing rubbish of all descriptions into the same bin – eggshells, egg cartons, avocado skin (always with the bloody avocados), not a thing separated. I don't have the energy for this today. Although I must admit it is nice being in the buzz of the apartment on a Sunday morning. It's so different to down home. I feel very . . . liberated.

'You're lucky, Aisling,' Sadhbh calls from the

kitchen. 'I was nearly going to drink your Diet Coke. I've an awful head on me.'

Jesusmaryandallthesaints, she's right. I bought two cans of Coke in the chipper and put one in the fridge when I got home so I'd have it for the morning. Genius move. Drunk Ais can be very good to Hungover Ais sometimes.

Sadhbh saunters over to the couch and passes the deliciously cool tin to me. 'Are you all right here, Aisling? You're very quiet. Are you in bits?'

Well, look, if she's going to ask.

'John has a new girlfriend.'

'He doesn't!' Sadhbh gasps, and both Elaine and Ruby look up from whatever vegan masterpiece they've put together.

'John has a new girlfriend,' Sadhbh parrots over to them, and they gasp too. Sadhbh pulls it together almost immediately and says, 'And so what? You were out on a date last night, weren't you? The only reason you haven't gone on Tinder is that your dad wasn't well. Fuck him. And her, for that matter.'

I appreciate her enthusiasm but I just can't get the idea of John's big safe arm around someone else out of my head.

'How do you know, Ais?' Elaine and Ruby have come over to the couch, crouched low around me in sympathy, almost like they're paying their respects. 'Who told you? You didn't . . . see him?'

'I met his housemate Piotr out and had a drink with him after Barry left. He told me.'

'The big eejit. Why didn't he just say nothing?' Ruby chimes in.

'I suppose I was there on a date, so he thought it was OK. He seemed a bit pissed off with me, to be honest. It was all a bit of a mess.'

'Well, at least you know he'll go back and tell John you were there with someone else. That looks great. He's not the only one back in the saddle.' Sadhbh is determined to make the best of this, clutching at anything positive at all to say.

'Thanks, girls. I just wish I could stop thinking about it. I was having nightmares about the three of them. John, Piotr and Barry were all throwing stuff at me. It was awful. My hair is in dreadlocks from the sweat.'

Elaine pipes up again. 'Jesus, this Piotr guy must have really gotten to you if you were dreaming about him as well, you poor thing. Do you know what you need?' She glances sideways at Sadhbh. 'A holiday.'

'Aisling!' Sadhbh nearly lifts us all out of it with an exclamation. 'We're going away to Berlin next weekend. Come with us!'

Next weekend? Are they mad? Imagine the cost of the flights for a city break at the height of summer. And where would I sleep? I can only imagine the converted prison cell turned 'bijou space' they have themselves booked into – or worse still, a hostel.

'Ah no, girls, you're grand, honestly.' I've never been on a holiday I haven't personally organised. Sure how else would you be sure that where you were staying was equidistant between the airport and the town square, or wherever the most restaurants and swivelly postcard kiosks are? You want to be able to hit as many points as possible. Museums, statues, bridges, Hard Rock Cafés – I always hit them all.

'Ah, go on. We've enough beds in our Airbnb and I bet if we shop around we'll get a flight handy enough. And that's all you need.' Sadhbh looks so excited.

'I'll think about it,' I hear myself say. 'I'm going back in for a lie-down.'

My bad sleep, what with the nightmare and the rogue fork, is catching up on me. I may go back to bed and watch my stories for a few hours. I have a *CSI: Miami* boxset calling my name. John has a *CSI: Knocknamanagh* T-shirt. One of my favourites.

'Do think about it,' Elaine calls after me as I head back to my room.

What feels like twenty minutes later, I wake with a jolt again. The light in the room is weird. I can't make head nor tail of what time it might be. I grab my phone from the bedside locker. 6.20 – I haven't slept all the way through to Monday morning, have I? I can hear the girls in the kitchen, clinking glasses and laughing. It's Sunday evening. I've been asleep all day. The *CSI* music is playing away on my laptop, for God knows how long. I obviously really needed a good rest.

Reaching for my phone, I'm slightly disappointed to see nothing from Barry. I thought he might at least have checked to see if I got home OK. Two texts and a missed call from Majella though. She must be apoplectic at this stage having not heard from me about the date. Sitting up in bed, I ring her back.

'Well, stranger,' she answers sarcastically. 'You're alive!' Her voice converts to a whisper. 'Are you still with him?'

'No, Majella! I'm in Portobello. I've been asleep half the day. Wrecked.'

'Oho,' she teases, 'wrecked, is it?'

'I came home on my own. Well, with chips.'

'Ah, did you have fun at least?'

'It was grand. A bit weird.'

I give her the lowdown on the whole evening, the drinks, the leg-touching ('go on ya boy ya,' she interjects), the encounter with Piotr, the revelation about John, my dramatic exit, the solo mission home, the chips. I stop talking and she's quiet.

'Well,' I push, 'wasn't the whole thing weird? I

was fairly floored with the news about John. I can't believe it.'

'I . . . I had heard something about it all right.' Majella sounds like she's talking into her jumper. 'Cillian told Deirdre Ruane that John was seeing someone. That's all he said though. I was going to tell you but I wanted to wait until after your date so you weren't upset. Sorry.'

'Piotr was the same! No information whatsoever. Why are lads so useless?'

'Was Piotr looking as well as ever?' Majella thinks everyone always looks well, to be fair. 'You should have just shifted him. That'd show John.' Majella is fierce het up altogether. Although in the next breath, she sounds reproachful. 'But that would be awful. His housemate, like.'

'Yeah. It would.' Shifting Piotr – there's an image I can't allow myself to conjure up. I'm absolutely roasting even thinking about it. 'C'mere, Maj, I'll go. I'm starving.'

I am starving and all. Sure I've eaten nothing since the chips last night. Weight Watchers Maura is always warning against the evils of eating after 6 p.m., but then at the same time she's always telling you not to go hungry. Make up your mind, Maura. She lost eight stone eleven years ago and has been maintaining ever since. Her sidekick, Jacinta, who looks after the money and the cards, looks like she was born seven stone and stayed there, rake-thin on a diet of fags and gossip. I was up the last time I weighed in down in BGB.

'Up a pound, Aisling, and you maintained last week. Are you counting everything right? How are the portion sizes?'

I mumbled something about my period and she gave me an encouraging smile and waved me on: 'That'll be it then. Sure you can't help it sometimes.'

I know I'm not fat but ever since Sister Assumpta told me in Fifth Year that I had 'grand thick ankles', I've been punishing myself, trying to be less beef to the heels. I have a feeling the girls have takeaway out there though, so Points be damned.

I was right. They do have takeaway – some swanky Thai place they're very fond of. Doesn't do chips. The range of stuff you can get delivered now is just out of this world. In BGB, you can ring ahead to the Chinese and ask them to have your chicken in black bean sauce ready for you to pick up. Here, you have all manner of cuisines at your fingertips. Sadhbh and Elaine have even been known to pay through the nose to order wine to the flat for extortionate amounts.

'Aisling, there you are. We were wondering if you might be dead. We got you some pad Thai. Not too spicy.' Sadhbh gestures towards the bag on the table in a 'go on, go on' kind of way.

'Wine?' asks Elaine, holding out the bottle of white.

'Sure why not?' I reach for a glass.

It's so cosy and nice and different to be doing this on a Sunday evening. Gal pals sitting around, curtains closed, me trying to throw an eye to *Call the Midwife* – the girls thought it was gas I wanted to put it on but they were open to giving it a go.

It's pissing rain outside so it looks like we had our summer yesterday. Mammy will have to take the cushions for the patio chairs back in. She put them out rather optimistically last weekend with the promise of a bit of good weather and she's been in and out like a yo-yo with them ever since. Several of her texts this week have focused on their current state of dampness.

The girls are chatting about their nights out last night, about how poxy it must be to give birth and would you be well even having children (there was a particularly harrowing labour playing out in the background on the telly), tactfully avoiding the subject of John or Barry or any of the mess. I'm grateful, and staring off into space when Sadhbh turns directly to me.

'Did you think any more about Berlin, Ais?' she coaxes, a glint in her eye.

'Do you know, I hadn't thought a jot more about it,' I say.

'We'd have such craic,' she continues. 'Wine and chats and whatever else, but in Berlin.'

'Will we look up flights?' Elaine's enthusiasm is infectious and before I know it, we're gathered around her laptop, trying to trick about seven different price-comparison websites into giving us the lowest fare. '€190, and it's on the same flight as us. You're not going to get much better than that,' Elaine says decisively.

'Will I get my card?' I'm on my third glass of white and feeling mad altogether.

'Get it! Get it! Get it!' the girls chant, and in a flash I'm in and out of my handbag and entering my details.

'Whoo! We're going to Berl-i-in,' Sadhbh and Elaine start to sing as I press 'confirm payment' and shout 'done!' I'll have to dig out my German verbs book.

22

'So according to TripAdvisor, the number one thing to do in Berlin is see the Reichstag.' I did German in Transition Year and I make sure to do a good throaty pronunciation so everyone knows I'll be taking the lead when it comes to reading menus, maps and the like. *Links, rechts, geradeaus.* It's all come flooding back. Frau Delaney would be delighted, God rest her soul. She used to tell me I'd a great ear for languages and I've always felt a sort of affinity with the Germans – so orderly, so efficient.

Of course my excellent pronunciation is falling on deaf ears since Sadhbh, who nabbed the aisle seat, is too busy trying to get the air hostess's attention. She was actually a bit quiet this morning in the taxi to the airport (I couldn't convince them the Aircoach is just as handy and far cheaper) and we haven't even reached cruising altitude when she's talking about ordering rosé. Across the way, Elaine and Ruby give her the thumbs-up and I say a little prayer to Saint Jude, patron saint of lost causes, to protect my liver this weekend as best he can.

'I know we're only going to be here for forty-eight

hours, but we should probably make an itinerary so we manage to do a few cultural things,' I continue, to nobody in particular. 'I've a pen and paper, so will I just put down Reichstag as number one and then use a map to cross-reference where the other sights are and sort of make a provisional route?'

'Um, it's not that kind of weekend, Aisling,' Sadhbh says, swinging around so hard she nearly gives herself whiplash as the air hostess – steward? – finally emerges from behind the curtain at the back of the plane, trolley heaving with clinking bottles, mega-watt smile plastered across her gob, eyes telling a different story. 'This holiday is about us letting our hair down, having a laugh. It's about you relaxing and getting out of your own head. I'm more interested in going on the lash than sightseeing.'

'Yeah, sorry, Aisling – I went to the Reichstag on a school trip ten years ago,' Elaine chimes in, pouring wine for herself and Ruby. 'Heidi, our friend who you'll meet tonight, has lived in Berlin for four years so she's going to bring us to all the cool new places.'

'We're going to an avocado bar tonight for dinner,' Ruby adds. 'I've been dying to try it for ages. Well, it only opened three weeks ago, but I've been dying to try it since then.'

Elaine nods, complicit as ever. An avocado bar? Give me strength. I was hoping to sample some leberwurst and schnitzel but I've a feeling that neither of them is vegan.

'So are we going to go to Berghain or what?' Sadhbh asks, knocking back the rosé and reaching for the button above her head, no doubt signalling for another round. I decide I better get on board if I'm going to survive the next two days and crack open my own mini-bottle. It's not even cold but no one else seems to have noticed.

'What's Berghain?' I say, hoping that it's the kind of place I can check in to on Facebook to look cultured and impress Niamh From Across The Road.

'A techno club in an old power-plant,' Sadhbh explains matter-of-factly, and my heart sinks. I should have known. 'Well, it's more than just a club, it's a super-club. The best club in the world, apparently, and virtually impossible to get into.'

I stare at her blankly. 'Why wouldn't we get in? Is it one of those places that discriminates against tourists? No dogs or Irish?'

'The door-policy at Berghain is notoriously tough,' explains Elaine from across the aisle, taking a gulp of her wine and leaving a long pause for effect. 'I was denied two years ago, and that was after queuing for three hours.'

I gasp involuntarily, clutching my hand to my craw. Elaine, denied from a club? Elaine, with her €200 white-blond highlights and poker-straight bob, which she has a standing appointment to get done exactly every six weeks, and her endless parade of ridiculously hip and often semi-famous friends? She gets into clubs in Dublin for free all the time, VIP sections and all, often rubbing shoulders with the likes of Brax from *Home and Away* or girls from *Corrie* over to pull pints of Guinness for the Sunday newspapers. It's not that she even tries – she just gets ushered up the line because she seems to be on first-name terms with every doorman in the Pale. Ruby explained it all to me once during an ad-break in *Fair City*. What kind of a club wouldn't let Elaine in?

'They like to make sure the crowd is diverse,' Ruby says diplomatically, patting Elaine on the thigh. 'There are plenty of hip clubs in Berlin but Berghain is rad because you never know who you're going to bump into – male, female, trans, gay, straight, young, old. Anything goes. That's what makes it so fucking cool, and better than any of the generic, homogenised borefests that are popular at home.'

'Er, right, I see,' I say, accepting another bottle of wine from Sadhbh, even though I don't see at all. The place sounds terrifying and I have no intention of setting foot inside it.

By the time we land in Berlin, the four of us are half-fluthered and it's only 11.30 a.m. I'm clutching the address of our Airbnb so hard that the scrap of paper has started to disintegrate in my hand but luckily Sadhbh has it on her phone. There's an app for that, as the ad goes.

Being away from Dublin has done wonders for my mood already and I'm feeling a bit flighty as we flag a taxi. I'd honestly love to know what these girls have against buses. It turns out that since Sadhbh, Elaine and Ruby are regular visitors to Berlin, my translation services are not required, so I slip my phrase book into my anorak pocket, sit back and concentrate on relaxing. It's nice to not be the organiser for once, even if I can't help but panic about, well, basically everything, including whether Elaine switched on the alarm when she left the apartment and where Berlin sits on the Global Terrorism Index. But, like I said, I try to relax. And I'm certainly not thinking about John. Or Barry. Or Piotr, for that matter.

The twenty-minute taxi ride from the airport is over before I know it and suddenly we're at our accommodation. After my initial reservations about Airbnb, I'm delira and excira that everything is as it should be when we meet our host, Heinz, and check in to our converted loft – 'industrial chic', apparently – in Mitte. I was full sure it was going to be a scam – you know how it is with the internet – but no, Airbnb is actually a real thing.

Sadhbh and I are first in the door so we nab the twin room just off the living area, which leaves Elaine and Ruby with the double on the mezzanine. I feel a bit bad but they did get the *en suite* and anyway they don't seem to mind. They're both very easy-going that way. We spend a good couple of hours opening every press and drawer in the place, trying to imagine the madsers who live there under all the exposed pipework and lightbulbs. Then we head out to the local *supermarkt* for all the essentials: spare tea-bags, milk, continental bread and cheese – although I make sure to hunt down a nice hunk of red cheddar for myself.

When we get back from the shop, I'm emptying my trusty backpack when Sadhbh appears with a bottle of airport vodka and demands that we toast our household's first international trip.

'Gals, let's make it one to remember – or not,' she announces and we all shriek and raise our glasses as Elaine heads for the stereo.

By 4 p.m., we've set ourselves up in front of the stereo and are fighting over who gets to control the Spotify playlist. My suggestions – Ed Sheeran, Adele, The Script, even Kodaline, for God's sake – keep getting vetoed, while Elaine tries to give me a basic introduction to techno in advance of tonight's attempt to infiltrate that god-awful Berghain place.

It's just noise to me, and there are no lyrics, so there's not even anything to shout along to. I'd listen to Nathan Carter over it any day, and I'm no Nathan Carter fan, despite what Majella thinks.

'This is pure shite,' I keep repeating as I try my best to dance to it while Ruby assures me that, if we do get in, my whole attitude to electronic dance music will change in an instant, such is the power of Berghain's state-of-the-art sound system. I remain sceptical.

At 7 p.m., the Getting Ready commences in earnest, which involves various hair and make-up stations being assembled around the loft. I try to join in but it doesn't take long to lash on a bit of foundation and a slick of mascara. I brought a trio of eyeshadow for blue eyes that I wheel out on special occasions but I have the three steps (one colour on your eyelid, one under your eyebrow and one mashed into your eyelashes – there's a diagram and everything) done in about six minutes.

Two hours later, they're *still* at it, passing around eyelash primers and contouring kits like their lives depend on it. Ruby even has a freckle pencil on the go at one point. I ask you! I wouldn't mind but they're all bloody gorgeous and don't need half of it. I check my watch – 9 p.m. That means it's eight o'clock at home – Daddy will be settling down in front of *Winning Streak*, hoping to see someone local on it. Against the odds, we've had several represent-atives from BGB spinning the wheel with Marty. I was even in the audience myself once, the night Mad Tom O'Brien won €8,000 and later put it all on BGB to win the county championship. The less said about that, the better.

When the doorbell finally goes at 10 p.m., it's the girls' friend Heidi – an old pal from college – ready to escort us to this famous avocado bar the vegans are so desperate to try. She has a few bottles of prosecco with her so after herself and myself are introduced, the toasts start again and we're back at it.

When the others finally get changed just after midnight, I'm fair taken aback by the rig-outs they've put together for the night that's in it – there's black vinyl skinny pants (Ruby), a backless silver jumpsuit that's also as good as frontless (Elaine) and a latex dress as seen on Gigi Hadid (Sadhbh). And don't get me started on the heels.

'You look like the Kardashians,' I go, and they're delighted so we all get into a selfie using Ruby's new phone, which is about the size of a football pitch (no wonder the battery only lasts forty-five minutes or so).

Of course nobody warned me that we'd be trying to get into the world's coolest nightclub this week-end, so all I have to wear are my navy bootcut jeans, my good Savida white shirt and the walking boots on my feet, but I'm too drunk to care. I slip on my going Out Out Hairband though, because I might not be a fashionista but I do have standards. It's far from avocados I was raised but I could eat a horse so I throw on my anorak and pray that chips are vegan and this restaurant is not too cool to serve them.

23

It came as no surprise to anyone that the vegan dinner didn't hit the spot for me, although I didn't say a word other than '*danke*' when my plate of glorified hedge-clippings arrived. I'm not saying that avocados aren't nice in principle, if you're looking to waste 12 Points on a fruit, but a dinner isn't a dinner without a potato in some form or another, especially if you've been drinking for fourteen hours and are desperate for a bit of soakage. When I let loose at a carvery, I've been known to load up on at least six types of spuds: roast, boiled, mash, chips, croquettes – even gratin if I'm feeling fancy. Christ, I'd kill for a carvery, I think to myself, salivating at the thought of roast beef and gravy.

'They're so good for you though,' Elaine is slurring across the table at me. 'Avocados. Full of potassium. And good fat.'

'Lads, I need potatoes. And meat,' I whisper back at her, sloshing some water into my glass and wondering how a vegan restaurant at 2 a.m. could be so loud and rowdy. 'I'm a growing girl.'

'Don't worry, Aisling – I know a good bratwurst

place on the way to Berghain. That'll sort you out,' Heidi says with a wink and I almost hug her.

But hang on, it's going-home time. I'm shocked that this restaurant is still serving booze, let alone food. We can't possibly be going on somewhere after this.

'We're not seriously still going to Berghain, are we? Sure it's nearly morning,' I say, aghast at the very idea. 'It sounds like the kind of place where you'd get roofied. And getting roofied is a major fear of mine.'

'I didn't wrestle myself into this dress to go home after a plate of avocado carpaccio,' Sadhbh says, topping up my wine. 'We're going – and we're going to get in too, if it kills me. Now, drink up everyone, or I'll be forced to roofie you all.'

Twenty minutes later, the five of us are crammed into a taxi, watching the bright lights of Berlin flash by as we speed out into the back-arse of nowhere to get to Berghain. True to her word, Heidi has delivered on the bratwurst front and I make short shrift of mine before Sadhbh is pushing a naggin of vodka into my hand. I have no idea what's up with her, but she seems to be on a one-woman mission to keep us all plastered this weekend. I can't fight it any longer – I'm pissed.

'You're a good friend, Sadhbhy,' I say. 'To Sadhbh, and her infinite supply of booze! *Ich liebe dich!*' I roar and everyone cheers, and shouts *'dich'* this and *'dich'* that, which the driver must think is pure gas.

*

Even though I've had a few sups of vodka during the journey, by the time we pull up outside the club I've kind of drunk myself sober and can feel my hangover starting to take hold in earnest, not helped by the deafening noise of techno echoing into the night. My mouth is dry and fuzzy and the familiar thump of a headache is threatening to force me into sneaking off home without the others. But I can't do it, not in a foreign city, even with my level of German. I'd surely end up crammed into an Aldi suitcase floating down the River Spree. Daddy would never forgive me.

'OK, I think we stand a good chance,' Sadhbh says, looking at us appraisingly after we all pile out of the taxi. I feel her eyes linger on my anorak but she says nothing and gives me a weak smile. This was an expensive anorak, I'm tempted to tell her. I got it in a proper outdoor shop. It has a detachable hood!

'Me and Heidi will go first,' she says, smoothing her plastic dress over her skinny little thighs which are about the same circumference as my ankles, 'and you hold up the rear, Aisling.'

'Fine by me,' I say, getting the hint, and we all stagger to the back of the queue, which is moving much faster than I hoped it would. 'By the way, my head is thumping so I'll probably just mind the bags if we get in. Which I hope we do, of course!'

It takes nearly forty-five minutes to get to the top

of the queue and by now, I'm feeling close to death and the sun is coming up. The nearer we get to the door, the tenser things become. Two lads about three groups ahead of us get turned away without so much as a 'by your leave' while a gang of Swedes after them are ushered straight in. There is a fierce smell of want off Sadhbh but the others are playing it a bit cooler. Elaine and Ruby are giving each other the odd peck and I have to admire their quick thinking. If it's diversity this crowd want, it's diversity we'll give them.

Suddenly it's our turn. As we watch an Asian couple ahead of us disappear inside, Sadhbh turns on the charm.

'*Guten Abend*,' she shouts with a smile. I'd give her accent about six out of ten.

'You're not getting in,' the head doorman, a big brute of a lad with a face full of piercings and tattoos, says, barely looking up from his clipboard. 'Next!'

I see Sadhbh's shoulders slump immediately and, hangover or no hangover, I can't let her get turned away from Berghain. She'll never live it down. It's plain to see Elaine still hasn't recovered from the mortification.

'Excuse me,' I shout, pushing past Elaine and Ruby and nearly flattening poor Heidi in the process. 'We've come all the way from Ireland, and we're going in there and we're going to dance to that,' I hesitate, 'music like our lives depend on it.'

Metal Face looks up again and I see him slowly take in my outfit from the toes of my sturdy Merrell boots (half-price in the January sales) to the top of my going Out Out Hairband. We lock eyes and I arch an *au natural* eyebrow, determined not to give him an inch. Feck him and his stupid nightclub and its rubbish techno. He should be glad of our custom, the ungrateful shite. There's a long pause and I think Sadhbh is going to pass out, she's trembling that much.

Slowly, a smile creeps across Metal Face's metal face and the atmosphere shifts ever so slightly.

'Normcore. *Sehr gut*,' is all he says, before standing aside and gesturing for us to go past him.

'*Go raibh míle maith agat*,' I call back, overtaken with a rush of joy and reverting to my usual Irish 'thanks', and with that, we're absorbed into the famous Berghain.

'Aisling, I can't believe you got us in,' Sadhbh screams, as soon as we're out of Metal Face's earshot. 'You are a fucking legend. What are you drinking?'

The other three are hugging me too and it's a nice feeling to be the cool one, for a change.

'Ah, it was nothing,' I say, playing it down. 'Sure it's only a nightclub. The Vortex plays better music,' and they're all in stitches laughing again, bodies swaying to the beat.

I have to admit, as nightclubs go, it's fairly impressive. The room we're in is huge – about the size of

Croke Park, no exaggeration – and there's dry ice and disco balls and lasers and the whole shebang going, while about 1,500 sweaty people in various states of undress bash into each other and don't seem to care. 'Revellers', I'd call them. I can't believe some of the things I'm seeing.

I take off my anorak and knot the arms around my waist – when in Rome and all that. But my head is properly pounding and I have to firmly decline the excessively frothy pint that Ruby pushes towards me.

'I can't,' I roar, trying to be heard above the music. 'My head.'

Behind me, I notice the others are huddled in a little knot. Out of the corner of my eye, I see Heidi pass Elaine a small plastic Ziploc bag, the kind a pair of handmade dangly earrings might come in at a market – but instead of earrings, the bag contains little white tablets. I blink and it's gone and they're looking normal again but I'm sure I saw it. White tablets in a techno club. Drugs! The girls are on drugs!

'You poor thing,' Ruby roars, looking at me and tapping her temple. 'Do you want to take something? I have stuff in my bag.'

This is the moment Miss Heneghan in Third Year Religion warned us about: 'One day, girls, you'll be in a nightclub and someone will offer you drugs and you have to say no,' she told us, about once a fortnight. 'Just say no.'

And here I am, in the world's best nightclub, thinking, 'What would happen if I said yes instead?' I know Elaine and Ruby take ecstasy tablets all the time. Pills, they call them, but I googled it and found a helpful thread on Boards.ie that a suspicious dad had started. And to the best of my knowledge, neither of them has ever gotten so high that they tried to jump off a two-storey building because they believed they could fly, which is what Miss Heneghan swore blind would happen. That reminds me, Majella was offered ecstasy at 2 p.m. in the dance-tent at Oxegen one summer. She only went in there looking for somewhere showing the All-Ireland Final on a big screen, although we decided it must just have been an undercover Garda trying to catch her out. He definitely didn't look like a drug pusher, she claims. He was wearing very clean wellies.

'Oh, go on then, you've twisted my arm,' I bellow at Ruby over the music and she gives me the 'OK' hand signal and dips into her handbag. Feck it. This is the one and only time I'll ever be in Berghain – I might as well go for it, I think, watching Sadhbh, Elaine and Heidi giving it socks, not an inhibition between them. It'll surely kill my hangover too.

Ruby hands me the tablet surreptitiously. It looks innocent enough, tiny in my palm, but Miss Heneghan told us a thousand times how addictive ecstasy is. 'It ruins lives,' she used to say. 'From ecstasy to agony in just one night.'

'Should I just take half, and see how I get on?' I shout into Ruby's ear.

She shakes her head furiously. 'Not at all, I usually take two,' she says, holding up two fingers and waving them at me. 'I have more if you need it.'

More? Is she mad or what? Before I can talk myself out of it, or panic that it might be cut with rat poison, I loaf the pill into my gob and start dancing with the others, who are chewing the faces off themselves and sweating buckets. I've seen enough *Ibiza Uncovered* to know it's important to stay hydrated when you're getting off your head, so I drink about six pints of water and make sure the girls get plenty into them too. And it turns out techno isn't so bad when you're mashed – plus, I can't stop thinking about the number of calories I must be burning with all the elaborate shapes I'm throwing.

It's not until about 9 a.m. that I finally run out of steam and I pull Elaine aside and explain that I'm fading fast.

'Ais, I can't believe you stayed going all night,' she says, hugging me again. She's been hugging me for about three hours, on and off. 'You're my hero. I fucking love you.'

'I love you too, Elaine, but I really need to get to my bed. I'm falling asleep on my feet here. And sure you must be in bits.'

'I am, I am,' she concedes, gurning away. 'Let's

call it a night. You played a fucking blinder, mate. You're one of the best people I've ever met, and I mean that.'

It's at that point that I realise that there are only four of us present and correct – we're missing Sadhbh. The last time I saw her she was chatting to a German lad with a beard and a woolly hat, despite it being about 200 degrees in here. The club has started to thin out and there's not sight nor sound of her anywhere. I beckon Ruby over.

'Have you seen Sadhbh? I think we've lost her.'

'Oh, she's fine – she left with that guy Max a little while ago.'

I think I'm going to pass out with the shock. She doesn't know Berlin well enough to be wandering the streets with strange men – I don't care if he looked a bit like Jamie Dornan. Did she not see him in *The Fall*? Tying people up and not in a sexy way.

'She *left* with him? Where did they go?'

'I don't know, back to his maybe? She told me she'd see me tomorrow. Er, today. You know what I mean. Don't worry – he's a friend of Heidi's. She knows where he lives.'

'Oh right. OK. Grand.' I suppose trying to get this lot on to a bus or U-Bahn in this state is pointless. Waste of a three-day travel pass. I turn to Ruby. 'Will you use that fancy phone of yours to magic up a taxi so?'

What little is left of our time in Berlin is spent sleeping, rehydrating, drinking tea and ordering food to the loft, facilitated by Heidi, who has taken up residence on the sofa bed. I don't so much as catch a glimpse of the Brandenburg Gate or the hotel where Michael Jackson dangled his baby, but I decide I'm fine with that. Sure I can always come back anyway and do the cultural stuff another time. Maybe take a day trip to a concentration camp. When Sadhbh eventually returns in the evening, on the back of your man's moped no less, she's as coy as anything.

'You look a bit more . . . relaxed than you did yesterday,' Elaine smirks, proffering the remnants of a vegan pizza, which Sadhbh rightfully turns her nose up at. 'Done anything lately that relieves stress?'

'I'm delighted you're not murdered, Sadhbh. Did you get his number? He was the stamp of Jamie Dornan,' I say approvingly, pouring my eleventh pint of fizzy water and tucking into an exciting new snack discovery: currywurst taytos. You couldn't pay me to calculate the Points in the massive bag I'm cradling, not with this hangover.

'No, no numbers were exchanged,' she says with a smile, kicking off her heels. 'And that's just the way I like it. I'm wrecked now though. How long have I been up?'

'You haven't been asleep yet, Sadhbh? Jesus, it's been nearly thirty-six hours! Get into that room now and have a lie-down. I'll bring you in some water,' I practically roar, equal parts flabbergasted and impressed. It's no wonder these girls stay so skinny: they burn about fifty thousand calories every weekend. It explains so much.

'Did you take more MDMA back at your man's?' Ruby says, not so much as asking as she helps herself to my crisps while I try to act like I don't care. I'm mentally counting them, of course. 'He had some seriously good shit.'

Cue furious nodding all round and murmurs of 'good shit' and 'seriously good shit'. I make a mental note to ask someone later what MDMA is. This trip has been a real eye-opener for me.

'Lads, you probably won't believe this,' I announce to the room, 'but last night was my first ever time taking illegal drugs.'

The girls exchange looks, obviously a bit surprised, and I have to say I'm flattered. I sometimes worry that I can come across a bit unsophisticated and sheltered.

'I know, I know,' I add with a shrug, 'but it's true.'

'Oh my God, Aisling, what did you take?' Ruby asks, breaking the silence.

'Well, just that one ecstasy tablet you gave me, but I think it was very strong . . .'

There's another pause.

'Ais, I didn't give you ecstasy,' she says, horrified.

'Have you lost your mind? I would never give you drugs. Unless you asked, of course. Then I'd give you, like, loads. Whatever you wanted. I was tripping balls last night but I would have definitely remembered corrupting you.'

Now I'm the confused one. 'The tablet you gave me? I was as high as a kite after it. I even started loving that god-awful techno music for a while there.'

Elaine's hand goes straight to her mouth. She's slapping her thigh and laughing so hard there's no sound coming out. If she doesn't take a breath soon, she might actually suffocate. What's the number for emergency services in Germany? 999? 911? 112? There should be a universal number, I think, not for the first time.

'Aisling, that was . . . that was . . . that was a paracetamol,' Ruby eventually gasps. 'You told me you had a headache!'

And she's off again. They all are.

I'm still feeling a bit embarrassed the next morning when we head to the airport after bidding Heidi a fond *'auf Wiedersehen'*. She's a good skin that one – we'll keep in touch. Ruby is still swearing on her mother's life that there was nothing stronger than paracetamol in that tablet, but I'm certain it had to have been Nurofen Plus at the very least. I floated the theory that one of the ecstasy pills had somehow escaped from her stash but she flat-out denied it was even possible. The others keep doubling over laughing intermittently but it's starting to get old now – although it's nice to see Sadhbh back to her normal self again. She was so mad to be partying the whole time. Fair dues to your man Max, is all I'll say. She's mad not to have given him her number – although I suppose she can always get it off Heidi.

Finally, the passengers for Dublin are called to the gate for boarding and like that, I'm straight up to the desk in a flash. We're flying Aer Lingus so seating is assigned, but I always insist on queuing as soon as the gate number is announced – that way, I'm guaranteed plenty of space in the overhead bins. The others don't even look up from their soy lattes and *Vanity Fair*s and *Vogue*s, risk-takers that they are.

Taking advantage of the free airport wifi (another reason to love the Germans), I open Facebook on my phone to make sure Sadhbh hasn't tagged me in any dodgy pictures from Berghain. I know she checked us in the second we got past old Metal Face. As is normal for a Sunday morning, my feed is flooded with pictures of Majella in various stages of drunkenness down in BGB. I throw a few likes and the odd 'lookin good, Maj' around until something in the background of one of the pictures causes my thumb to freeze and my blood to turn cold. She's in Maguire's – I'd know the back-bar anywhere. We were so young when we started going there with Maeve Hennessey, Sinéad McGrath and a few others – they used to call it the crèche. In the top left-hand corner of the picture, sitting just beside Majella's good red Michael Kors with the chain strap, is John, my ex-boyfriend John, head thrown back, mid-laugh. I can almost hear it now, just from looking at that tiny photograph. And next to him on the faded leather couch, the one I got sick into my hand on after the 2013 county championship, looking straight into the camera is Ciara. Ciara from Fibber Magee's in Tenerife.

24

I feel sick. Sick. Was there something going on when we were in Tenerife? Maybe that evening me and Pablo went on a fruitless search for Hula Hoops and left John in the bar singing 'If Tomorrow Never Comes' like his life depended on it? I had been trying to explain the virtues of the Irish crisp scene to Pablo and thought that if he could just experience a brown Hula Hoop for himself, his life would be changed. But the one shop that was open only had seven different varieties of regular old ready-salted taytos so I made an empty promise to send him over a consignment of brown Hula Hoops as soon as I landed back at home. All the while, was John back in Fibber Magee's, making promises of a different kind to Ciara?

Did he . . . did he *fly* her back home to Ireland because he couldn't bear to be without her for another second, now that his relationship with me was over?

Had they been secret pen-pals, sexting each other in the nip? Was she the Ciara Piotr met on the landing that Sunday morning? Or is he seeing *multiple*

Ciaras? Had they gone to our favourite restaurant, for the two-for-one pizza deal (ham for me, pepperoni for John, extra instructions to the waiter not to be sneaking any secret spicy stuff onto it)?

Had they fired on ahead watching *The West Wing*? John and I had been on season four when we split up and I haven't been able to bring myself to watch on. And besides, he has all the box-sets. I'm not going to get into illegal downloading and end up in court for three series of *The West Wing* and two episodes of *Love/Hate*. Those ads about piracy in the cinema are very effective. They're right. I *wouldn't* steal a handbag.

So many horrifying thoughts are going through my head, but standing out above it all is the greatest betrayal of the lot: Majella. There in the same pub with them. Drinking with them probably. Making best friends with Ciara. Showing her the best spot to stand at the bar in Maguire's to get served. Sharing her Diet Cokes with her. The betrayal is too much to bear.

Behind me, on the hard metal seats, the girls are in various states of airport stupor, looking like they plan on being the last people on board the flight. Already the queue has started to move forward, and I mindlessly hand my passport and boarding card to the smiling Aer Lingus woman, barely managing a smile as she parrots, 'Thank you. Next! Thank you. Next!'

The man behind me is being told he's going to have to check his hand-luggage because it's too big and I'm too shook to even feel smug about it. I invested in the perfect lightweight cabin-bag three years ago before a weekend in London to see *The Lion King* with Majella and it's been my trusty travelling companion on weekends away ever since. Elaine's bought so many geometric scarves in Berlin that there isn't a hope her bag is going to be let on but I haven't the wherewithal to be fretting about that now.

I'm the sixth person onto the plane so I stow my little suitcase easily and slide into my window seat. Sadhbh will eventually be in the one beside me if the girls ever actually make it on board. I've lost the wifi now but I don't know if I'll be able to sit through the entire flight without doing something, anything. I'm going to text Majella. I can't believe she was hanging around with John's new girlfriend. I don't trust all that 'free roaming' carry on, but I need to know. I'm going to text her and damn my phone bill to hell.

What'll I say though? Will I play it light and breezy and ask if I missed anything over the weekend? Or will I land her with an '*I saw you!*'?

I type out a few variations, barely even noticing the people streaming onto the plane, failing to stand in from the aisle and shoving their jackets into the overhead compartments, despite the rules. Eventually I settle on 'Hiya Maj. On way home now. Great weekend. I saw u were out last night with John. Pics on FB. Were u talking to him?'

There. She's going to know I've seen. She's going to have to explain herself. God, I hate this. I hate all of this.

I turn my phone over on my lap so I can't see the screen. A watched toaster never pops, as Mammy says. But I keep flipping it back to see if she's texted me back. Nothing. Six minutes now since I sent the text. She's probably lost the bloody phone again, the big hames, I think unkindly.

Here comes Sadhbh down the plane towards me, managing to look so swish in just a grey sweatshirt and black leggings. Of course she has on a clangy necklace made of spoons or something and a base-ball cap too. I'd look like I was on day-release in that get-up but she just looks effortless. The man in the aisle seat hoofs himself out of it to let her in, and helps her to shove her suitcase into a spot she some-how finds in the overhead bin opposite us. Sadhbh calmly removes his three jackets and a duty-free bag bursting with Ritter Sports to make enough room and hands them to his family sitting beneath, win-ning them over with her serene smile and 'I hope you don't mind' cock of her head.

She lowers herself into the middle seat, exhaling loudly. 'Oh, thank God. I'm wrecked. You don't mind if I snooze, Ais, do you?'

She's already pulling her headphones from her handbag and removing her cap to replace it with an eye-mask. I never really sleep on planes because I'm afraid I might miss the dinner, if there's one going. Donna told me that she and the hubby were so wrecked coming home on a very early flight from their honeymoon that they missed the complimentary meal and I wasn't able to stop thinking about it for weeks. There's no dinner scheduled for this flight home to Dublin but you never know when a trolley with nuts or something might be wheeled out.

I'm kind of glad we won't be chatting on the flight actually. I feel very much on the verge of tears and wouldn't mind a silent weep as I look out the window. Don't they say planes make you more likely to cry anyway? Something about the altitude and the idea that you might die at any moment. Sure that'd get anyone's nerves up.

I flip over my phone one last time to check before the steward comes after me for not switching to flight mode. Nothing from Majella. As I turn off the phone, the man behind me removes his shoes and wedges his besocked feet into the gap between the wall and the side of my seat. I face the window and a silent tear slips down my face and onto the sleeve of my good anorak. It's going to be a long flight.

*

None of us checked bags, so getting out and off the plane in Dublin is a pretty painless exercise, even with Elaine's bag of scarves weighing her down. I did think I had left my travel pillow behind me and had to go back for it. It was €13 in Argos, so I will not just 'get another one', thank you very much, Ruby. Turns out I had squashed it into the bottom of my handbag, but I was so distracted that I had lost track of it. It takes a while for my phone to re-align itself to Ireland and what with all the rushing to the taxi queue – I'm too tired to even suggest we just get the Aircoach – and jamming of the bags into the boot, I'm in the passenger seat before I see the text from Majella. The driver is yammering away to me about American politics and the state of the world and the three in the back are pretending not to hear him. I just throw him the odd 'mmm hmm' and 'oh really' and turn my attention to the phone.

'Hiya Ais. Glad u had a gr8 time. Yeah I was out n he was der I wasn't rly talking to him. Any craic frm Berlin?'

Ugh, I'm so infuriated. Why is she being so blasé about it? Tell me everything, for God's sake!

'He was with a girl we met on hols. What was she doin in Maguires???' No beating around the bush here. I'm gripped by madness and injustice.

'Ah Ais don't b worrying about it. He's seeing her I think. Didn't want 2 upset u n sure you've been out

237

wit Barry. Don't b upset. I wasn't talking to them. Leave them off.'

So much for a best friend. Blinking away hot tears, I fire back 'glad u had such a great wkend. See you whenever' and shove the phone into my handbag.

I feel so hard done by, and kind of . . . wild. Yes, I went on a date with Barry but only because John seemed to have forgotten I existed. Not a word from him when Daddy was sick. And now it turns out he's going out with someone we met on holidays – before we had even broken up. And Majella has been in their company, breathing their air and probably talking to her and thinking what a fab new best friend she's going to be. It's all so unfair.

Pulling up to our apartment block, I fling €30 at the driver, not even waiting to gather up the offerings from the girls in the back, who are all in a bit of a post-holiday daze. They pile out of the car, Ruby too. Wouldn't you think she and Elaine would be sick of the sight of each other by now? Once we're inside, I fling my bag into my room and come straight back out, pacing up and down and around the kitchen island.

'Ais? What's wrong?' Sadhbh asks, coming out of her room to put on the kettle. 'You're like a madwoman.'

I feel like I've been going on about John for so long, for so many months, that I'm loath to even breathe his name again. They must be sick of hearing about him. Sadhbh rarely talks about lads, and I've literally never heard Elaine or Ruby mention a guy. I feel like, at twenty-eight, I'm too long in the tooth to be raging about exes and jealous of girls in pictures. But I can't help myself. I feel like I'm going to hop a saucepan off a wall.

'John has a new girlfriend and he had her down in BGB at the weekend. And Majella was with them. And it's a girl me and John met on holidays.'

Sadhbh stands there, struck dumb. 'Woah, *what*?'

'There's a picture of them on Facebook. All in the local. Lovely and cosy.' I'm spitting tacks. Give me a bloody saucepan to throw.

'Met on holidays . . . ? Out with Majella . . . ? Down in your pub?' Sadhbh doesn't know which morsel to cling onto first. She opts for the safest one. 'Have you asked Majella about it? I'm sure she wouldn't do anything to hurt you, would she?'

'I texted her. She says she wasn't out with them, just in the same pub as them. But it all looked very cosy.'

'She probably wanted to tell you in person that she'd seen them.' Feck off being rational, Sadhbh – I need you to be outraged and on my side! 'And what do you mean you met the girl on holidays? What the hell?' That's more like it.

'She worked in the pub we went to. She actually used to go out with someone John knows from down home. From the club.' I can see Sadhbh looks confused. 'The GAA club,' I qualify.

'Ah, I see. But she's not from down home?'

'No, she's from Wicklow.' I spit it out like Wicklow is a place only murderers and hussies hail from. 'They must have been the right pals after the holidays. He was probably only delighted when we broke up. I think I remember them making friends on Facebook on the last day in Tenerife. Never thought anything of it.'

'Ah, I'm sure that's not true, Ais. And look, you *did* break up. You've moved on too.'

'I just can't imagine going home now. What if she's there all the time? What if Majella makes friends with her? I don't want her around.'

Sadhbh moves in for a hug. 'Ah, you poor thing. Don't you have us now? And we'll go down there and show them who's boss anyway.'

The idea of Sadhbh and co. down in BGB is enough to make me squeeze out a weak smile.

25

'Are we ok Ais?' I turn the phone upside-down on my desk and then, on second thoughts, slip it into my handbag.

I haven't spoken to Majella in four days. She's sent three texts since Sunday and I've ignored them all. The first one was apologetic. The second one was angry – she called me a hypocrite, reminding me once again that John isn't the only one who's moved on. The third is the simple 'Are we ok Ais?' I would say we're very much not OK, Majella, you gom. I think it's probably the longest we've ever not spoken. We've had so few proper rows that I can actually remember them all.

There was the time in Fifth Year that she wrote a note to Orlaith Farrelly, saying that I thought I was 'it' because Conor McCormack sat beside me on the bus on a Foróige youth club trip up to Dublin to see *The Lord of the Rings* – but Orlaith Farrelly showed me the note because she was a trouble-making rip. I couldn't believe Majella thought I thought I was 'it'. The absolute cheek.

There was also the time I didn't tell Majella about

Shannon O'Shea's house-party for her twenty-first in Knock because she was going through her Gold-schläger phase and I was sick of holding her hair back while she puked her ring. The gold flakes rip open your throat so you get drunk faster, you know? Fierce stuff altogether. Actually, Conor McCormack was a catalyst in that row too – Majella was still trying to get into him and she was raging she might have missed her chance at the party.

And then there was the time Majella did finally shift Conor McCormack in the back-bar in Maguire's and I was still smarting that he had never actually lobbed the gob on me, despite what I believed to be out-and-out flirting about orcs and what not on the Foróige bus several years previous, and she overheard me telling Amanda Carey that Maj was going to 'loooove' herself even more now. The only thing worse than saying someone thinks they're 'it' is saying they 'loooove' themselves. I didn't really think Majella 'looooved' herself but jealousy is a terrible blight.

All in all, they were all fairly minor incidents and we never stayed mad at each other for long. This is different. We're not kids any more, fighting over liking the same boys and accusing people of being up themselves. She's made a fool of me. Images of her and Ciara clinking glasses and throwing their heads back for mutual laughs dance through my head. Projections of Majella telling me, 'She's actually really nice, you'd really like her' months down the line run like icy blasts through my mind's eye. I suppose deep down, I don't really know what I expected Majella to do to Ciara. She was hardly going to glass her in the pub or throw her under a truck on Main Street, Ballygobbard, but I just feel betrayed and stupid.

I glance up from my desk and catch Barry staring at me through the glass wall of his office. I haven't heard anything from him since the date and I'm a bit confused about it all. He smiles and looks away when I catch his eye, and I'd be lying if I said it didn't give me a little bit of a thrill and a momentary distraction from the Majella/John/Ciara fiasco. Sure who wouldn't enjoy being eyed up by a big ride with lovely teeth? He might ask me out again. Maybe I'll ask *him* out. The next date might not end up with me bizarrely drinking with Piotr this time. I wonder if Piotr has told John about seeing me out that night. I wonder if Piotr . . .

'Earth to Aisling!' It's Laura, brandishing a file for me to look at.

Laura is the new Donna. Well, she's at Donna's old desk. She's certainly not a new Donna – Donna wishes. Laura is going out with someone who maybe once played for Leinster and she's mentioned three times since she started here that she went to boarding school. She looks like she was born in a Range

Rover, and not the type of one that's carpeted in nuts for the calves or shite from the fields. She definitely calls her Mammy 'Mummy'. Sure she probably owns her own skis. Imagine how much extra Ryanair must charge for them.

I can't wait to tell Donna about her. We're going for an early bird later. I never thought I'd miss her but I do and, truth be told, I'm looking forward to seeing her. She wants to meet at some sushi place on the northside so I better take a look at the menu online first. It can't all be raw fish, can it? And the price of it for something that's not even cooked. I ask you.

'Aaaand katsu curry for yourself.'

I don't really know what katsu is but curry sounds like it has to be cooked so I went for that. I've already asked the girl twice to bring me a knife and fork because it will be some craic if I have to try to scoop this up with chopsticks. Donna has gone for sushi and she's making a big play of knowing what to do with her sticks but I'm anticipating some tuna flying across the restaurant and braining someone.

Donna says she's well, and confides that she's actually like a pig in shite not to have to go to work every day. It might be the best thing that ever happened to her, she says. She'll have to get another job, of course, but she got a good pay-off from our place and she's always banging on about how well Martin does, so she's not too worried.

She looks a bit worried though, despite the optimistic chit-chat, and it doesn't take long for the mask to slip. 'I didn't do it though, Aisling. I know I didn't.'

I go along with her and tell her it must have been an error in the system and didn't they need someone to blame and sure can't she go to the cinema in the afternoon now if she wants or sail around the shops on weekday mornings with countless bored assistants smiling at her, waving rich hand-creams in her direction because she can obviously afford them if she's not in work on a Tuesday at 11 a.m.?

'How's the hen-planning going?' I change the subject because I know she'll have at least ten minutes of chat about dildos and plastic flutes.

'Oh, mighty. I've twenty T-shirts ordered with our *Fifty Shades* nicknames on them. I'm Doggy-Style Donna. I was getting to go for Dirty Donna but that's not very Christian Grey, is it? Suzanne is Spank Me Suzanne. The other bridesmaid is Finger Me Fiona.' I choke on a bit of katsu at this one, which is very nice to be fair to it. 'And I'm after getting Missionary Michelle for Suzanne's workmate Michelle because she didn't bother getting back to me about what name she wanted on it. You snooze, you lose.'

'Is . . . is Suzanne's mam not going to be there?

Are the T-shirts not a bit much?' I'm trying to imagine Mammy being asked to wear a 'Mount Me Marian' top, and failing miserably.

'She is, she thinks it's gas. She's Balls-Deep Bernie.' Balls-Deep Bernie. I've heard it all now.

Talk turns to the new developments in the office since Donna's been gone. I fill her in about Laura, and Donna does an involuntary intake of breath when I mention the Leinster player and the Mulberry handbag, which looks real, to be honest with you. Majella has a fake Mulberry that she got in New York for $200. She had to climb into the back of a van with a Chinese lad and drive around to a back-alley to get to the good stuff, but she's an old hand at that. She got a wallet for me while she was at it. I palm the wallet now as our dinner draws to a close and I try furiously to catch the eye of the waitress, who seemed very disappointed a few minutes ago when she took away the funny-looking tea I hadn't asked for and hadn't touched. They better not charge me for it. It was green and not a drop of milk to be seen.

'Bye now, Donna – sure I'll see you soon. Enjoy the hen.' I hug her goodbye outside the restaurant, before heading for Dunnes on Henry Street. I've a shumper with me I want to return – too tight in the arms even though it's a fourteen. *And* it was strangling me. Sure I'll run in now before I head back to work. If Barry does ask me out again, I wouldn't mind having something new to wear and at least I'll be able to fend Sadhbh off before she has me in some kind of bubble-wrap dress.

Ten, ten, eight, six, ten, twelve. Not a sixteen to be had. Maybe I'll ask if they've any in the back, although how often is it that you just get a useless young one who tells you it's 'just what's out'? Oh wait, here's another few here. Twelve, eight, fourteen, sixteen – hallelujah. As I go to pull the shumper (lovely creamy-yellow shirt collar and cuffs sewn into a pale-blue jumper, very summery), someone else is pulling at it too.

'Sorry now . . .' I start, looking straight up into the eyes of Ciara. Tenerife Ciara.

My cheeks immediately flame up, so fiery that I can nearly feel the heat in my eyeballs. The rest of Dunnes falls away from my peripheral vision like something from *The Matrix* or that film with Leonardo di Caprio I couldn't make head nor tails of, and all I can see is my little hammy hand clinging on to the hanger and her staring me in the face, as I'm rooted to the spot.

'I found the towels.' A horrifyingly familiar voice comes from somewhere off to my right, where I can only see scudding shapes and hear the ringing of tills and the shouting of a toddler. It's like something from a nightmare. It's John. He's found the towels.

'Oh.' He stops dead. I want to just drop every-thing and run, but I can't. 'Ais. Hiya. I mean, how are you?'

'Hiya,' I hear myself say. Is that me speaking? It must be. 'Grand, just back from Berlin. You know yourself. Getting a few bits. Spend spend spend.'

I'm babbling. I don't know where my eyes are going. John is kind of uselessly gesturing towards Ciara, who has dropped her hands down by her side and looks like she wishes she could impale herself on an adjacent rack of leggings.

'You . . . do you remember Ciara?'

'I do.'

Silence. It probably only lasts two or three sec-onds, but to me it seems like the length of two ice ages. Glaciers sliding by and everything.

'I've to go.' I announce suddenly, turning on my heel and walking blindly in the direction of what I hope is an escape route.

I see the great expanse of the exit and speed through it, followed immediately by the ear-piercing shriek of a security system. I'm still carrying the shumper. I'm still clutching the hanger. Turning back towards the shop, I fling it in the direction of the nearest rack, des-perate to get out of there but at the same time conscious that shoplifters *will* be prosecuted. We've all seen the posters. Not today, Satan, as Majella would say.

The relief when the cool air hits my face is

unbelievable. I had never felt so trapped in my life. What are the chances? What were they doing there? Were they shopping together? He was holding hand-towels. Why was he buying hand-towels? How many times did I beg him, Cillian and Piotr to recognise the glorious difference between drying your hands on a nice clean hand-towel and the stinking damp ones they've been using after their showers for at least six months and just draping around various parts of the bathroom? 'Sure amn't I clean when I get out of the shower?' Cillian protested once, and I gave up on trying to get them to accept hand-towels into their lives.

And yet here was John now, buying his own. What a bloody gent he turned out to be for his new love, Ciara. What a kick in the face.

26

'Lads, I just got the weirdest text from Mammy. If I didn't know better, I'd say she was hacked,' I announce, walking into the kitchen of the apartment on Saturday evening. It's been three days since I came face-to-face with John and Ciara and I'm only now starting to string together proper sentences instead of blubbering some word-salad about towels and shumpers.

'Well, don't leave us hanging,' Sadhbh says, looking up from one of her high-protein, low-carb concoctions, obviously delighted to have a normal conversation with me again.

'Paul's finally shown up as an extra in Summer Bay?' offers Elaine, which is a good guess, but not right in this instance.

'No. Well, not that I know of anyway. No, Mammy has invited you both down to BGB on the bank-holiday weekend . . . for brunch.' Mammy! How does she even know what brunch is? I bet bloody Niamh From Across The Road has been in her ear again.

'I'm game,' Sadhbh says straight away. 'I can't believe

we still haven't been to BGB. I want to order a whiskey in Maguire's and get a dash of Coke for free. And I definitely want to grill your dad about the cow you bought with your Confirmation money. I can't comprehend it.'

'Ha ha,' I go, regretting the day I ever told them that story. I still haven't lived it down, no matter how many times I've tried to explain that where I'm from, a heifer, especially if it's in calf, is a solid and very common Confirmation-money investment. I made a packet on it in the end. But it always falls on deaf ears and they just end up creasing themselves laughing.

'How about you, Elaine?'

'I wouldn't miss it for the world. Tell your mom thanks a mill and ask if we can bring anything.'

'Right so,' I say, texting Mammy: 'Theyd luv to. Wat time? Wat can they bring? xx'

Mammy is back on immediately – she must have had the phone in her hand. 'Gr8 stuff pet. Tell them 2 just bring demselves. See u all at 3pm on Sunday so. I'll have the spare room ready xx.'

Three o'clock is a bit late for brunch, but I hold my tongue. I've told Mammy more than once how great the girls have been to me the last few months so I know this invitation is her way of saying thanks on behalf of the family. She'll be stressed now that they've said they'll come, I know she will, even though it was her idea.

'See u soon. Don't go 2 ne trouble now. Btw Elaine is vegan. Google it xx.'

'How are relations between you and Majella?' Elaine asks between mouthfuls of quinoa or spirulina or whatever Deliciously Ella has tricked her into cooking this week. 'Still frosty?'

'That's an understatement,' I reply, sticking my Marks & Spencer Count on Us chicken curry (4 Points) into the microwave. 'I still haven't forgiven her.'

I can feel the betrayal bubbling up inside me at the sound of her name. But at the same time, I'm desperate to tell her about the Run-in of Horrors in Dunnes.

'I wasn't making it up – I'm dying to finally see Ballygobbard,' Sadhbh goes, changing the subject briskly.

'Oh, I'll show you all the sights. The handball alley where I got my first shift. The moving statue in Filan's car park – it hasn't moved in a while, don't be getting excited. The underground bunker where Mad Tom apparently keeps 400 tins of Batchelors Baked Beans and a commode, ready for Doomsday. Sure you won't want to come back up to Dublin – you'll meet a nice farmer with road frontage and that'll be the end of you,' I add, winking at Elaine who's too busy looking down at her phone to notice. Probably sending one of those Snapchats to Ruby. They're always at it, those two.

*

My suspicions about the state of Mammy's nerves are confirmed when she rings me at work the next day.

'Aisling, we're having the kitchen painted this week. Daddy wants to go with Magnolia again but I'm sick to the teeth telling him it's the source of all depression in Ireland. Will you have a word, love?'

'Mammy, tell me this has nothing to do with the girls coming down,' I whisper, fake-typing, trying to make it look like I'm on a work call. 'They're not going to notice the colour of the walls.'

'Not at all, love – it's just a coincidence. Honestly. Sure we haven't had the place painted since Paul's Confirmation. It's desperate. Will you say it to your father about the Magnolia? Úna Hatton has me convinced that a light grey would be much nicer. Trout's back or Mouse's Pelt, or something, she said it was called in the paint catalogue.'

'All right, all right, I'll do my best. Now, I have to go,' I hiss, shouting, 'I'll have that on your desk on Monday' for good measure before hanging up. I don't think anyone has noticed, but you can't be too careful given how volatile things are at work at the moment. Time-theft is a genuine problem.

By Sunday morning, Sadhbh and Elaine have worked themselves into a frenzy about their impending pilgrimage to Ballygobbard.

'It's because you and Majella talk about it so much,'

253

Sadhbh tries to explain, while cramming her swish Samsonite wheelie case into the back of the Micra.

It's rare she leaves Dublin, and when she does, it's only to go to festivals or surfing in Sligo or some other wholesome outdoorsy activity you might see on an ad for rashers and sausages. God only knows what she has in that bag. I notice she's invested in a pair of those expensive Hunter wellies and involuntarily roll my eyes.

'In my head, it's going to be like one of those quaint, picturesque villages in a BBC drama where the murder rate is, like, two hundred per cent higher than Detroit,' Elaine adds, slipping into the front passenger seat. Little sleeveen didn't even bagsy it. 'All granite farmhouses and rapists and guards who look like David Tennant.'

'Lads, you're in for a rude awakening,' I snort, pulling out of the underground car park. 'We've never had a murder; people in BGB die from old age or boredom.'

It's 2.59 p.m. when we pull up outside the house and as well as being delighted with myself for timing the journey perfectly, I'm also feeling a bit anxious. As we exit the Micra, I'm trying to see the homestead through Sadhbh and Elaine's eyes. They immediately ooh and aah over the low granite walls around the house (a divil to get over when you've had one too many West Coast Coolers), the rolling green hills in the distance and even Tiger, who's in her usual spot on the kitchen windowsill giving us evils. The air is fragrant with fresh-cut hay and the sound of bird-song is, I must admit, glorious. I suppose it's not a bad auld spot.

'Christ, the Irish countryside is gorgeous,' Elaine says, raising her ridiculously oversized sunglasses to get a better look and inhaling deeply. 'No filter required.'

Sadhbh already has her phone out snapping pictures of the Front Field and the Far Field in the distance when the back door bursts open and Mammy comes blustering out, a tea-towel over her shoulder. I wonder if my eyes are deceiving me but no, she's definitely wearing make-up, which she normally saves for special occasions. It's actually Wedding-Level Make-Up. *And* she's had a blow-dry.

'Right on time as always, Aisling,' she says, enveloping me in a hug and the familiar scent of Red Door. 'And you must be Sadhbh,' she says, correctly identifying Sadhbh, 'and Elaine, the vegan!'

'Guilty as charged,' Elaine says. 'Thanks so much for inviting us, Marian – it's so nice to get away to the country.'

I knew they'd call her by her first name. I just knew it.

'Not at all, girls,' Mammy says, ushering us inside.

'It's the least we could do after all the support you've given Aisling up in Dublin. We've missed her but sure we're delighted she's getting on so well. And her practically running the place at work! Isn't it gorgeous out?'

And we all agree that the drying is second to none.

27

Well, she wasn't lying when she said she was freshening up the house – it looks like the Considered by Helen James section of Dunnes puked on it. There are baskets and brass candlesticks and earthenware pots in a neutral palette as far as the eye can see. She's even bought a tasteful new kitchen table and chairs to replace the old Formica thing I had all my childhood birthday parties around. The spot where Tiger's pristine bed once lay now boasts a five-foot fiddle-leaf fig and I know this is the final straw for our relationship – That Bloody Cat will know it's all my fault and never forgive me, even though she never set a paw in it. Úna Hatton, I have to hand it to her, has faboo taste. No surprise there. It's the Protestant blood.

'Where do you want us, Marian?' Sadhbh asks, approaching the table, which looks as if Helen James, whoever she is, set it herself.

'Oh, wherever you like, love,' Mammy says, coming in with the milk jug. 'Make yourselves at home now.'

'Where's Daddy?' I ask, looking around, genuinely

worried that she's banished him to the sitting room because he doesn't blend with the new decor.

'Up the yard, but he should be here any minute. I have him well warned.'

'I love your table settings, Marian,' Elaine goes, in that charming way she has about her – such a pro at chatting up mammies. 'And the flowers. Are they from the garden we saw on the way in?'

'Oh, well, thank you very much, Elaine,' says Mammy, going slightly pink. 'They are indeed from the garden. I'm not the green-fingered one though. That'd be Daddy. Now, will you have a glass of milk? Fresh in this morning.'

'Er, no thanks, I'm vegan,' Elaine replies. 'Sorry, when you say the milk is fresh, do you mean, like, it came from the cow today?'

'You're on the farm now, girls,' I laugh, filling my glass to the brim.

'So this milk is genuinely raw?' Sadhbh goes, gesturing at the jug. 'That means it still has all the enzymes, fatty acids – everything? It's unpasteurised? My personal trainer told me he buys this stuff for €2 a pint on the black market. You could be making a fortune selling it at farmer's markets on the south-side, Marian. The yummy mummies are *obsessed*.'

Just then, the kitchen door swings open and Daddy shuffles in, wearing his Medium Good Jumper, which means he hasn't been doing any manual labour up the yard and was probably ordered outside for his own safety. I'm hoping it's a sign that he's taking Dr Maher's advice seriously and slowing down, at least at the weekend, all-clear or no all-clear. Tiger is immediately all over him, slinking around his legs, and he pretends to swat her off as I make the introductions and the girls tell him how much they're dying to see BGB and ask him all about the farm and whether he has any heifers going cheap. Lick-arses, the pair of them. He's looking a bit pale but not too bad, and I make a mental note to set aside some time later for worrying.

By the time Mammy serves up the food, it becomes clear the concept of brunch hasn't made it to BGB yet. After a starter of vegetable soup, followed by roast beef with three kinds of spuds (and a porto-bello mushroom for Elaine) and then a trifle, Mammy confesses she thought it was just a new word for 'a whole heap of food'. Sadhbh admits that Mammy is ninety per cent right.

I was fairly relieved myself. Since I've been staying up in Dublin more, I've come to realise what a scourge brunch culture is. If I've been Out Out or even just out the night before, the last thing I want if I drag my carcass to a restaurant is bloody eggs Benedict or some kind of hipster pancake nonsense.

No thanks. Sunday dinner, served any time between 12 and 3 p.m., should be a roast.

Later, after a good brisk walk around the farm, Daddy gives us a lift into Maguire's, and I realise that I haven't been in there since those June evenings with Maj. That has to be a record. Not that it's changed, mind. It's jammed, with everyone back home for the bank-holiday weekend. The GAA lads, a few from Knock Rangers and BGB Gaels are at the bar – always first in and last to leave – drinking cans of cider when we walk in and we exchange friendly nods, although I notice that none of them run over to ask me how I am. Very telling. No sign of John, thank God – they must be cutting silage this weekend.

'Aisling! The old stranger returns,' Felipe shouts across the bar when he spots me. 'And who have you brought with you, eh?'

'Well, Felipe. These are some friends from above in Dublin. Sadhbh, Elaine – meet Felipe, the best barman in BGB.'

'Ah, Aisling, you're too kind. West Coast Cooler and a pint glass of ice, is it? And for you, girls?'

'Two double Jack Daniels and Diet Cokes,' Sadhbh says without hesitation. Elaine and I exchange a look. She's been drinking like it's going out of fashion since Berlin. Or maybe it was before then?

I can't really remember, but something isn't quite right.

'Grand, ladies – I'll drop them down to you.'

We make our way to the back of the pub and I direct the girls to one of the corner tables I know will give them a good vantage point. I can feel their questions coming. I nod a few 'hellos' and 'wells' along the way and wave at Sinéad McGrath, who can barely meet my eyes. No doubt she and John's Ciara are best mates now. At least she has the good grace to be ashamed of herself.

'Aisling, is that a framed picture of a load of Roses of Tralee outside this pub?' Elaine can't contain herself.

'It is. They were down here in 2008 – look at the sashes. As you can see,' I say, pointing out several other blown-up photographs of the women in front of various BGB landmarks, including the church, 'it was kind of a big deal. My brother Paul is in the background of the one outside the ladies'. You can't miss it.'

I feel my phone vibrating in my bag and make a grab for it, Daddy's pale face swimming into my mind. But it's not Mammy – it's not even a call. It's a text – from Barry.

'Hey Ais, wat u up to for de BH?'

Barry actually texts quite a bit, truth be told – always hoping I'm well or wondering if I'm out. He's mentioned going for dinner or to the cinema too, but we still haven't managed to pin down a day.

'Where's your man from?' Sadhbh asks, snapping me back to reality, nodding her head in Felipe's general direction. 'That's definitely not a local accent.'

'He's Brazilian,' I explain. 'There's actually a thriving community over the road in Knocknamanagh. Felipe's younger brother Luís is on the county team – his right leg is legendary. If you want to try authentic Brazilian food, not that shite you can get in Temple Bar, I could bring you over to Foguiera for lunch tomorrow. Felipe will even whip you up a caipirinha now, if you like? They get the good rum in specially.'

The pair of them are looking at me now like I've sprouted a second head and I know why: they assumed that Ballygobbard was going to be a bit backwards just because it's rural. OK, from where I'm sitting, there are a few auld lads wearing tweed flat-caps and nursing pints of Guinness like they're straight off a postcard from the fifties but I can also see Tessie Daly in the snug with Sumaira Singh, who's originally from India but who took over the local nursing home about thirty-five years ago. Sumaira manages to put in a few hours every week in the charity shop as well and regularly sends a tinfoil-packed plate of samosas home with Mammy because she knows Daddy goes mad for them. And leaning against the bar talking the ear off

Paddy Reilly is Vasile Alexandrou, who was born here but who goes to Romania at least twice a year because he says the air over there is nicer. He set up his own water-divining business in the seventies – 'If there's water there, Vasile Alexandrou will find it' – and his brother was part of the anti-terrorism unit during the Troubles. His daughter, Ioana, was in the year ahead of me and, to this day, is the only girl in the Pres ever to get 700 points. Sure, according to Mammy, there are three Patricks in Junior Infants this year and two of them are black.

'I suppose I wasn't expecting the crowd in Maguire's to be so . . . diverse,' Sadhbh eventually says, after Felipe drops down a bag of King taytos along with the drinks because he knows I love them. 'It's so beautiful down here, and everyone is so nice. I'm starting to see the appeal of country life.'

Elaine snorts. 'Sadhbh, are you pissed already? You wouldn't last five minutes in the sticks.'

'I really think I would,' she insists, putting down her glass for emphasis and sloshing whiskey and Coke on her white three-quarter-length culottes. 'I do most of my shopping online anyway. And I'm trying to cut back on eating out. I could grow my own vegetables, maybe get some chickens. Make baby applesauce and settle down with a nice vet, like Diane Keaton in *Baby Boom*. Actually, no – bad example . . .' And she trails off.

'You've lost your mind, babe,' Elaine says, not letting it go. 'The phone signal is shit. There's no Deliveroo. There's no place to even get a coffee here.'

I nod. My first instinct is always to defend Ballygobbard – it's like when you slag off your family but nobody else is allowed to say a bad word against them – but it's all true, although there are rumours that Eamon Maguire is looking for planning permission to add tea rooms to his hospitality empire. You'd have to assume there'll be coffee too.

'Listen, Sadhbh, I used to think it didn't get any better than BGB,' I say, leaning across the little round table, 'but I realise now I was wrong. It's a nice town, but there's a lot to be said for the anonymity of the Big Smoke and nobody knowing your business.'

'That's true,' she concedes after a long pause. 'Fag?' and we all head out to the smoking area, me stashing the bags and coats under the table as usual. You can't be too careful, even in BGB.

Three hours, six West Coast Coolers and at least a bottle of Jack Daniels later, we're still outside. It didn't take long for the GAA lads to migrate out to the girls and they're taking turns trying to convince them that they'd both be better off down here than in Dublin. Cyclops – Eoin Ó Súilleabháin – is making a serious play for Elaine, but she's having none of it and keeps having to remove his wandering arm from the back of her seat. Meanwhile, Pádraig Nolan is telling Sadhbh about the time Father Fenlon came over to the house to do the Stations of the Cross. Jenny Nolan was off to Canada for the year the next morning so he offered to do confession while he was there. The house was fairly rammed, so the only place Pádraig's mammy could put the priest was on a garden chair in the bath, behind the shower curtain. Sadhbh is literally bent over laughing.

'He's not making it up, I was actually there myself,' I confirm. 'Kneeling on the bathmat, telling him how I'd taken the Lord's name in vain three times that week. He gave me twelve Hail Marys and as I was leaving, a full bottle of Pantene fell right on his head. Serves him right. This was only about three years ago, I should add.'

Sadhbh looks like she's going to burst a blood-vessel she's laughing so hard, before she suddenly realises it's just after twelve and insists on buying shots for us all 'before the bar closes'. It adds up to eleven sambucas, but she has the MasterCard gone to Felipe before I can stop her and explain that Maguire's doesn't stop serving until the place is empty. It's like international waters in all the pubs in BGB since the Garda station closed. That's why half of Knock comes over at the weekend.

*

It's gone 3 a.m. when the place finally starts to clear out. When the lads get the message that the girls have no interest, they start calling Terry Crowley, the local taxi, to come get them and let poor auld Felipe, worse for wear himself, start piling stools on tables. It's not long before we're the last three standing, save for Paddy Reilly asleep with his head on the bar, half a pint still in his hand.

It's only when I'm distributing the girls' bags and coats from where I have them stashed under the seat that I realise that Sadhbh is crying silently, tears streaming down her face. I don't even know how long she's been like that.

'Jesus. Sadhbh, what's wrong? Did one of those big eejits do something to you?' I ask, horrified, nudging Elaine who's rooting through her bag, no doubt looking for her phone, which is on the table in front of her. 'I'll bloody kill them. Which one was it? Philip Johnsie? Cyclops? The Truck? Baby Chief? It was Baby Chief, wasn't it? He wouldn't leave you alone, I saw him at you for the past hour. He's nothing but a . . .'

'No, no! God, no, Aisling. It wasn't Baby Chief. They were grand. Really funny in fact,' she replies, smiling but crying at the same time. 'That was probably the most I've laughed in the last month. It felt really fucking good, actually.'

'Then what's going on? Is it because you just spent nearly €60 on shots for people you don't know?

Listen, it's happened to the best of us. Majella does it once a week. I'll go halves with you if you want?'

'No, I wish. I wish it was something as easy as being overdrawn,' she sniffs, taking a drag on her rollie. I notice she's shaking a bit and I take off my good pashmina and throw it over her skinny little shoulders. That's the good thing about having more meat on your bones – I'm always running warm.

Elaine is suddenly back in the land of the living, phone in hand, but she's not as empathetic as me. 'What the fucking fuck is going on with you, Sadhbh? Mate, you've been acting really weird recently. We've all noticed.'

She looks at me pointedly and I nod. Sadhbh *has* been acting weird. She called in sick for three days last week and barely came out of her room the entire time. I also heard her pacing around the apartment late at night. And Ruby told me she caught her eating a cheese toastie the other day – like, made with real cheese, not her usual dairy-free shite.

'Is it about work?' I ask, running out of ideas, but she shakes her head. 'Then what? What's going on, Sadhbh? As Mammy always says, a problem shared is a problem halved.'

'If you don't come clean, I'm just going to go ahead and assume you've developed a drug problem, Sadhbh, because you're exhibiting all the same symptoms my cousin Imogen did before we found out she was smoking crack,' Elaine is shouting now, off on a rant. 'This is a safe space. And Imogen has been clean for three years now – she's managing a Supermac's in Limerick, staying away from the temptations of Dublin.'

Neither of us is prepared for Sadhbh's eventual response.

'I'm pregnant. OK? I'm seven weeks fucking pregnant,' she whispers hoarsely, and now she's crying harder than ever, her body racked with great big heaving sobs, snot running down her face.

Even in my foggy drunken state, I know this is not good news. She doesn't even have a boyfriend. Elaine is immediately up and hugging her, but I know it's not congratulations she's saying. She's telling her it'll be OK. She's telling her she'll support her, she'll be there for her, do whatever she can to help, give her money, whatever she needs. I'm rooted to my stool but my eyes automatically dart to Sadhbh's hands, half-drunk caipirinha in one and cigarette in the other. I can't help it. She catches me and I don't look away in time.

'Oh don't, Aisling, for fuck's sake,' she says between sobs. 'I'm hardly keeping it.'

28

'Was it . . . was it the lad in Berlin? The MMDM lad?' 'M-D-M-A!' Elaine shouts, exasperated, unable to help herself. 'And sure how could it be him? She said seven weeks. Oh Sadhbh, it's not . . .'

'Stop stop stop, don't say it.' Sadhbh continues to weep.

She doesn't even have a boyfriend. How did it even happen? You hear stories of people being caught on the hop, but it's usually only the biggest dopes like Christina Haughey (I actually do believe her when she says it was a Spanish sailor – the child is very dark). Seven weeks. I rack my brains, but nothing about Sadhbh even going on a date springs to mind. In fact, I can't remember the last time she even mentioned dating. I suddenly get a flashback to First Year, when Majella had me fully convinced you could get pregnant from sitting on the toilet directly after a boy, and Sister Assumpta told us to always put a book on a lad's lap before sitting on it in case his sperm – she whispered the word 'sperm' – somehow got on you.

We stumble down the road away from Maguire's, into the encroaching darkness of the country night.

I could probably chance Terry Crowley for a lift but I don't want him seeing this drama and reporting back to all and sundry in his pitch-and-putt group. It would only be a matter of time before it spreads to the set-dancing gang and sure then it would hit the Tidy Towns Committee and that would be the end of that. It will be a bit of a trek home, but the fresh air will probably do us good and I don't want Mammy and Daddy hearing the roaring and shouting and crying.

'Is it really such a bad thing?' I offer in what I hope is a helpful tone, shining the torch from my phone onto the road ahead of us, pointing it here and there for potholes and unexpected dips. 'I mean, we're a bit old for it to be scandalous to have a baby. You're nearly thirty!'

'I don't want to have a baby,' Sadhbh sobs. 'I don't know if I ever want to have a baby and I definitely don't want to have this one now.' She stops dead in her tracks. 'Ah Ais, you're not about to turn all sanctimonious on me, are you?' She cries even harder and carries on marching up the road.

'God, no, not at all,' I splutter, trotting after her, feeling instantly like a dope. It hadn't even crossed my mind that she point blank mightn't want it. Sure I was already thinking about buying it a tiny hurl. It's something I've never really had to think about, what with John and I always doubling up with condoms and anti-babby pills to be extra careful. I don't know if I could ever do it myself, truth be told, but on the other hand, I just can't imagine being made to have a baby I didn't want. Sure you wouldn't know what you would do until it happened to you. We've never talked about it at home really but I'd have been killed if I came home sixteen and pregnant. Or any age and pregnant. Daddy would be a fan of keeping your politics between yourself and the polling booth, but not a fan of single mammy Ais, I don't think. Come to think of it, Mammy swiftly switched from Radio One to Lyric one Sunday recently when they had someone on talking about abortion, so I can guess which side she'd come down on. Who am I to judge anyone though? I'd absolutely hate Sadhbh to think I was judging her so I need to make sure she knows I'm with her, no matter what. I catch up with her on the road.

'You're just so upset that I thought maybe you were sad at the thought of it,' I apologise.

'I just . . . I just didn't think it would be *this* sad.' She stops to do another big crying breath. You know the ones, a great big shudder. 'I thought if it ever happened to me it would be as simple as getting on the plane and just doing it. A few days away, get it seen to and then back to normal. But it's such a big deal. The whole thing is such a big deal and I'm so thick with myself for letting it be such a big deal. I thought I would be . . . better at this.'

'Ah, Sadhbhy.' Elaine's voice is soft. 'It's not as if it's something anybody is *good* at. You're allowed to be sad.'

'I'd be in bits,' I say.

I would be. I just don't know if I could do it if I found myself in the same situation, no matter how many times I told myself it wasn't a big deal. But if Sadhbh wants to have an abortion, then she has to. And we'll mind her.

'So, is it Stephen's?' Elaine gently pushes.

Stephen? Who in all that is holy is Stephen?

'Yes,' Sadhbh crumples back into tears, nearly falling sideways into a ditch in the process.

'Who is Stephen?' I practically shout at Elaine, who sighs.

'You know Holly, the girl who used to live in your room? Well, she didn't move out because she was going to teach yoga in India. She moved out because Sadhbh was riding her boyfriend, Stephen. Have you told him?' she asks Sadhbh.

'Why would I tell him? I'm not seeing him any more. I'm not going to have it. The whole thing is over.'

Silence on the road apart from Sadhbh's sobs and hiccups. I'm struck dumb. Perfect put-together Sadhbh. Almond-milk Sadhbh.

'Holly and Stephen decided to give it another go, because he and Sadhbh swore it was a once-only thing. But obviously not.' Elaine doesn't sound harsh – she sounds sad, probably spurred on by Sadhbh's quiet sobs as she trips along behind us. 'I suppose they couldn't stay away from each other.'

God, don't people do awful things to each other? Poor Holly. And poor Sadhbh. And poor everyone.

'Car!' I shout suddenly, as glaring headlights peep over the crest of a bump in the road in the distance. 'Get in, get in, mind the ditch.'

Sadhbh and Elaine are shrieking like banshees, clambering onto the grass verge in their mad boots, sinking into the muddy softness. I flash my phone's torch ahead of us, so the car knows we're there. It's absolutely flying. Probably Mad Tom out practising his doughnuts in the Subaru or stealing pallets for another one of his get-rich-quick schemes.

'My hair is stuck,' Elaine is shouting, trying to twist away from a branch sticking vindictively out of the hedge.

'I'm sinking,' bleats Sadhbh, as dubious ditch juice threatens to crest the top of her boot.

The car flies by and I yank the two of them back out onto the road, creasing myself laughing at the state of them and shining the torch into their faces. Elaine's usually immaculate hair is like a haystack and Sadhbh's porcelain face is blotchy and red. They've looked better. Elaine starts laughing with me and before long, the three of us are hooting into the darkness like demented owls.

'Come on,' I gesture uselessly in the pitch-dark, wiping tears of mirth from my eyes. I'd say my carefully applied coat of mascara has made some journey south at this stage. Poor Sadhbh's Kylie Minogue eyeshadow, or whatever it is, is all over her face. 'We're nearly there. I'm dying for toast.'

Good old Daddy has left the gate open for us, although I'd say it nearly killed him, what with his good lawnmower and the variety of power tools he was swizzed into buying in Aldi in the garage ripe for the taking. Never mind that there's a padlock on the door. There's a key left under the second plant-pot at the back door. It's not the best hiding place but the lock on the door is so tricky that any burglar would be long caught before he was able to jiggle the handle just the right way to get it open.

After shushing the girls up the driveway and around the side of the house, I unlock the door with minimum effort, hissing at them to 'take off your shoes' and 'straight through to the kitchen'.

Elaine spies an armchair in the corner beside the Aga and swings into it thankfully, plonking down before I can warn her about That Bloody Ca ... *meeeeyoooowwww*. The cat is gone like a shot, shrieking as it fires past me out the door.

'Jesus Christ,' pants Elaine, thankfully unscathed. 'This is like effing Jumanji.'

I shush the girls again, listening to make sure the racket hasn't stirred Mammy and Daddy in their room at the end of the house. All quiet.

'Toast?' I announce, and set about making a few rounds, pulling the butter dish out and flipping on the kettle. Mammy has left out a lovely loaf of seedy bread. I'd say she spent a fortune on it.

'Is bread vegan?' I ask Elaine, who's still recovering in the armchair.

'I'd eat the batter off a chicken ball right now, to be honest,' she answers.

Sadhbh is very quiet, looking down at her nails.

'Are you all right, Sadhbhy?' Elaine asks gently.

Sadhbh does another one of those shudders you do when you've been bawling for hours and it's all bawled out of you. 'Yeah. I'm grand. I just can't believe I have to get a bloody abortion.'

29

Mammy is in full flow again the next morning, crashing and banging around the kitchen, the smell of sausages and rashers (poor Elaine) wafting up the stairs when I peel my eyes open and fumble for my phone on the bedside locker. 9.11 a.m. Mother of God. Sure we're only in the bed a few hours. I wonder whether Sadhbh and Elaine are alive or what. They're in the spare room across the landing, smothered under an avalanche of cushions Mammy must have decided she had to have for the visitors. She had a Yankee Candle she's been saving for three years (Christmas present from Paul) lighting in the bathroom yesterday too. I'm surprised she hadn't ripped out the sink and toilet and installed brand-new ones for the occasion.

I lie back in bed and take a look around the room I've called mine for so many years. A curling poster of Ryan Giggs overlaps one of Gareth Gates on my wall. Rewants from the odd time Filan's would get in a batch of *just its* and we'd go mad hanging exotic celebs on the walls. John used to say hanging up the

Giggs one was sacrilegious to the parish and the county – but if he was allowed to fancy any number of RTÉ weather ladies, I was having my poster. Giggs was a fine thing in his day.

All the notes me and Majella used to send each other in school are under the bed in a Roses tin and everything Marita Conlon-McKenna has ever written is on my bookshelf. I still reach for *Under the Hawthorn Tree* for a bit of comfort. Also sitting on the bookshelf is a photo of me with the Bishop on my Confirmation Day, standing beside a bush outside the BGB church. I have a fierce amount of freckles and am wearing green culottes and a floppy hat. I thought I looked the business. On my bedside locker are a few opened letters from the Credit Union and the bank – I don't get much post at home any more but it's usually opened 'by accident' by Mammy because it 'looked important'. My one pair of Susst jeans are still in the chest of drawers. I'd totally wear them today if I could fit back into them. They've a lovely flare on them and I like a bit of a flare, no matter what Sadhbh says.

I can hear her and Elaine chatting in the room across the way now, probably roused by Mammy's enthusiastic scrambling of eggs. They said they'd probably get an early enough bus back to Dublin. I'm going to stay down another night and drive into work first thing Tuesday morning. The peace and quiet is nice sometimes and last night was fairly hectic.

I pad across to them and stick my head in the door. 'Hiya, girls. Are . . . are you all right, Sadhbh?'

'I'll live,' she sighs heavily, placing two cotton-wool pads on her eyes, probably to stop them looking like footballs from all the crying.

'Mammy has breakfast on if you want some before you go? Sure follow me down.'

Mammy is fully turned out again for her second meal with the Dublin visitors. The make-up is toned down a bit but there's a hint of mauve eyeshadow going on, and she's definitely wearing new shoes. And I'm fairly sure the toast is on a Denby plate she's liberated from the cabinet in the Good Room.

She looks up from the black pudding as I come into the kitchen. 'Ah hello, you're alive.'

'It's not that late, Mammy.' It's half nine. On a bank-holiday Monday. Just because she and Daddy have never been known to stay in bed past seven . . . apart from the times Daddy couldn't get out of bed at all.

'Are the girls up?' She sounds a bit strange.

'They are. They'll be down in a minute. I'm going to drop them in to get the bus back up. They're nice girls, aren't they?'

'They are.' She still sounds strange. Probably the stress of the visit and the relief at it nearly being over.

'Where's Daddy?'

'He's gone back for a lie-down.'

Before I get a chance to question her, Elaine and Sadhbh push the kitchen door open, all smiles and 'hiya Marians' and politely turning down the panoply of things they wouldn't dream of putting in their bodies. Sadhbh is very quiet but Mammy gently coaxes her into having some tea and a sausage in a bit of bread. She's sought out some grapefruit so Elaine's only delighted. Absolutely mad.

Before long, the girls have packed up their snazzy overnight bags and are bidding Mammy and Daddy (who's emerged from the bed again) all the 'byebye-byebyes' in the world before getting into the Micra for their lift. Elaine didn't quite manage to make it away without the other half of the grapefruit wrapped up in tinfoil but at least neither of them have sausages about their person.

As we pull out of the driveway, I look at Sadhbh in the rear-view mirror. 'Are you really OK, Sadhbh? Do you need anything?'

'I'm grand. I'll be grand. My sister lives in London. I won't be the first making this visit to her and I won't be the last.'

And we ride the rest of the way to the bus stop in silence.

Mammy is sitting in the kitchen when I get back, changed back into slightly more everyday attire.

'Sit down here and talk to me. You never sit down and talk to me any more.'

I suppose she's right. We're not huge on the heart-to-hearts. We chat and we fight sometimes and we've supported each other when things are tough, but we don't really go in for deep sharing. And since I'm up in Dublin more and more, we don't get to catch up as much as we used to.

I pour myself a cuppa from the freshly boiled kettle and sit down opposite her. 'What'll we talk about so?'

She pauses, and takes a breath. 'Is Sadhbh all right, Aisling?'

I can feel my cheeks burning slightly, defensively. 'What do you mean?'

'I heard ye, last night. I heard ye talking after ye came in and the cat went squalling out of the kitchen. I wasn't being nosy. I got up for the toilet, that's all. Ye were louder than you thought.'

'Well, then you probably heard. She's not really all right. She's pregnant. She . . .'

'She's going to have an abortion,' Mammy interjects softly but matter-of-factly.

280

I feel an immediate and unexpected instinct to fiercely protect Sadhbh, kind of surprising myself with the way I round on Mammy.

'Ah, don't start. She can do what she likes. She doesn't want to have a baby. You don't understand.'

I've never really discussed topics like this with Mammy. I just assumed she'd be a bit funny about it so I never brought it up, and wouldn't you be mortified talking about doing the deed in front of your parents?

'Why wouldn't I understand?' She looks a bit wild-eyed. 'Sure didn't I have one?'

30

I'm floored. She's floored me. Abortions aren't for my mammy. They're for other people. Other people, and Sadhbh. 'Oh, Mammy. When? What happened?'

Thoughts of her first standing at the top of the stairs, raw potato in one hand, bottle of gin in the other, but not being able to go through with it. Images of her with a little suitcase clambering onto a boat alone on a cold and foggy evening crowd my mind. Snapshots of her being madly in love with some chancer who wouldn't marry her despite her father going after him with a pitchfork . . . no, I'm losing the head altogether.

Poor, young, beautiful Mammy. She's wearing a chic head-scarf in my imagination. And maybe red lipstick. Although I've never seen her wearing lipstick in my life.

'It wasn't all that long ago, pet. 1995. Me and Daddy decided together.'

1995? Sure I was . . . six. I was alive. I'm floored. Completely.

If these kitchen walls could talk, they'd tell tales about the time Daddy exposed Mammy for trying to serve oxtail soup that was three years out of date. 'It's grand', she insisted indignantly. 'It's only a suggestion of a date.' He still laughs about it every time we have soup. Mammy hates waste. These walls would point to the press above the radio that has about twelve years of bows from our Christmas box of Ferrero Rocher, carefully saved 'just in case'. They'd give a running commentary of the rows Paul and I have had with Mammy, begging her to buy fizzy orange and free us from the drudgery of the diluted stuff. But I never thought they had any secrets from me, that they'd tell me I hadn't been privy to hushed conversations about an abortion. Mammy and Daddy's abortion.

'Remember the time you stayed with Auntie Sheila? You and Paul? You were six and he was two. You might not remember.' I *do* remember. Auntie Sheila had chocolate-chip ice cream. The luxury.

'You lost your first tooth while we were in Liverpool. You were so sad that we had missed it. Not as sad as we were though. We went to Liverpool and I had it and I cried and I left it all behind me.'

'Why did you do it?' I had to ask.

'We had no money for another baby. The mortgage was strangling us. The Celtic Tiger was a long time coming to a farm in Ballygobbard. Do you not remember the hole in the floor of the Renault?'

I did remember. The car was so banjaxed we had

to lift our feet up when it rained. We didn't have a load of money growing up, but look, nobody did. We were grand, I thought. Sure everyone's yearly holiday was a week all packed into the same room in a B&B in Dungarvan. Daddy swearing blind that he didn't need a map and that it was normal that it was taking us four hours to get to whatever sacred stone or thatched cottage was on the agenda that day and Mammy doling out the 99s at petrol stations to keep the peace.

'It was hard enough to scrape together enough to go to Liverpool at all,' Mammy continues. 'I was going to go on my own but Daddy said we'd make it work. And we did. You should have seen the hole we stayed in. Cigarette burns in the carpet and some loola up half the night roaring about someone stealing his underpants.' She almost raises a smile, and then turns to me, sad again. 'Do you think I'm awful?'

'No . . . no, Mammy. I just . . . I just didn't think people . . . well, parents really did that.'

'Sure aren't your parents people, Aisling?' She's not angry, she's just . . . right. They are. 'I was ashamed of myself, make no bones about it. I still am a bit. Sure why wouldn't I want another baby? I was married. And didn't I already have two dotes? Why wouldn't I want another one?'

She turns a tea towel over and over again in her hands, still wearing the ever-present apron. She's Mammy. But she's a whole other person now too.

'Granny had just died and I was fierce down about it. The blues, Dr Maher called it. He gave me tablets and told me to go out for a few walks. And I'd had the baby blues with Paul. I was in a bad way. And I had to work hard, and so did Daddy. We didn't want another baby. We couldn't have another baby. We had our babies. And when I went to Dr Maher again, I knew I was pregnant. I told him I didn't want it, I couldn't have it, and he told me I wasn't the first and I wouldn't be the last. He told me where I could go and what I could do.'

'Oh Mammy, you poor thing.' The tea towel is still going ninety and I impulsively reach over and grasp her hand, squeezing it so hard. Her hands are somehow soft and rough at the same time, and her fingertips are nearly shiny from years of hot roasting tins and sinks full of scalding water.

I've always thought about abortion as a thing that desperate young girls have to do. A thing that girls I don't know have to do. But it's a thing Sadhbh has to do. It's a thing Mammy had to do – she's not just aprons and tea towels and oxtail soup.

'Why didn't you ever tell me before?'

'Well, I suppose I was afraid you'd think that maybe we didn't want you either.'

Oh. That hadn't even crossed my mind. Sure she's mad about us, isn't she?

'And we did want you. Very much,' Mammy adds

hurriedly. 'But our little family was complete and we were very happy with what we had. It was an accident. Sometimes no matter how careful you are, it happens.' She's right. Only I took serious heed of the warning about the pill being only ninety-nine per cent effective, I could have been letting John come at me with his lad uncovered. It could have been us.

I'm thinking of all the times I begged her for a little sister and wince a bit. Paul was grand but he was a boy and useless and uncooperative when it came to allowing me to dress him up like a doll and push him up and down the driveway in a wheelbarrow masquerading as a pram. I think of all the times this has been on the news and in the papers and how she's reminded of it every time.

'What do you make of it these days? You still go to mass. It must come up there?'

I don't mind a bit of mass myself, truth be told. It's nice and peaceful. But I usually save it for Christmas. Great for a bit of gawking and speculating, and also excellent for eyeballing everyone's Good Coats and spotting who did the dog on it at Christmas Eve drinks in Maguire's.

'It does. And I wish it didn't. I believe in God, but mass can be hard.'

Jesus, imagine if the parish priest knew about Mammy. Would she be cast out the side door of the church? Would they be on the hunt for someone else to hand out communion at mass? Nobody hands out communion like Mammy. She's nearly as good as Father Fenlan.

'And sure it's everywhere now. The young ones think it's their fight. And it is, now. But it's a fight that's been going on for years. I just wasn't much use in helping.' She sounds wrecked.

'Ah, Mammy. Don't say that. It's not your job to change things.'

'It shouldn't be yours either, Aisling. But you can help Sadhbh. The poor craythur. Look after her.'

'Does Daddy know you're telling me?'

'No. I don't know if he'd mind but, well, when he was sick he talked about it a bit. Said the idea of dying made him think about it. Made him sad about it. I suppose he was thinking about his life. He was off his head on tablets anyway. Kept calling me by the cat's name. But I haven't mentioned it to him since. When it comes on the radio or telly we just wait it out or turn it off.'

Well, that explains the occasional lunge at the radio. Poor Mammy. And poor Daddy. What a tale.

And she's right. I will help Sadhbh. I'll hold her hand and fill her glass and make her hot-water bottles and tell her as many Mad Tom stories as she can handle. I'm not sure if she's heard the one about the night he pitched head first into a flowerbed of Tidy Towns subsidised pansies and was only found the next morning by two young ones on their way to school. They thought he was dead he had such a grip on the can of Guinness in his hand. He was right as rain. And Sadhbh will be too.

31

The whole week I can't stop thinking about Mammy, fretting and agonising, and the pair of them on the sad plane to Liverpool. I keep picking up the phone to ring Majella to talk to her about it and then remembering that we're not talking. It would be so much better if we'd bumped into each other in Maguire's at the weekend. But she's gone to the Gaeltacht for three weeks to earn a few extra bob as a teacher. To be honest, I'm surprised they had her back after last year's incident with another teacher on a deserted minibus.

Mammy suspects me and Majella aren't talking but she told me she's due back any day. I've missed our daily texts and chats and her stories about shifting Donegal guards and waking up on boats.

I have a nagging feeling that I've probably blown the whole picture thing out of proportion. It wasn't Majella's fault John and Ciara were in Maguire's. I suppose I just needed somebody, anybody, to blame.

I pick up the phone to text her: 'Maj, are u up in Dublin this wkend? Can I take u for lunch? I'm an awful gom, I know.'

She's back in a flash. 'Ok gomface, Bishop's Head in Phibsboro on Sat at one? Ur payin.'

Good old Maj.

Lunch turns out to be brunch, of course. Who knew there were so many ways to cook bloody eggs?

I decide to leave the car and bus it over to Phibsboro from Portobello, making sure I have all combinations of change counted out so I can produce the exact fare, whatever it is. The amount of times I've had to trek to Dublin Bus on O'Connell Street to get those little refunds sorted. Such a waste of a day but sure you have to do it.

Before I know it, I'm shouting 'thank you' and hopping off just outside the place Majella has had the foresight to book us into. Good thing too, because the queue is out the door. I'm feeling a bit, I don't know, nervous as I scan the room for Maj but I quickly spot her at a tiny little table near the back and I'm nothing short of delighted to see her big mad head, even though she's clearly wearing last night's make-up and a man's hoodie.

'Well, Ais, any craic?' she says, standing up, and we hug. It's definitely not something we'd normally partake in but today it feels right. The stand-off is officially over. Normal service can resume.

'Ah, you know yourself,' I say, 'not much,' and I pick up the menu.

It's my worst nightmare – granola as far as the eye can see and not a single potato product in sight. But I know I'll be safe enough with the all-day breakfast, even though it inexplicably contains avocado (and infinite Points). I just pray that the beans – homemade, not from a tin, and more's the pity – come in a separate receptacle. God knows beans have no business oozing around a fry. Unless it's a Full English you're after, and sure then you may as well just throw in the towel altogether. Majella orders the same, and a third bottle of ginger beer. She's clearly hanging, as well as taking advantage of the free lunch. Sorry, *brunch*.

'Good night?' I ask, nodding at the hoodie and raising my eyebrows.

'Very,' she says with a coy smile. 'His name is Mikey. A plumber from Cavan, but not tight in the slightest. I gave him my number, but I just realised I must have left my phone in the taxi. It's on silent and everything. Oh well.'

Some things never change.

'So, what's going on with you? How are the girls? I heard you had them down in Maguire's on bank holiday Sunday. Mad Tom told Daddy he nearly took you all out on the Knocknamanagh Road.'

I hesitate and she cops it straight away. That's the thing with Majella and me – we know each other inside out. The night I lost my virginity to Denis Kernan at a house party after his Debs, she was having an early night and she said she woke up at exactly 2.25 a.m. and sat bolt upright in bed. She just knew, somehow. There's no use in trying to keep a secret from her, not that I ever would. I'm about to confide in her about what's going on with poor Sadhbh when something stops me. I wouldn't want someone talking about me like that over their seventeen-grain toast. So I half laugh and lean forward.

'Oh, we just got *so* ossified in Maguire's. I'm afraid we might have been the talk of the town.' There's nothing Majella loves more than a 'I was so locked' story. She thrives on them.

'Oh lovely.' She rubs her hands together. 'Go on. Did anyone score Baby Chief?'

Sadhbh might have thrown him the eye if she hadn't been so upset. Sadhbh. She's flying on Monday. Her appointment is for midday. She told work she was going to stay with her sister for the week, might even take in a show or two.

'No, but he had his eye on Sadhbh all right. She was having none of it.'

'Oh, I'd say he did. They've never seen the likes of the style of that pair I'd say.'

Our chuckles fade out, replaced by silence. I start trying to fish actual leaves out of my tea to make it drinkable. Whatever happened to a good old-fashioned teabag? I'll get up early and make Sadhbh a lovely cup on Monday morning before she goes. It's the little things and they'd be trying to swizz €4 out of her for one in the airport.

'About your one Ciara, Aisling,' Majella says abruptly, breaking into my thoughts about Sadhbh. She's looking across the restaurant, not meeting my eye. 'I should have told you I knew about her and that I'd seen her in BGB. I'm sorry about that. Honestly, I am. I'm an eejit.'

'No, it's my fault. I made too big a deal out of it,' I say, as the server, beard almost down to his knees and tattoos as far as the eye can see, arrives with the food. '*I'm* sorry. Let's just move on. I'm sure they'll be very happy together. More power to them.'

Haven't I little to be worrying about, when you think about it? There's Sadhbh taking herself across the Irish Sea and I'm fretting about something I should just let go.

'Er, what are you talking about?' Majella looks confused.

'Well, it's obviously serious, Majella. I bumped into them in Dunnes the other week. Together. Buying hand towels, probably for their lovers' nest.'

It still stings a bit, try as I might to martyr myself into not caring.

'Slow down, slow down, Ais. What makes you think they're shacking up?'

'The feckin' towels!' I hiss, exasperated. 'And he's

already brought her home to meet Mel and Fran. Jesus, it'll be wedding bells next. I'll never be able to show my face down home again.' OK, so I do still care. I'm not made of granite. But why do I care? Sure aren't I better off? Living the high life with my new friends in Dublin. Expanding my horizons. Spreading my wings. I'm lucky.

Majella laughs. 'Ais, I know for a fact that it's *not* serious. Ciara didn't meet his parents – she was down in Knock for the tractor run, God only knows why. She was actually staying with Yvonne Stapleton. Ciara went out with her brother, James, for a while a few years ago. OK, she and John had met up in Dublin but they just ran into each other in Maguire's when everyone came to BGB after closing time. Sounds like she followed him down here, if you ask me. I couldn't tell you what they were at with towels though.'

'Oh. Right. I see.'

Just then the food arrives, so I have a couple of minutes to digest what was just said as Maj starts slamming sausages between slices of artisan sourdough bread and horsing them into her. So John and Ciara aren't necessarily *together* together.

I let the information sink in and try to gauge how I feel. Happy? Indifferent? Relieved? What was that quote I shared on Facebook this morning? 'Smile, you're alive.' Smile and stop being such a miserable gom, more like it.

'Are you OK?' Maj asks between bites. 'Listen, I swear that's the last time I'll ever mention John. He doesn't exist any more, as far as I'm concerned.'

'Yeah, totally, I'm completely fine,' I say. 'It's all old news now.' I smile. 'And sure me and Barry have been texting a bit outside of office hours. There's talk of another date. Sure we'll see. It's mad – he seems quite keen.'

'Why wouldn't he, Ais? You're a catch! Fabulous arse. I'm delighted for you.'

My smile widens. Look how alive I am!

My bag is hanging off the table on one of those handy little hooks that keeps it from getting dirty and I feel the vibration of an incoming call on my knee, just as I'm about to ask for the dessert menu. I'm tempted to let it go to voicemail – Maj and I have plenty to catch up on and I feel gripped by my new 'Smile, you're alive' fever. Maybe I'll go into town and buy a pair of mam jeans. Although, it could be Sadhbh, and I don't want to miss her. When I retrieve it from the special phone pocket inside my bag, it's Auntie Sheila's name that's flashing up on the screen. I point at it and throw my eyes up to heaven so Majella knows I have to take it.

'Hiya, Auntie Sheila, how are you?' I say, standing

up to slip out the back door, mentally preparing some excuse that will allow me to hang up after ten minutes max. Auntie Sheila can talk – for days, potentially.

'Aisling, it's your daddy, pet,' comes her voice, shaky down the line. 'They've rushed him into the General. You need to come down now, love. Is there anyone who can come with you? Now.'

I hold on to the back of a seat to steady myself. Majella has already copped that something is wrong and is signalling for the bill while simultaneously mouthing 'what is it?'

'Majella is here,' I say, sinking back into my chair. 'We're on our way.' My phone slips on to the floor just as the bill for our €43 hipster breakfast hits the table. 'It's Daddy.'

32

What is it about Irish hospitals that the floors, the walls and the ceilings all look like they're made of the same stuff? Flecky lino, shiny with age, applied to every available surface, making you feel like you're travelling through some kind of sixties time-warp tube, with the smell of antiseptic pumped in for ambience.

Daddy is in intensive care. I always imagined intensive care to be like something out of *ER* or *Grey's Anatomy* – one person in a dimly lit room full of monitors and cables and blinking lights and mysterious and terrifying beeps, handsome doctors zipping in and out, fresh from trying it on in a linen press. It's not like that at all. Daddy's on a ward. There are five other people in the room with him, in various desperate states. There are monitors and cables and lights, but there are also scratchy blankets and the hushed voices of other visitors and his slippers lying uselessly on the ground beside his bed.

When I walk into the ward, Mammy is sitting on one of those impossibly huge hospital chairs – the ones that kind of look like thrones, upholstered in shiny black pleather, and weigh about two tonnes, which seems impractical in a place where moving chairs around is an almost constant activity. I remember the chair politics at visiting times when Paul was in to get his appendix out.

Paul.

Has anyone told him?

Auntie Sheila is on a less impressive chair beside Mammy, more like one you might have swung on in school. She rises silently when I approach, gesturing grandly towards the seat and mouthing 'no, you sit down there, go on now, sit down, good girl', and slipping towards the door, miming a cup of tea.

The ward isn't dimly lit at all – the opposite, in fact. Light is streaming in through a huge wall of windows down the end. The curtain is half-pulled around Daddy's bed but some of the other patients look like they're nearly cooking where they lie. I sink silently into the chair and Mammy turns with a start to face me.

'Hello, Aisling.'

'Hi, Mammy. What happened?'

'He just collapsed last night. He wasn't feeling right in the evening and then he went down like a sack of potatoes in the hall. I couldn't lift him. I had to get Paddy Reilly in to help me. I called an ambulance and Auntie Sheila and they brought him right straight into A&E.'

'And what did they say was wrong?' But I already

know what's wrong. Look at him lying there, swollen with medication. It's back again, worse than ever.

'They did the scans. Oh, it's bad, Aisling. It's eating away at his poor brain.' She's not even crying. She just seems kind of resigned to it.

'Why didn't you ring me before this, Mammy? For God's sake!'

'Don't give out to me, Aisling. Not now. I didn't want you flying down here in a panic before we knew what was going on. Dr Timmons was in with him earlier.'

'And?' I feel weirdly calm. Like, this is the worst thing that's ever happened to me but at the same time I'm already accepting it. There's two custard creams on a saucer on the bedside locker – 3 Points each. Hospital custard creams wrapped in clear plastic, doled out with tea in an effort to make things a bit better. They haven't been touched.

Mammy glances at Daddy, as if to make sure he can't hear us. He seems out for the count. He's wearing his good pyjamas. Going Out Pyjamas, he'd call them, loving his joke.

'She wants to see us both.'

Dr Timmons is as shiny as ever, hair swaying like one of those Pantene ads where they're nearly giving themselves whiplash swinging around. I can feel the bad news radiating off her, even though she's smiling and gesturing for us to sit down. She's got decent chairs. She'd want to.

'So Seamus is unfortunately back in with us again,' she trills in her doctor voice. 'He's not very well at all really, is he?'

Mammy and I shake our heads in agreement, like obedient Junior Infants.

'I've had a look at his scans, and I think at this stage there's not really much more that we can do. This has come back so much quicker than we could have imagined, and any further treatment at this stage would be counter-productive, I think.'

I know what she's saying, but at the same time she can't be actually saying it, can she?

'Do you understand what I'm saying to you, Marian? Aisling?' Still in her doctor's voice but lower now.

'He's going to die.' My Daddy. My strong Daddy. Lying there in his Going Out Pyjamas and his slippers waiting for him.

'Yes,' she says gently. 'I would say it's a matter of weeks, or maybe even days. He's gone downhill so so quickly. I'm so very sorry.'

'Ah God,' Mammy gasps. 'Ah God, the poor fella. The poor man. Ah God. Ah God help us.' She starts to sob and I put my arm around her.

'Stay in here as long as you need,' Dr Timmons pushes a box of nice Kleenex towards us. Fancy, like the chairs. 'You have a brother abroad, Aisling? You might want to see if he'd like to come home to be with the family.' And with that she glides from the room silently.

I've never felt more alone. My Daddy. My safety. My heart. He minded me all those years and I only managed to mind him for a fraction of it. My Daddy. I stare at my hands. Aware that Mammy is quietly weeping beside me, but unable for the time being to stop repeating 'my Daddy' in my head. What does the world look like without him in it? Does he know what's happening to him? That bit kills me. Does he know he's going? Is he sad? Does he know I'm sad? Who's going to mind me? Who's going to mind us? The tears start coming thick and fast.

Mammy paws at my hand and I grasp at hers. How long have we been sitting here? How long can we sit here? Surely Dr Timmons will be hovering around outside, waiting to get in to get an exotic salad out of her desk drawer for her lunch.

'C'mon, Mammy. We'll go back to him.'

'Will you tell Paul, Aisling? Will you ring him? He has to come home.'

Oh God, poor Paul making that ridiculous flight home on his own, with nothing to face into only this, hellish stopovers in Dubai or where have you, and nobody to be nice to him.

'I will.' How are we going to get through this?

*

Auntie Sheila is sitting beside Daddy's bed when we get back. She's cleared the custard creams but sure she probably has at least another seven little packets in her bag, siphoned off from various abandoned tea trays. She takes one look at Mammy's face and her own one crumbles. She knows.

'God help him,' she whispers, repeating Mammy's mantra.

It's like everyone in the hospital has suddenly been given a memo about our bad news. A nurse comes in to check on Daddy's pillows and sees that we're back, and kindly whispers about sourcing another chair. I perch on the edge of his bed in the meantime, gingerly sitting on the harsh blue blanket, afraid to hurt or disturb him. What do we do now, like? What's the procedure when you're told someone is going to die? Is there a special place they send them? Or will he be coming home with us?

Mammy's voice breaks through my train of thought as she babbles to Auntie Sheila. 'For luck, I had the place painted for Aisling's friends coming down from Dublin. At least it will be fresh for the funeral. I won't have to do another big job on it.'

Funeral. How can she be thinking so rationally? Daddy's funeral. The dread of such an occasion sinks deep down to my toes. Everyone in the place looking at us and feeling sorry for us, and funeral homes and coffins and graveyards.

'Aisling?' She's talking to me now. 'Will you see if you can get Paul? Will you be OK to talk to him, pet?'

The last we heard from Paul, he was heading for those Whitsunday Islands with The Lads. He doesn't know one single Australian yet, but at least he's finally left Sydney after drinking the city dry of Bulmers and pints of milk. He has a mobile he's sharing with three others so I should be able to get him on that. It's probably around midnight over there.

The last time I was talking to him, it was winter but it was still twenty-three degrees and sure you'd get scalded in that. 'You'll get scalded in that,' I told him. But he assured me that he and the lads had invested in 'factor fuck off' and are well on their way to matching the colour on their forearms with the rest of their bodies. There was a bit about the Whitsundays in the *Irish Independent Weekend* a few weeks back so Mammy cut it out and put it on the fridge. She and Daddy were thinking of maybe going to Australia if Paul ended up staying there for a couple of years. She'll hardly go now.

I'll go out to the car to ring Paul, I think. I don't want to do it in front of Mammy – or anyone really – and I need to prepare what I'm going to say. I drove me and Majella down to the hospital in the Micra after she bundled me into a taxi in Phibsboro and ordered the driver to get to Portobello as fast as his Prius would take him. She threw some things in a bag for me and tried to insist on driving but she's only on her provisional and it took her two goes at the theory test. She wanted to stay with me in the hospital too but she couldn't come into the intensive care ward and God knows how long she'd be waiting. Her brother Shane collected her in the Subaru – so they're probably in a ditch somewhere. Shane has four points on his licence from speeding and Majella's mammy has given up trying to get him to stop smoking hash in the garage.

I make it out of the hospital after only being stopped twice to be asked something – a new record. (I'm often mistaken for a nurse on account of my kind, round face. People feel compelled to ask me for more pillows and if they can get a telly in their rooms.) I get to the car park in a bit of a trance, trying to remember where the hell I parked the car when we arrived. As I navigate the rows of vehicles, I realise with horror that there are 'Have you displayed your ticket?' signs everywhere. I haven't. I haven't displayed my ticket. We were so flustered when we arrived that it never even crossed my mind to pay for the parking.

I finally spot the car, wedged between a jeep and a kerb. And adorning its front passenger wheel is a big, shiny, yellow clamp.

33

'Well, it looks like they finally got you.' A familiar – and awkward – voice wafts down from behind me, from behind where I'm sitting like a big eejit on the kerb, crying silently onto my hands.

'That's not like you, Ais. Very careless,' he laughs nervously, coming around to face me, and stopping dead in his tracks as he clocks the state I'm in.

It's John. My John.

'Jesus, it's only a clamp, Aisling. It's not the end of the world.'

Of all the things in all the world that could have happened, he had to find me sitting here on the ground of a hospital car park, crying because I've just been told my Daddy is dying. Could I not just be left alone with my dignity and my clamp?

'It's not the fucking clamp.' My teeth are gritted. 'Although that's not helping. What are you doing here anyway?'

Of all the car parks in all the regional hospitals in the country he had to walk into this one. Just go, will you? Just go, I think to myself.

'Daddy got kicked by a bullock,' he shrugs. 'In

the hand,' he adds hurriedly. 'Not in the head or anything. I had to drop him in for a scan. I think he was protecting his you-know-whats. Is . . . is that why you're here? Is it your Daddy?'

I nod down into my chest. 'He's not well at all . . .'

I can't even get it out. Bursting into tears, I bury my head in my knees, willing him to get into his car – the jeep beside mine, of course. How did I not clock that it's his father's? – and leave me be.

John shuffles his feet on the ground, makes to come towards me and then changes his mind, stammering, 'Ah, Ais. Ah, don't be crying now. It'll be OK.'

I can't even tell him it won't be OK because I can't get any words out. I have to get away from him. It's too much. It's too much to be sad about. I push through my legs and stand up, muttering, 'I have to go,' and walk quickly away from him back in the direction of the hospital.

'Aisling! Ais!' he calls after me.

But I'm leathering away from him now. And I never even rang Paul.

Just before I reach the cavernous glass porch entrance and the half a dozen smokers studiously ignoring the 'No Smoking' signs outside, I duck down a small path leading into a garden at the side of the hospital and pull out my phone. Willing Paul not to answer, I take a deep breath, trying to blow away the great big cries building up inside me.

Five rings, six rings – he's not going to answer. And then a click and a voice from very far away.

'G'day, Aisling, you big pain in the hole! What's the craic? When are you coming to see me?'

'And was he OK, the poor craythur?'

Auntie Sheila has appointed herself chief tea-getter and all-round comforter. We've been beside Daddy's bed for hours now. He hasn't moved much, just opened his eyes a few times and gestured for water, which we give him through a little straw. Dr Timmons came around about an hour ago and said they'd be looking to keep him comfortable, and would do everything in their power to make sure he wasn't in pain.

Paul had been morose on the phone, berating himself for not coming home in June, when Daddy got sick again, occasionally calling to the lads he was with that he had to go home: 'Look up flights there, Mossy – I have to go home.'

The sound of Mossy slapping him on the back. 'We'll get you home, head. Don't worry.'

'Paul is coming home to see you,' Mammy leaned in to Daddy, talking to him like they were just in the front room waiting for *Prime Time* to come on, eating Good Biscuits Mammy forgot she bought for Christmas and hid in her wardrobe behind a hat she bought for Tessie Daly's daughter's wedding but never got up the gumption to wear.

Daddy doesn't open his eyes but just raises his eyebrows in acknowledgement. I wonder if he knows. Is he with it enough to know what's happening to him? It hits me that the idea of him knowing is devastating. There's nothing I can do to help him. It's not like I can just make him go to Dr Maher and get whatever antibiotic he's firing out that month. This is final.

Auntie Sheila is making noises about 'maybe we should go' and 'long day' and 'need your rest'. But no nurse has been by to tell us it's time to go. The ones who've taken over for the evening shift have obviously gotten the hospital-wide bulletin about our bad news and have just smiled sympathetically. That was Mammy once – helping some strangers through their pain, asking had they enough pillows and guiding lost old women back to their beds. It's another world.

'You have the car, haven't you, Aisling? I'll go with Sheila.' Mammy looks wrecked.

I wouldn't mind a bit of time in the car on my own, truth be told. Excellent space for a good cry and maybe a stop in a petrol station for whatever chocolate costs a zillion Points. If ever there was a time to eat my feelings, this is it. Weight Watchers Maura is always warning about the dangers of 'eating your feelings', but I don't think an apple and a glass of water and waiting half an hour are going to help this time, Maura. Just have the Bounty, Maura. You never stop going on about them.

I sit with Daddy for a bit longer.

For some reason, what I know now about Mammy and the abortion makes me even sadder still. Daddy was her confidant in that. They had been through that terrible time together and now he was leaving her alone. I suppose I had only ever really seen them as Mammy and Daddy before. Parents, not as people with their own separate relationship and hopes and dreams and jokes and lives. It's finally time to grow up.

He looks so peaceful and he doesn't seem to notice when I eventually decide to call it a night. I head out of the hospital towards the car, stopping suddenly. Oh feck. The clamp. Fighting the rising panic and injustice of it all, I fumble my phone out of my bag. My understanding is that you have to ring up and pay them there and then and then they'll come and take it off for you. Daddy always told the cautionary tale of Mad Tom taking a hacksaw to a clamp and ending up having to pay for clamp and all. Now, I've seen Mad Tom driving around with a handmade tax disc, so the idea of him paying over the odds for a parking violation was hard to accept. Still though, better safe than sorry.

But as I approach the car, I see that someone has already attempted to scrape the frankly over-the-top sticker from the passenger window and as the pitiful hospital car park shrubs part, I can see that the clamp is gone. A guardian angel? Mad Tom?

There's a piece of paper stuck behind the windscreen wiper. It's a ticket from the parking machine. Not only did someone remove my clamp, but they've paid for my parking. I can't believe some gouger didn't make off with the ticket. Oh, there's writing on the other side.

'Now u can pretend it never happened. John'

34

Dr Timmons had said it would be weeks, but we didn't know we'd only have days in the end. I dipped into my Emergency Fund to get Paul home in time to say his goodbyes, and fill Daddy in on the latest comings and goings in Summer Bay. Every hour, he seemed to slip further away from us. By the end, he was almost completely sedated when he eventually passed on that Wednesday, a wet, quiet night in August, all of us crammed into the room to say our goodbyes.

He'd told Mammy a while back that if it ever came to it, he wanted to be waked at home and so I made up the spare room, put a little bunch of pansies – his favourite – on the bedside locker and held Paul's hand when Eamon Maguire and Young Eamon Maguire brought in the body. He was wearing his Good Christmas Suit and looked, well, grand, considering.

By the second day of waking, I'm wrung out, not just from the crying, but from holding it together in general. My jaw is aching from a combination of fighting back tears and smiling at appropriate moments. Everywhere I look, there's a kind face, a soft handshake, a pat on the back, someone to tell me what a fine man Daddy was, how fond they were of him, how much the parish will miss him. Who'll provide the sheep and cow for the live crib at Christmas now? is a common refrain. Daddy always had them good and clean. No better man to convince Mammy to let a ewe into the good bathroom.

In the past forty-eight hours, from the most unlikely sources, I've learned more about Daddy than I had in the previous twenty-eight years. It was news to me that, shortly after meeting at a dance in Knock, he and Mammy broke up when she went to Dublin for her nursing training, but he won her back by writing her a letter every Friday. My Daddy! An auld romantic. And I found out as well that he was briefly the lead singer in a local Dickie Rock tribute act called Mickey Mock and once toured the country supporting Joe Dolan, with a young Mad Tom hauling the band's gear from dance hall to dance hall. The craic was mighty, according to Peadar Gorman, my old primary school principal-slash-Mickey Mock bass player. It also emerged from somewhere – Paddy Reilly, or one of Daddy's other friends who I saw wiping away tears with frayed jumper sleeves – that Daddy played centre forward when he was a hurler himself. Just like John.

A steady stream of mourners has been passing through the house and I'm fortified by the support of the community. I know Mammy is too. Mel and Fran took me aside in the back kitchen to explain that John had a microchip emergency at work and that's why he wasn't here. Costing the company hundreds of thousands a day it was – he couldn't possibly abandon ship to come down, and wasn't it desperate? I just nodded. I'd been doing a lot of nodding. Keeping on, you know – for Mammy's sake. Majella's been great too, whipping coats out of people's hands as they arrive and putting them on my bed. There wouldn't be such a queue in Coppers on a Thursday night if she was working the cloakroom.

Naturally, I've been all over the funeral preparations and glad of the distraction. Hymns have been chosen, readings decided and I've narrowed down contenders for the offertory procession to eight good candidates – cousins, mostly. But I'm worn out boiling the kettle and offering around cups of tea and I can't remember the last time I ate, or what it even was – although at a guess, I'd say it was one of Úna Hatton's little triangular ham sandwiches. She puts fancy relish on them, in case anyone forgets she's Protestant.

I haven't managed to look at my phone in hours, the sheer number of WhatsApp notifications making me anxious. I've seen Elaine's name pop up a good few times, and Ruby's. Barry's too. But when it starts to ring and I cop Sadhbh's picture, I know I have to answer it, so I grab a little brandy and nip out to the garage to sit on Daddy's beloved ride-on lawnmower. There's a patio heater out here some-where too. Aldi strikes again.

'Ais?' I can barely hear her, but I don't know if it's because someone inside has started belting out 'Danny Boy' or because she's far away.

'Hiya, Sadhbhy. It's good to hear from you.' The brandy feels hot against the back of my throat when I take a sip.

'Oh, Ais. I'm just in the door and Elaine told me about your dad. I'm so, *so* sorry, Aisling. I wish she'd told me when it happened, I would have called sooner.'

'Jesus, you don't have to apologise. You've been through enough yourself. How are you after . . . everything?'

'I've been better,' she replies with a hollow laugh. 'I had the . . . procedure . . . and everything appears to be fine. Medically speaking. Happy to be home though. Are you OK? How's your mom?'

'She's all right.' I sigh. 'She's doing great, consider-ing.' Mammy's on autopilot, truth be told, red-eyed and a tight smile pasted on her face as she shakes hand after hand.

Sadhbh's voice is wobbly and immediately I think about Mammy and what she went through twenty years ago, and here's Sadhbh dealing with the same thing. I'm surprised by the anger I feel bubbling up inside me about the journeys Mammy and Sadhbh had to take, and I take another gulp of the brandy. Daddy's good stash. He'd go mad.

'Ais, do you need anything? Elaine said the funeral is tomorrow. Do you have something to wear? Something black, I mean? If you've left anything here tell me and we'll pack a bag.'

Poor Sadhbh. She's only in the door after having an abortion and she's already worrying about me and my clothes. She's unreal. I think back to when she first told me, that night we were fluthered in Maguire's, and so much has changed. I drain the last of the brandy.

'Sadhbh, I want to tell you something. It's something I haven't told anyone else, but I want you to know.'

'Ais, you can tell me anything,' she says.

'Mammy . . . *my* Mammy . . . she had an abortion too. She told me just before Daddy died.' I spare her the details about the overheard conversation. It doesn't matter.

There's a pause. 'Poor Marian,' she says. 'It's not an easy decision.'

'It's not,' I agree. 'But she and Daddy made it together.' I start to cry again and I hear Sadhbh on the other end of the phone, sobbing along in solidarity. We stay like that for a few minutes before saying we'll see each other tomorrow and byebyebyebyebyebye. What a lady she is.

'Aisling, *craythur*, how are you?' Auntie Sheila corners me when I get back inside, where the drinking part of the wake is now in full swing. She's been checking on me all day when she's not sitting beside Mammy, quietly holding her hand, whispering names into her ear when she clearly hasn't a notion who a mourner is. Dr Maher gave Mammy something to help her sleep and I really hope she takes it later. 'Do you want to get out of here for a while, love?' Auntie Sheila asks. 'Paul and myself will mind your mother. You haven't had a minute to yourself in days. Go on now.'

She's right. Between the frantic supermarket sweep through Penneys to get Paul suited and booted in black and all the funeral organising, I've been mithered. The thought of hopping in the Micra for a good private cry and a chance to decompress sends a jolt of relief through me. The brandy was only a small one anyway.

'Would you mind, Auntie Sheila? I'm worn out trying to remember the names of all the second cousins. They all look the same to me.'

'Not at all, love. Why don't you take a spin up to Dublin? Go out for a meal with Sadhbh and the other one who won't eat meat?'

I was more thinking a quick trip down to Smith's River for a few lungfuls of fresh air and some peace and quiet, but now that she's put the idea of Dublin into my head, I can't shake it. Although it's not the girls I want to see – it's John. I want to thank him properly for doing his knight in shining armour bit after I got clamped. The more I think about him, the more I realise I have to leave immediately or I'll change my mind, so I grab my Michael Kors, wrap a few sambos in tinfoil – save me stopping somewhere to eat – and slip out the back door.

Outside, I pass Tiger sitting on the kitchen windowsill, looking forlorn. That Bloody Cat will miss him as much as any of us – and like that I'm off again, my already dry and burning eyes somehow producing more tears, my nose running like a tap.

By the time I reach the outskirts of Dublin, I've found a little corner of peace. I forgot how much I love driving, especially on the open road. The freedom of it. I could go anywhere – well, anywhere with good street lighting. The twinkling lights of the Dublin skyline feel welcoming and I turn up 'Don't Stop Believin'' on the radio. One small-town girl, and one lonely world. This is how I used to feel turning left down Main Street, Ballygobbard – completely at ease. And I realise that I now have two homes, each offering me something I need, and each missing one thing to make them complete: John. John is home to me, wherever he is. Is this how Mammy and Daddy felt about each other, all those years ago? I suppose it is.

When I turn on to his road, I'm sure Saint Anthony himself must be guiding me because I'm spoilt for spaces. It's only when I'm reversing into a spot right outside No. 57 – jackpot – that I realise all the other cars have permits on their windscreens. Has it really been that long since I've been here? I suppose it has. The feckers have finally done it. I won't be taking any more chances, so I end up having to drive around for another fifteen minutes before I find somewhere safe and free to park.

As I'm getting out of the car, I cop that I'm shaking and I don't know whether it's from dehydration or tiredness or nervousness. Is this an ambush? I haven't even texted him to tell him I'm coming. But my legs carry me on, not giving a shite about what my brain is trying to say. All I know is that I *need* him.

As bold as you like, I ring the doorbell and hear it echo inside. Brzing! Brzing! I'm imagining the narrow hallway, the bang of damp hitting my nostrils when he opens the door. Will he be surprised to see me or will he have somehow sensed that I was coming? I haven't even thought about what I'm going to say, or whether I'll even say anything. Just the thought of pressing myself into his big, warm chest is keeping me going. Despite all the BGB versus Knock nonsense, Daddy was mad about John and I know the feeling was mutual. They weren't shy about declaring it at Mammy's sixtieth when we all went back to the house and the good whiskey was produced. Not that either of them would admit it afterwards, of course.

I'm mid-sniffle – a good, loud one – when the door swings open without warning. But it's not John standing on the 'Nice Underwear' doormat I campaigned for years to bin, it's Piotr. Again! Why does this keep happening?

He looks like he's just woken up from one of his early-evening naps, his blond hair messy and flat on one side, two-day-old stubble on his jawline making it look good and angular. I feel a drop of snot slip out of my nose and down my chin, and his blue eyes follow it until it hits the toe of my new black suedette ballet-pumps, bought specially for the funeral.

'Piotr, hi,' I stammer, retrieving a balled-up tissue from my sleeve and giving my nose a discreet blow. 'Sorry if I woke you. Is John here?' My voice sounds unfamiliar.

'Aisling. Long time no see. I don't think John's about. Come in, I'll just check upstairs.'

He stands aside and I hesitate slightly before brushing past him. I haven't seen him since that night in Grogan's when he told me he thought John took me for granted, and then dropped the Ciara bombshell. I shiver just remembering it.

'John?' he roars, nearly lifting me out of it. 'John? You up there?'

We both freeze. But there's not a peep in the house, save for the pounding of blood in my ears. It's so loud I'm sure he can hear it. Now would be the right time to step back and leave.

'Yeah, he must be still at work,' he says, stifling a yawn and stretching. His T-shirt rises up slightly and my eyes wander to the waistband of his boxers, just visible above his jeans. John is more a boxer-briefs man than a true boxers man. He says they're the most comfortable and they give the lads a bit of support too. I was never a fan, if I'm being honest.

Piotr and I are now standing about six inches apart and neither of us has said anything for at least two minutes. I know we're alone because Cillian is back down in BGB practising 'Amazing Grace' on the accordion, as per my explicit instructions. He kept making a balls of the second verse when I made him perform it in the calving shed this morning.

'Do you want a coffee, Aisling? A cup of tea? You were always more of a tea woman, weren't you?'

He's giving me a half-smile and the devil on my shoulder is deafening. 'Stay, Aisling. It's only a cup of tea. You're actually gasping for one.'

I'm so relieved to be away from home, the mourners, the body, that I'm tempted. Would it be so bad? A quick cup, maybe one of those nice Polish biscuits that Piotr gets in the post from his mammy. I might as well hang on anyway, in case John appears. He could be on his way home.

No, I should go. What am I thinking? It's been nice to get away but I'm needed at home. I've been gone close to two hours now. Paul won't have a clue where the Good Biscuits for the VIP relations are and we still haven't decided who's doing the eulogy. I should be re-filling the Burco boiler and offering neighbours cans of Guinness, not standing here in a hallway in Drumcondra, thinking about Piotr's underwear, and my father's body still warm. Christ, what would happen if John found out? They share a wall – let's leave the sharing at just that.

'Yes. Please. Tea, please.' The words spill out and once the seal is broken, I can't stop them. It's like when you go to the toilet after your third pint of Coors Light and after that you're up and down like a yo-yo. I'll never forget the time Majella broke the seal in Maguire's just before a three-hour bus trip to Slane to see Red Hot Chili Peppers. She must have seen about twelve ditches before we eventually got there.

'My father . . . he died. It was Wednesday. Brain tumour. It was very quick in the end. We're all still in a bit of shock.' I stop. 'Can I smell the milk?'

'Aisling, I'm so sorry,' Piotr says quietly after a pause. 'I know how close you were. You talked about him a lot.'

My hands fly up to my face and I'm in floods again, head bent against the pain and injustice of it all. Piotr immediately steps forward, gathering me into his arms, gently shushing me. I lean into him and sob, inhaling his unfamiliar scent. He's not wearing any deodorant, no aftershave, nothing. There's not even a whiff of Brylcreem off him. He smells masculine and slightly sweaty and suddenly I decide I'm not ready to get back in the Micra. I don't want to think about Paddy Reilly at home digging Daddy's grave, or Mammy watching *Winning Streak* by herself for infinite Saturday nights, or Paul on a plane back to Sydney, his holdall in the overhead bin heaving with Taytos and black pudding and teabags.

I extract myself from Piotr's grip and blow my nose, embarrassed that I went to pieces in front of him. We make our way down to the little kitchen and he busies himself with teabags and cups and all the rest of the paraphernalia, making small talk about the new parking situation on the road and the way it's brought the neighbours together, united against Dublin City Council, the pack of gougers. The way he says 'gougers', you'd think he was born and bred and buttered here. He's easy to talk to and a good listener. No Polish biscuits unfortunately, but I produce the ham sandwiches and he's delighted.

'Was it peaceful, the end?' he asks, helping himself to one. 'For your father?'

'It was,' I say, sipping my tea. Good and strong. 'We were all there with him and I think he knew.'

'My father died three years ago. It's not easy.'

'Oh Piotr, I'm so sorry. You never mentioned it.' I'm mortified that I never offered my condolences. I'm always first in line at a funeral, arm outstretched, ready with the 'sorryforyourtroubles'. Have I ever really sat down and had a conversation with Piotr, in the two years he's lived here? I don't think so.

'It never really came up,' he says with a shrug. 'But I will tell you this: the pain becomes bearable. You'll get through it. I hope you're looking after yourself, Aisling.'

The pair of us sit there quietly for a minute, drinking our tea and finishing the last of Úna Hatton's sandwiches. I haven't thought much about my future, bar getting through the next twenty-four hours, supporting Mammy and Paul, but suddenly the thought of Daddy not being there to walk me down the aisle or kick the tyres when it's time to upgrade the Micra hits me like a tsunami and I need to get back in the car. I need to get home.

'Er, thanks for the tea, Piotr,' I say, standing up. 'Can I leave this here for John?' And I produce the envelope containing €80 from my bag. No note, just the cash. He'll know what it is.

'No problem, Aisling,' he says, reaching for it, gently brushing my hand. And then he sort of stops, his hand still on mine. We both look down at it. And he's looking at me now with those husky eyes, looking straight into my soul, searching for something.

Before I know it, I'm overcome with a desire to kiss him, so I stand up on my tippy-toes and gently press my lips against his. I close my eyes and imagine what might happen if he responds. Would we kiss for a while in the kitchen, my arse pressed up against the table, in danger of knocking our mugs off? Would I let my hands wander around inside his T-shirt? Would he go up my top? Would he lead me up the stairs and into his bedroom?

He's definitely responding, his lips parting, hips moving forward, locked against mine. But hang on, what about John? We shouldn't be doing this. It's too soon: too soon since the break-up, too soon since Daddy. I'm not in my right mind, I'm mad with the grief. But Piotr is pulling me closer now, his hand on the back of my head, and I'm finding it hard to stop myself. It feels good to be wanted.

No! I can't. We can't. I stop and pull away, holding him at arm's length. His pupils are so dilated that his eyes look almost completely black. I can't help it – I steal a quick look at his crotch. Yes, he's definitely into it. But we can't. It wouldn't be right.

'Piotr, I'm so sorry,' I say. 'I didn't come here looking to do this.' And I'm gathering up my coat and firing rolled-up balls of tinfoil into the bin and cups into the sink like my life depends on it. Let *him* rinse them and put them into the dishwasher. I can't stay in this house a minute longer.

'Ah don't, Aisling. Stay for a while – we can just talk. I've missed you, you know?'

But I barely hear the last bit because I'm gone into the night, weak with shame, weak with want, and wondering why John is never home when I need him.

35

Word on the street is that Daddy's funeral was the biggest the parish has seen in ten years, testament to his standing in the community. Majella was right there beside me through it all, and I heard her name singled out more than once for her emphatic reading from the Book of Ecclesiastes. I saw faces in the crowd that I never imagined would make the trip down to BGB: Laura and the girls from work, Donna and Martin, even Barry – all among the figures decked in black that I don't quite remember talking to. Barry gave my hand a good long squeeze outside the church and said he'd be in touch. I do remember that. Back at the house, I saw Mammy and Sadhbh hugging tightly, each promising the other one she'd mind me.

In the days afterwards, Mammy and Paul and me slipped into a comfortable little routine, getting up, taking care of the farm and generally spending as much time together as we could. Where before we'd been in and out to the hospital in shifts, passing like ships in the night, we now made an effort to be there for each other – physically, at least. I was terrified to leave Mammy by herself for more than the length of a shower (four-point-five minutes – I'd given up using conditioner without Sadhbh's good influence), just in case she needed me to open a jar or wire a plug. And Paul had slowly begun to take over from Paddy Reilly, who'd been keeping the farm ticking along. Every evening, we'd all convene in the sitting room after dinner to watch old episodes of *Mrs Brown's Boys* and *Who Wants to be a Millionaire?*, shouting out the answers and drinking tea and eating cream crackers with butter. *Home and Away* wasn't even considered. It's too soon.

But after ten days at home, work beckons and on a rainy Sunday evening, I find myself hoofing my stuff into the Micra, just like old times. Sadhbh and Elaine are poised and ready to order in a pizza – I just have to text them when I'm passing the Red Cow. There's not a spare hole in the wine cooler, I'm told. Tessie Daly had taken me aside outside Filan's earlier to assure me she'd be dropping in daily to check that Mammy was taking all her tablets and to make sure that Paul was slowing down on the rashers. He had a new appreciation for them after their scarcity Down Under and it was in danger of putting him in an early grave. Auntie Sheila's also on the case so I know they're in good hands.

I spent all day dreading having to say goodbye to Mammy, but in the end, it's not as awful as I'd anticipated. I vow to come down every couple of days to check on them and I think that helps.

Mammy pretends she's keen for me to get back to Dublin. 'You can't stay here for ever,' she says, and I just nod, holding in the tears for when I'm alone in the car. We hug – we've been hugging a lot more lately, and talking too – and I promise to call her as soon as I arrive in Portobello.

After checking my oil, Paul shoves two litres of fresh milk into the boot for Sadhbh's personal trainer. And with a slap on the boot I'm gone, looking at them both in my rear-view mirror.

My key is barely in the door when the girls appear.

'Ais, it's so good to have you back,' Sadhbh says, elbowing off Elaine to be the first to hug me. 'The place hasn't been the same without you.'

'It certainly hasn't been as clean,' Elaine adds, and we all laugh and it feels good and genuine and not like the laughs I've had to fake watching *Mrs Brown's Boys* – honestly, I really don't get that programme. There is just too much innuendo.

I give the place a quick once-over and it's spotless. Fair dues to them, I have them well trained. Before I know it, they've relieved me of my bags and whisked me onto the couch where the wine is already poured. Five minutes later, the pizza arrives and we settle in for a catch-up.

'Thanks so much for coming down to the funeral, girls,' I say, helping myself to a slice of ham and mushroom, which I know they ordered especially for me. They know how I feel about ham. 'Mammy was delighted.'

'Oh God, it was nothing,' Elaine says, pushing a glass of wine into my hand. 'Was it awful? You were so poised, Ais. He would have been proud.'

'It was pretty awful,' I admit, 'from what I can remember. It's all a bit hazy now.'

'How's your mom?' Sadhbh asks.

'She's coping. I think she's still in shock. I'm gone now, and the visitors have eased off, so I think the next while is going to be hard. But she has plenty of support. Our neighbours have really rallied around her.' I pause. 'I still can't believe he's gone.'

'I'm so sorry,' Elaine says. 'Truly.'

'How's John, Ais? You must have seen loads of him,' Sadhbh inquires.

'John never showed up at the funeral,' I say quietly. 'I really thought he would. He never even appeared in Maguire's for a few sandwiches afterwards. That's it now as far as I'm concerned. The final straw.'

'That was bad form,' she says, shaking her head in disbelief. 'And he'd definitely have known, right? I mean, the news wouldn't have passed him by somehow?'

'Are you mad?' I squawk. 'The whole parish was

out. I was talking to his parents at the wake. They told me he couldn't get down for it, but I assumed he'd be there for the actual thing. Oh, he knew all right, but maybe he just wasn't arsed being there.' Saying it out loud makes me realise how ridiculous it is. The more I think about it, the angrier I get.

'The things men do,' Elaine says, rolling her eyes, and I realise I haven't had a chance to tell them about my run-in with Piotr. My moment of madness. *Our* moment of madness.

Majella's take, when I told her over a cuppa the morning after the funeral, was that it was as well we didn't go through with it, out of loyalty to John. I think Piotr would have done it though. Were they ever really friends, Piotr and John? Housemates who enjoyed watching telly together and drinking cans, yeah – but not real friends like Sadhbh and Elaine and me. What would me and Piotr mean to John, if it had come to it?

'Any word from Barry?' Sadhbh asks, snapping me out of it.

'A few nice texts here and there. He said he wants to go out again, when I'm ready.'

'Are you still interested?' Elaine asks, passing me another slice of pizza. I think back to the night in Grogan's. I was having a great time with him until bloody Piotr ruined it all. Bloody Piotr and the waistband of his sexy boxers making me think impure thoughts. I decide to come clean.

'Yeah, I think I am. No, definitely. But did I mention the . . . run-in I had with John's Polish housemate? Remember the lad who ruined my date with Barry because he let the cat out of the bag about John and Ciara? Him.'

They're both looking at me, agog. How is it possible I have this much gossip and drama? It's so not me. Although, come to think of it, despite all the hoo-ha with Barry and the date we went on, Piotr is the first – and only – lad I've kissed since John. Aside from John, he's the only lad I've kissed in *seven* years. How did that happen?

'Hang on, hang on, hang on.' Sadhbh is squinting at me now, clearly regretting her third glass. 'You need to give us some more details.'

'OK,' I go, taking a sip of wine. 'The day we found out about Daddy I got clamped outside the hospital.'

'Aisling!' Elaine cries. 'You didn't! You've never gotten clamped. It's one of your claims to fame.'

'I know, but under the circumstances, Elaine, these things happen. I was in bits, like. Anyway, I bumped into John in the car park – his father got a kick in the hand from a bullock – and he ended up sort of saving the day. And then after the wake, I was a mess. I needed to get out of the house, so I drove up to John's to give him back the €80. Neither a borrower nor a lender be – Daddy had it bet into me since I started earning pocket money. Sure I had to honour him. But in the end, John wasn't there. Piotr answered the door.'

I've never had such a rapt audience in my life, not even when I was Holy Mary in the second-class nativity play and caused the donkey, played by Megan O'Doherty and Lorna Clarke, to collapse when I sat on it. You could hear a pin drop. Eventually it's Sadhbh who breaks the silence.

'And *what*? Jesus, don't leave us hanging.'

'We . . . we kissed. I kissed him. We kissed each other. It didn't go any further but God, I'd say it could have. He probably thinks I wasn't in my right mind.'

'And were you?' Elaine asks tentatively. 'In your right mind?'

'Well, no,' I admit. 'I was in bits. Literally blubbering away to him. There was snot everywhere.'

Elaine is nodding along. 'Do you like him? Do you *fancy* him?'

Good question. Do I genuinely fancy Piotr? I mull it over. Well, yeah, I suppose I do. He's a lash. I'm surprised at my quick conclusion.

'Well, yeah, I suppose I do,' I say, pouring more wine. 'He was sound to me that night in Grogan's. He said I was always too good for John.'

'Do you fancy him more than Barry?' Sadhbh asks. 'Now be honest.'

'I don't know. Like, it would have been awful if

something had happened between me and Piotr. And he would have gone for it, I think. He didn't seem to think of John . . . Oh, I just don't know.'

'And, if I'm reading this right, you still have feelings for John?' Sadhbh asks.

'No. Yes?' I'm confusing myself now. How have I ended up in this weird love . . . square? I thought they only happened on telly. 'I had feelings for John until very recently,' I eventually admit. 'But I'm actually disgusted he didn't come to the funeral. Majella was livid.'

'Is he still with your one, Ciara?' Sadhbh asks. 'Maybe that's why he wasn't there. Maybe she feels threatened by your history? I'm just hypothesising here.'

'No, definitely not. According to my cousin Cillian, they were only seeing each other very casually. They never even went away for a Groupon weekend.'

We all sit staring at each other for a minute. I'll be the first to admit it's a lot to digest, especially since we've drained a second bottle during our conversation. I glance at the clock – twenty past ten. Nearly time for me to call it a night.

'So,' I say, helping myself to the last slice of pizza, 'any news with you two?'

'Well, Elaine is engaged,' Sadhbh says casually. 'Does that count as news?'

36

Suddenly it all made sense – Ruby's omnipresence in the apartment, the shared Netflix account, the way they were always finishing each other's sentences, wrapped around each other on the couch, literally burning money with their posh scented candles out of Brown Thomas's. The bedroom situation in Berlin, for God's sake – I don't know why I didn't see it sooner. I suppose I always thought lesbians would be, I don't know, butch? Neither of them even has short hair. But once I got over the initial shock, of course I was only thrilled for them. Love is love – isn't that what we all agreed in the referendum? I still have the badge to prove it.

I'm mulling over my chances of being a bridesmaid and the probability of the meal being vegan when I arrive at PensionsPlus the following morning, relieved to have something to take my mind off everything. I'm hoping that I don't run into Barry, because just one kind gesture and I know I'll be in floods. The grief has been sneaking up on me at the most unlikely times – I passed an old man pushing a toddler on a swing on the walk in here and completely broke down. Daddy would have made the best grandad. My sadness intensifies when I think of how my own future kids have been denied him and I blink back the tears.

I'm only in the door of the building and on my way to the lift when I swear I see Donna heading into the Big Boardroom – the serious one in the lobby, reserved for visiting dignitaries and people selling cheap books and calendars. But it can't be her, can it? What would she be doing back here? I only catch the back of her head, but the hair certainly said Donna and so did the gait. Now, if I could only get some audio of her eating an apple, I'd be sure. The boardroom door closes softly but then I hear it. It's muffled, but I'd know the opening strains of 'Girls Just Wanna Have Fun' any-where. What the blazes is going on?

I manage to get upstairs without bumping into any of the girls, whose sympathetic smiles might push me over the edge. For luck, Laura isn't in yet and I slip into my seat virtually unnoticed. Already nine o'clock and I haven't cried yet, if you don't count the little hiccup on my walk – not too shabby. A few people pass my desk and give me sad nods and little smiles. I hope they don't make a big deal about me being back. I hate a scene.

As soon as I log on to my PC, I email Sadhbh for the inside scoop on what's happening downstairs. Her response is immediate: 'Just found out myself.

Not sure why she's here but she's lawyered up. It's something big.'

Something big? It has to be about the Dutch bank account fuck-up. But I would have thought Donna might have contacted me if there was any news. I check my phone: nothing. Well, nothing from Donna. There *is* a text from a number I don't know though.

'Aisling, I hope ur ok. I'v been thinkin abt u. I kno how hard it is. Got ur nmbr from Cillian. Piotr.'

Piotr. I think back to that night in Drumcondra. What came over me? In hindsight, I was mad with the grief, out of my mind. But when I remember his sexy stubble and that flash of taut tummy, I must admit that, to quote Elaine, I also had the horn for him. And he's been thinking about me.

My instinct is to text Majella and ask her what to do but I stop myself. It's time for me to start making my own decisions, taking control of my life, figuring out what I want – for me, not for anyone else. I know it would kill John if he knew, and I know it would kill John if anything else were to happen. I could hurt John if I wanted to. But would I hurt Piotr too? Would I hurt myself? I put the phone down. Maybe I'll reply later.

Just then, Sadhbh's name pops into my inbox and her email is straight to the point: 'Meet me in the disabled loo in 2.'

Jesus, whatever it is can't be said on email. She's

obviously worried about a paper-trail. I reply 'ok' and head straight for the toilets.

I knock when I get there, and she opens the door just enough for me to sidle in. This is all very clandestine. I feel like I'm in an Agatha Christie novel, except this one is set in a Dublin office block.

'Donna didn't do it,' Sadhbh hisses, her eyes wide. 'The money was moved at 2.13 p.m. on Tuesday the twenty-fourth and she has proof that it couldn't have been her.'

'Whaaaat? What's the proof?' I go, anxiety rising in my stomach. If it wasn't Donna, who could it have been? Not me, surely?

'A receipt. From the Kilkenny Shop. Apparently she was returning an unwanted wedding present. The reason she didn't come forward until now is that she was skiving off on company time. That's why she left herself logged in. Somebody else did it using her PC.'

The relief washes over me. Thank God. It definitely wasn't me because it wasn't a simple clerical error – Donna was framed.

One thing doesn't make sense though. 'Why did she come back with a lawyer? It's not like she was fired in the end – she was let go with a big pay-off.'

'I suppose it kind of suited her at the time to take the money. And it suited them too. And maybe she thought that it could have been her fault, so it was easier just to go in the end. But it turns out it's followed her around and she's struggling to even get an interview in any of the other places. So when she realised she could exonerate herself, she jumped at the chance.'

'Fair dues to her.'

'I know!' Sadhbh says, fixing her eyeliner in the mirror. 'I didn't think she had it in her. You need balls to take on a multi-national, even if it's just this one.'

'Did she say what she was returning, just out of interest?'

'She said it was a set of awful Orla Kiely placemats and matching coasters. Now, I better head back up. More intel as I get it. Apparently they're going nuts over in London.'

Donna, you wagon.

I'm just turning the corner to head back to my cubicle when I spot him: Barry. He's coming out of the lift but by the looks of him, he did twenty laps of the car park before he got in. He's pale and sweaty, his tie hanging loosely around his neck.

Here it comes now, I think, preparing myself for the arm touching and the 'how *are* you?', with the emphasis on the 'are'. I'm going to make a show of myself blubbing, I just know it. But instead of a hug, he grabs me by the hand and half-drags me into the stairwell.

'Jesus, Barry, what's wrong?' I say, when the door closes behind us. 'You nearly reefed my arm out of it there.'

338

'Ais, I'm so sorry – I know this is your first day back and you've got a lot on your plate but I have to tell you something. I don't want you hearing it from anyone else. It looks really bad but I can explain.'

'Explain what? What are you talking about?'

'It wasn't Donna who made the fuck-up,' he sighs, wringing his hands dramatically.

As usual, I pretend not to let on that I'm one step ahead of him. 'Really? Then who was it?'

'It was me.'

Now, *this* I'm not prepared for. 'It was *you*? How, Barry? Why did you let Donna take the fall for it?'

'It was just a simple mistake, Aisling. A decimal point in the wrong place. It wouldn't have been such a big deal if the money didn't just disappear into thin air. I couldn't lose my job, not when it looks like I'm headed for a divorce. My bitch of a wife is going to bleed me dry. The courts always side with the woman.'

I notice now that he's twirling his wedding ring on its finger and I start to feel a bit sorry for him. Money does sometimes get accidentally transferred to the wrong account, but it's usually easy enough to retrieve. I was erroneously paid a tax refund twice a few years ago and I couldn't give it back fast enough. Not everyone is as honest as me though. And framing someone else for it is a step too far – I don't care how white his teeth are.

'I thought Donna was a safe bet to pin it on,' he goes on, stammering a bit. 'Did you know she's the MD's niece? She gets away with bloody murder. I never for a minute thought she'd get the sack over it. We were both working on that file, so it was easy enough to change the timestamp on the transfer application and then log on to her machine to confirm it. I thought it might teach her to stop leaving the office on company time. Time-theft is just as bad as what I did. Worse, actually.'

Donna is the MD's niece? Well, that *does* explain a lot. And I did read that time-theft costs Irish businesses something like a billion euro every year.

'Why are you telling me all this, Barry?'

'I've just come clean about it to Head Office, but it looks like I'm going to lose my job anyway,' he says, obviously pissed off that his honesty hasn't gotten him far. 'I wanted you to hear my side of the story before the rumour mill kicks off. You're a special girl, and I want to stay in touch, no matter what.'

God, he looks like he's going to cry. And sure everyone makes mistakes. I go to reach out to grab him in a hug when suddenly the door swings open and Sadhbh appears, followed by the woman of the moment, Donna. And she's bulling.

'There you are,' Sadhbh squeaks out of the corner of her mouth, her eyes darting between Barry and myself. 'We've been looking for you everywhere, Aisling.'

'Aisling, don't you listen to a word this fucker is telling you!' Donna roars, booting the door closed behind her with her heel. 'Do you know what he's just admitted to doing? *Do you?*'

Barry is practically cowering in the corner, and I don't blame him. Donna is so incandescent with rage that it looks like she's grown a foot since I last saw her. She's probably been imagining this scene for months, in fairness to her, coming face-to-face with the prick who framed her and cost her her job. I'd be spitting bullets myself. Although *I'd* never have stayed logged in on my PC while I was swanning around town returning perfectly lovely wedding presents, but that's neither here nor there.

'He just told me, Donna,' I confirm, giving Barry a good dose of side-eye. 'I can't believe it. But people make mistakes.'

She just nods. Sadhbh is on the brink of breaking out the popcorn. This must be like Christmas for the HR girls. She's always complaining that nothing exciting ever happens, bar the odd positive drug test or personal hygiene problem.

'And is he still trying to get into your knickers, yeah?' Donna continues.

Now it's my turn to look embarrassed, as does Barry, who's very quiet all of a sudden.

341

But there's no stopping Donna. She's literally spitting out the words. 'Has he told you the old sob story about the wife? About how she cheated on him and how she's going to take him to the cleaners in the divorce?'

I nod.

'It's all bullshit, Aisling. All of it. He's a fucking sociopath.'

I turn to Barry, who, for some reason, is still here. He just shrugs, like, 'who are you going to believe, Aisling, her or me?'

'So you know the *Fifty Shades* hen that I was planning for, like, months?'

Oh Christ, not the hen again. And I love nothing more than a cheeky two nights in Carrick-on-Shannon. 'Donna, please, no more,' I say, holding up my hands. 'I can't take any more about the hen. I'm sure it was great . . .'

'I met her, Aisling. I met Barry's wife, Michelle, at the hen. Missionary Michelle. She works with my cousin Suzanne. Isn't it a small world, Barry?'

Sadhbh stifles a squeal, while Barry looks ashen, holding the wall to steady himself. I don't know what Donna's about to say, but I know he doesn't want me to hear it.

'Oh, she told me all about you, Barry,' she continues, hand on her hip, obviously enjoying every second of this confrontation. 'How she threw you out of the house three months ago, after she found out about all the cheating. How it started with *Room to Improve* all right, but it was *you* with the camerawoman. And how you've kept going since, racking up notches on your bed post – at least six other girls that she knows about. And she *never* cheated on him, not even once, despite what he's been going around saying.'

She turns to me then. 'His best mate Cian grassed him up after Barry here came on to his girlfriend. And he has a very specific type, don't you, Barry?'

Barry is shaking his head now, as if he can't believe this is actually happening. Neither can I, to be honest. I look at my watch. Not even 10 a.m. yet. It's been quite a morning.

'Do I want to know what this type is?' I eventually venture, my voice quiet. 'I have a feeling you're going to tell me anyway, aren't you, Donna?'

'The type is *you*, Aisling. They're all Aislings of some sort or another. Michelle got a good read of every single one of them on Facebook and Instagram and whatever. Country girls with kind faces and a fondness for kitten heels. He must get off on it, the big sicko.'

Donna throws her hands up in the air in an I-told-you-so way and now it's my turn to face off against Barry.

'Is it true?'

You could hear a pin drop.

'Not all of it, Ais. I swear,' he says, looking at me in desperation. 'Look, my mother left us when I was just a kid. She was a nurse, born and raised in Louth. Matronly, from what my father told me growing up. I was always attracted to that type of girl, until I met Michelle. She was from Dublin, glamorous and cosmopolitan – she wears make-up and goes spinning twice a week – but I've always wanted a nice country girl, someone I could watch the GAA with, who'd go to a colours night with me, someone sturdy and sensible. I have a weakness for them.'

'He's sick, Aisling,' Donna scoffs. 'You're sick, Barry.'

I know Donna is trying to be a good friend here but I can't help feeling a bit offended by her shrieking. Like, at least two men currently fancy me, thank you very much. OK, one is some kind of odd predator with a penchant for seducing 'sturdy and sensible' girls, but she could tone down the 'sicks' a bit. Nothing wrong with a kitten heel and a bit of cop-on.

Thankfully, Sadhbh steps in. 'Barry, I would advise you to go and check your email.'

'What's going to happen?' he asks.

'I'd imagine there will be an investigation, same as what happened to Donna. Although what you did was far worse than simple negligence. You could be looking at jail-time.'

She takes me by the arm and turns on her heel

and leads me towards the door. Thank Christ, I'm gasping for my cup of tea.

On the way past my desk, I stop to pick up my mobile. A missed call from Auntie Sheila, and suddenly all the Barry drama feels trivial. Has something happened to Mammy? Or Paul? I hit redial and she answers after three rings.

'Is it Mammy?' I blurt out.

'Oh, she's fine, love, she's fine,' Sheila assures me in her comforting sing-song voice. 'She's having a lie-down. There's nothing wrong – I was just ringing you with a little question. I hope it doesn't upset you now.'

Upset me? After the morning I've just had? I doubt it.

'It's John. Your John. I wanted to get him a little present but I haven't a clue what he'd like. Any ideas?'

'Why the hell are you getting John a present?' I say, incredulous. Could I be on one of those reality-TV prank shows, I wonder, looking around my cubicle. *Punk'd* or one of those? It would explain a lot. I rifle through the leaves of the fern on my desk for cameras. Nothing.

'I need to get him something from the family, to say thank you. He was such a wonderful support on the day of the funeral.'

John, a wonderful support on the day of Daddy's funeral? She must have the wrong John because if my memory serves me, there wasn't sight nor sound of him to be seen.

'Wh . . . what did he do? I didn't see him anywhere at the funeral?' I hope she's not having a senior moment.

'Well, didn't he mind the house when we were gone sure? And not only your house – he had the bould Mad Tom going up and down the Knocknamanagh Road keeping an eye on the Hattons, the Murphys, even the Cusacks. He rang your Mammy and offered. Did she not tell you? He knew how important it would be to your Daddy. Now, I was thinking, would he like a bottle of Jameson?'

Epilogue

'Do you want a swig of my naggin, Ais? I've a bottle taped to my leg. Emergency wedding stash.' Majella goes to hoik up her bridesmaid dress to retrieve the bottle as she exits the bathroom stall, but I wave her away. Sure I'll have a glass of wine in my hand before I know it. We're back in the Ard Rí. It really wouldn't be a Knocknamanagh–Ballygobbard wedding if it wasn't in the Ard Rí.

'Did I tell you John texted me this morning? He said he was looking forward to today and seeing me.'

'Ah, the big dote, he did not. That's very sweet. Were you nervous about seeing him?'

'I wasn't until I walked up the aisle and there he was. I forgot how good he looks in a suit.'

'I know. A man from Knock has no business having shoulders that broad.'

John certainly had cut quite the figure standing up at the altar, waiting, the early afternoon sun bringing out the bit of ginge in his new hipster beard.

'I suppose the groom looked good too.'

'He did. Sinéad is a lucky girl.'

It hasn't even been a year since I was here before,

here with John, with me wishing for our own Big Day. So much has happened. So much has changed.

And now here we were again, celebrating Sinéad McGrath and Jimmy Clancy's wedding – Jimmy, one of the big men on the Knock team, Sinéad, Majella's cousin and BGB Gaels camogie captain. I counted three guards of honour with hurls already today, and we haven't even had a bit of dinner yet.

John is here, of course. He's one of Jimmy's grooms-men. But we're not here together. We're . . . friends. Maybe we're more than friends. We're texting. We don't know what we are. I just about know what I am. Plenty of time for 'we'.

Majella is already changing out of her strappy bridesmaid sandals in favour of one of the pairs of flip-flops left in a basket for the guests. A lovely touch.

'It was a grand ceremony, wasn't it? Not too long.' She tucks the offending shoes behind a bin, never to be worn again. 'And they got the weather too – fair dues to the Child of Prague statue.'

It was a lovely ceremony, although I did think the 'Live, Love, Laugh' aisle-runner was a bit much, even if it is one of my own personal mottos. I'm sur-prised Father Fenlon allowed it. He was very sniffy about the Phil Collins we played at Daddy's funeral, but Mammy insisted. She was so defiant about it that morning in the kitchen. 'The church has enough say on things. Seamus is having his Phil Collins.' They both loved Phil Collins. 'Groovy Kind of Love' came out the year they got married and any time it ever came on the radio, in the kitchen or the car, Daddy would sing it tunelessly at her. So we swayed to that at his funeral, and cried. It was fierce sad, but lovely.

Watching Sinéad sweep up the aisle with her dad earlier was hard too, but sure we all float on. Isn't that what Elaine is always saying? Elaine and Ruby's wedding will be next. Me and Sadhbh are going to be bridesmaids. Sadhbh already has cracked ideas about the dresses. She's been banging on about 'industrial chic'. I'll have to put the foot down. I'm not wearing a dress made of spanners.

'Come on and we'll get a drink!' Majella drops the hem of the bridesmaid dress back down to the floor, covering the flip-flops. Nobody will be any the wiser.

Sinéad and Jimmy have gone all-out. Two sweet carts, a lad doing caricatures – although he seems to only be able to do one face for lads and one for girls, so I hope she isn't paying through the nose for him – and they arrived at the reception in a brand-new John Deere tractor after the obligatory photo shoot at the GAA pitch. A wedding dress and a pair of football boots – a classic snap if ever I saw one. The whole wedding party is back now, so that means John must be floating around somewhere.

The texting has been on and off. I've seen him a

good few times at home, on the farm. He's been helping Paul get a few things in order and Mammy has said he's called in on Wednesdays after training more times than she can count. We're shy and awkward around each other, like we're twenty-one again and only capable of proper interaction when we're eight drinks down and going in for the shift. We haven't been alone together yet, or out together, or really had anything beyond shy texts and meek meetings in Mammy's kitchen or out in the yard. I catch sight of him now, striding towards the groom with a pint, nodding 'hellos' and 'there you are nows' to people as he goes.

It helps that I've been coming down home more too. Things between Mammy and me are good now, better than I ever remember them being. I think our problem is we're more alike than either of us would care to admit. Oh, Daddy made a good buffer, but without him we've discovered that we both love a row. And when it's over, it's over. She's even talking about coming up to stay in Portobello – she wants to get her colour done with an image consultant. She read something about it in the *Farmer's Journal*. Úna Hatton told her she's definitely an autumn but Tessie Daly has her convinced she's a spring. She told me that if she doesn't find out for once and for all, they'll go for each other. And Sadhbh is only desperate to weigh in. The best thing about our new-found friendship, though, is the stories Mammy tells me about the old days, when she and Daddy were courting and everything was a bit . . . simpler. Piotr and our kiss occasionally cross my mind, but I push the memory as far back as it will go.

John's looking well today. Between the beard and the suit with the skinny legs, you'd nearly forget he was a bootcut jeans and piss-catchers man through and through. And I'm looking well too. Sadhbh insisted on coming with me to get an outfit for this wedding, and pawed away any attempt I made at grabbing something lacy with sleeves. She has me in trousers – *trousers* – at a wedding. Well, it's a jumpsuit. When she first suggested it, I thought she meant a giant babygro like the matching onesies Majella gets for us every Christmas in Penneys, but instead she reached into a rack and pulled out a sleek black yoke with an almost indecent neckline. She made me try it on and do you know what? It didn't look bad. In fact, it looked lovely. I drew the line at her suggestion that I get some neon accessories to 'set it off', but Majella told me I looked 'very Colette Green', which is the highest compliment ever. I'm wearing a Colette Green deodorant actually. She has a whole range of 'deodo-scents' in pharmacies around the country, making a fortune off them. She was on the *Late Late* recently and I had to try to explain the concept of bloggers to Mammy.

I check what table I'm on for the meal. They're named after Eurovision sings. A lovely touch. 'Rock 'n' Roll Kids': it looks like a good crowd – Maeve Hennessey, Jenny Nolan and Deirdre Ruane. Majella is at the top table, of course, and John. They're 'Hold Me Now'. 'Why Me?' looks like the rowdy bunch – Eimear Flanagan, Baby Chief and that lot. They've at least two bottles of Buckfast under the table-cloth. Sinéad has cleverly laid on some mini-quiches and chicken skewers while we wait to sit down though, so the leylandii may be safe yet. Nothing worse than a feed of drinks on an empty stomach to bring out the madsers.

'Aisling! Hello! Aisling!'

Who the hell is roaring at me?

'Jimmy Magee! Sam Maguire! *Conas atá tú*? That means "how are you?" *Conas atá tú*?!'

It can't be.

'It's me!'

It is. It's Pablo. Pablo from Tenerife. Behind the bar in the Ard Rí and waving frantically at me through the throng of people waiting to get served. He beckons me to move down to the end of the bar, and meets me there.

'Pablo! Hi! What are you doing here?'

'I came to visit John. The Lada, she die. Maybe I stay always. I want to play hurling! I play for the county some day! I want to beat the focking Kilkenny Cats! John help me to stay and give me tips. My game is good, he says.'

So John and Pablo must have stayed in touch.

John is getting him playing hurling and here he is, roaring his pidgin-Irish at people in the bar of the Ard Rí. Something about it warms my heart so much I feel like crying.

'Well, it's mighty to see you, Pablo. Four vodkas and two Diet Cokes, please.'

'Who's your man at the bar, Ais?' Majella's at my side before I get back to the table with the drinks, her interest is piqued. 'He's very exotic-looking.'

'That's Pablo. We met him in Tenerife. He's . . . he's a friend of John's, I suppose.' But she's already gone like a shot, making a beeline for the bar, ready for some hard-core introductions.

The dinner is lovely, even though Sinéad and Jimmy have gone out on a limb and put some kind of raw duck on as their starter. Smoked duck salad – sounds like another word for raw, if you ask me. I still haven't come to terms with sushi, so I'm not sure how to approach the idea of raw duck, but sure look at me here in my trousers and my no plus-one. And do you know, it's actually delicious. There's orange in the salad too, which is obviously some kind of mistake, but sure I'll say nothing and hopefully Sinéad won't find out. No point in ruining her day.

I don't see John at all during the meal. Well, I mean, I see him. He's right there, across the room. But I don't get talking to him. I catch his eye once or twice and look away shyly, remembering his text to me this morning about looking forward to the day. I had butterflies in my stomach thinking about seeing him. I wonder if we'll get chatt . . .

'*Here*, Ais.' A furtive whisper breaks my reverie and a glass full of fivers lands in front of me. The traditional betting on the speeches is well underway and the glass is moving like the clappers around the table with each utterance of the word 'thanks'. By the time we get to the Father of the Bride speech it's already passed me four times. Sinéad's dad says lovely things, and it's hard to hear. Majella catches my glistening eye and gives me a wink and a smile. I turn my eyes to John and he's watching me too.

I had the couple pegged as a 'Thinking Out Loud' pair, or maybe 'All of Me', but to my surprise, their first dance is to 'First Day of My Life', straight out of left-field. Jimmy always did have a bit of an indie vibe about him. He's been wearing skinny jeans for at least two years and has been known to break out the guitar and 'Wonderwall' after a session. Legend.

And so they sail around the floor to the plinky-plonky guitar and the flashes are going off and the wedding party is joining in and Majella is hanging over the bar, making Pablo give her his tie, even though she should be on the dancefloor. Sinéad will kill her.

'Dance?'

John's shuffled up beside me. Shy and awkward

and without a bridesmaid to dutifully turn around the floor, he holds out his big soft dry hand and we wordlessly circle the dancefloor as the plinky-plonky man sings, '. . . but I realised that I need you, and I wondered if I could come home.'

'Will we get a drink?' he whispers into my ear as the song ends. I could have stayed dancing for ever, to be honest with you. But the Grease megamix is surely not far away and I wouldn't mind a bit of quiet-time with John. Pablo expedites the drinks in record time for his number one man, who fires a grateful '*olé*' at him, and we find a nice deep windowsill to perch on.

'Well, remember the last time we were here?'

His deep sigh and slight nod tells me that he does. 'Ais, I'm sorry. This is lovely and all, but it's just not for me. The Ard Rí wedding and the plot of land and taking over the farm from Daddy or you taking over your farm at home. I didn't want that. I loved you . . . I . . . I love you. But I just wasn't thinking about that, and I wasn't ready to join you on the fast-track to it.'

Seven years is hardly a fast-track, and I'm a little bit hurt – but I suppose he's right in a way. I never gave him any reason to think it wasn't what I wanted. Sure it's only recently that I've started to realise that maybe that isn't what I want. Who knows what I want now? I still don't really know. I just want to feel happy and safe and maybe throw an eye to the soaps a few times a week.

Not that there's anything wrong with settling down home. Plenty of people do, and are so happy and content with the way they end up. If I've learned anything over the past few months, it's to live your life the way that makes you happy. You never know when . . . oh, he's still talking. This is the most talking about his feelings I think John has ever managed.

'. . . and I'm sorry about the Ciara thing. She got in touch when she got home and I suppose I was lonely and she liked me. But, Aisling, she was terrifying. So . . . so enthusiastic about everything. That day we met you in Dunnes, I was just trying to go to the cinema and she had us shopping for towels. I was full sure she was going to somehow move in with me without me realising it.'

I laugh, despite myself. He just looks so worried about coming home and finding Ciara in the bath with his jocks on her head.

I miss him too. So much. There's so much he's missed. Imagine the craic we could have if we stopped worrying about this stuff. Imagine we just had a lovely flat together in Dublin and feck what anyone else is doing. After seeing how much Sinéad and Jimmy have obviously spent on chair covers, I'm double-blessing myself that at least I'm not planning a wedding. Maybe we could go on another holiday – and make sure it's on the beach this time. Double bed, normal-sized kettle – a fancy place. No pressure, no expectations. I've wasted so much time worrying about what other people have and what other people are doing. And when it comes down to it, who cares? This is the first day of my life, indeed.

He's looking out at me from under his furrowed brow, big brown eyes searching mine and the big soft hand holding mine so tight. I smile and reach up and touch his unfamiliar beard, and bring my lips up to meet his.

'Aisling and John's turn! Aisling and John's turn!' Majella is well-oiled and Pablo's tie is around her head.

The caricature lad is in high demand, set up beside the midnight feast of triangle sandwiches and cocktail sausages. He's been churning out couples portraits to beat the band, adding a county flag here and a fascinator there to distinguish between one generic cartoon face and the next. John laughs and moves towards the now-vacant chair and pulls me down on his knee.

'Make it a good one, lad,' he calls to the artist. 'We might frame it one day.'

Four minutes later, and your man is done. He

puts the date at the bottom with a flourish and hands us our very own Knock/BGB version of a photo-booth memory.

A generic John with his brown eyes, new beard and big hands, and beside him, with her natural kink and flushed cheeks, a complete Aisling.

Acknowledgements

Thank you to our families and friends for their love and support. Thank you to those early readers: Áine Bambrick, Breda Gittons, Richard Toner, Sarah Kisch, Eoin Matthews, Ciara Brennan, Gavan Reilly, Louise McSharry and Fiona Hyde.

Thank you to our old pal Sheloa Nichols, to original Aisling Louise Keegan, to Emily Coffey for Geraldine, and to Conor Nagle from Gill Books, who insisted we do it.

Thank you to India and Esme, for sleeping. Thank you to everyone who offered words of support and encouragement; we can't name you all, you'll get notions.

And finally, to the Aisling community, keeping her lit every day.